COALESCENCE

DRAGONFIRE STATION BOOK 3

ZEN DIPIETRO

PARALLEL WORLDS PRESS

COPYRIGHT

COALESCENCE (DRAGONFIRE STATION #3)
COPYRIGHT © 2017 BY ZEN DIPIETRO
This is a work of fiction. Names, characters, organizations, events, and incidents are either products of the author's imagination or used fictitiously. Any resemblance to actual events, business establishments, locales, or persons, living or dead, is coincidental.

All rights reserved. No part of this publication may be reproduced, stored in a retrieval system, or transmitted in any form or by any means (electronic, mechanical, photocopying, recording, or otherwise) without express written permission of the publisher. The only exception is brief quotations for the purpose of review.

Please purchase only authorized electronic editions. Distribution of this book via the Internet or via any other means without the permission of the publisher is illegal and punishable by law.

ISBN: 978-1-943931-08-8 (print)
Published in the United States of America by Parallel Worlds Press

DRAGONFIRE STATION UNIVERSE

Dragonfire Station Book 1: Translucid
Dragonfire Station Book 2: Fragments
Dragonfire Station Book 3: Coalescence

Intersections (Dragonfire Station Short Stories)

Selling Out (Mercenary Warfare Book 1)
Blood Money (Mercenary Warfare Book 2)
Hell to Pay (Mercenary Warfare Book 3)
Calculated Risk (Mercenary Warfare Book 4)
Going for Broke (Mercenary Warfare Book 5)

Chains of Command Book 1: New Blood
Chains of Command Book 2: Blood and Bone
Chains of Command Book 3: Cut to the Bone
Chains of Command Book 4: Out for Blood

To stay updated on new releases and sales, sign up for Zen's newsletter at www.ZenDiPietro.com

1

Fallon sat in the *Outlaw*, waiting for the right moment to detach from the belly of the *Nefarious*. Piloting her little race car of a ship always got her blood pumping. She and her team were closing in on the class-six cruiser and she itched to get to the big moment.

Finally, they got into range. As she initiated the separation she barked, "Ross, break left!"

She dropped just in time to avoid getting hit by the much-larger *Nefarious* as her old combat instructor banked hard. Then she broke right, allowing the two to double-team their target.

"Hawk, energy charges!"

She imagined him over there leaning into the console while the *Nefarious* fired on the cruiser. Meanwhile, she used the *Outlaw*'s size to maneuver close, positioning herself alongside its docking port. She allowed herself a whoop of success when she achieved capture of the smaller craft.

"Target acquired," she announced to her teammates on the other ship. "Nice job."

Rather than board the vessel, she released it. "We can do it faster, though. Let's try it again."

She imagined Hawk's groan of frustration and smiled. "Acknowledged," Ross' voice came back over the voicecom after a brief pause. "Resetting the drill."

"Doing the same here. You ready to go again, Per?" Her gaze went to the cruiser, piloted by Peregrine and Raptor.

Peregrine's voice came over the voicecom. "Let's do it."

THREE MORE PRACTICE runs had Fallon sure they could pull off the maneuver in a real firefight. Which ticked one tactic off her list and left a few dozen more. She had big plans for her team, and she wanted them to be ready for anything.

"You're shaping up," she teased Ross after they'd docked the three ships on the stem portion of Dragonfire Station and gone aboard. She'd had to work at reframing her view of him over the last few weeks. When he'd brought her team proof of Krazinski's betrayal of the PAC, he'd been a former authority figure, but now, he was just an older colleague, and a part of her team.

"And you're a relentless taskmaster." Hawk eyed Fallon with disdain.

"Like you'd want her any other way." Peregrine smirked.

Hawk's blue eyes twinkled. "Well, you got me there."

Fallon and Ross fell in behind Peregrine and Hawk as they walked down the corridor. Raptor trailed behind.

Ross remarked, "I'm already twice the pilot I was when we started a week ago."

"Flatterer." Fallon narrowed her eyes at her former instructor. "That's a good way to make me suspicious. But you don't give yourself enough credit. You're a decent pilot."

Since recovering her memories, she'd had to reconcile her new acquaintance of Ross Whelkin with her older recollections. She'd briefly experienced an odd sort of double vision that caused her to experience a sense of duality. She'd mostly reconciled her two perspectives, which was a relief.

Ross smiled at her. For an older guy, he was good-looking in a beachy way. "Nothing like you. You're one of the best pilots I've ever seen. I always knew you were a fantastic fighter, but piloting skills came as a fun surprise."

"I didn't realize you were unaware of my flying abilities."

He shook his head as they arrived at the lift. "Details on BlackOps are need-to-know. I didn't need to know. Once you guys left the academy, I was out of the loop."

The lift opened.

"I'm hungry enough to eat mandren," Hawk said, and led them onto the lift. "Anyone want to hit the boardwalk for some dinner?"

"Sure, unless you're serious about the mandren." Raptor grimaced. "The smell of that stuff turns my stomach."

"Just an expression," Hawk assured him. "How about you two?" He looked from Per to Fallon. He could have added one of his mock-sleazy leers just for kicks, but he was all seriousness. For the moment.

Per nodded, but Fallon had to decline. "I have to meet with Captain Nevitt."

"Better you than me." Hawk slapped her on the shoulder.

"Your support is underwhelming."

Raptor and Ross chuckled.

The lift stopped and the door opened to Deck One. Hawk patted her shoulder, gently this time. "You'll do fine."

Per gave her an encouraging nod as she passed on her way out of the lift. Raptor smiled at her as the doors closed.

Fallon steeled herself as the lift ascended to Deck Five. She'd gotten a better understanding of Hesta Nevitt, but it wasn't every day that Fallon asked an upstanding PAC captain to commit treason and turn her station into a rebel headquarters.

This would not be an easy conversation.

F ALLON ACTIVATED the chime for Nevitt's quarters. She wondered what the captain thought of her request to meet there. She'd never even seen Nevitt's personal living space. At the least, she hoped her request had given the captain some forewarning of the seriousness of their meeting.

The doors swished open and Captain Nevitt stood there in all her formidable glory. "Chief." She gave Fallon a deep bow that indicated respect, and Fallon bowed yet lower, showing great esteem.

As the doors closed, Nevitt gestured Fallon to the seating area. "Judging by that bow, you're about to ask me for something big. I assume you're sufficiently recovered to follow up on whatever that might be?" She eased into a tall-backed chair with the air of a monarch sitting on a throne.

Fallon resisted the urge to get a good look at the captain's living space. She kept her attention fully on Nevitt as she settled across from her.

"Yes. It was kind of you to give me time to get my bearings. But it's been over a week, and we can't lose any more time."

"Of course. So say whatever it is you so clearly do not want to say."

Fallon considered leading into it gradually, but doubted Nevitt would appreciate the evasiveness. So she dove right in. "I want to set up a rebel headquarters here on Dragonfire."

Nevitt's eyebrows moved toward her hairline. "Is that all?" Her quiet words blistered with sarcasm.

"Before I left here, you said you wanted to join the upper echelons of the PAC, so you could make changes for the greater good. This is your chance."

Despite the bombshell, Nevitt remained composed. The time she took to respond was the only indication of the magnitude of what Fallon had laid on her.

"And you have a plan to do that?" Nevitt sounded skeptical.

"Not a precise plan. More like an agenda of potential tactics, each of which will require their own contingencies. But I need to get your approval before we go deep into the logistics."

"What if I say no?" Nevitt's gaze didn't waver.

Fallon met her eyes. "Then we select another, less ideal site. Someplace less protected, where we have fewer assets and allies. But we'll still go after Blackout."

"And if I say yes?"

"Then you'll be putting the lives of everyone on this station in jeopardy. You'll become an enemy of the state. And you might just save the PAC from intergalactic war."

The quiet of Nevitt's quarters roared in Fallon's ears as she waited for a reply.

"Agreed." Nevitt snapped the word out like a stinger blast. "But I have some conditions."

"State your terms."

"Protecting this station and the people on it will be among your top priorities. You will remain security chief here." She ticked off the points on her fingers as she went. "You will not fail to fix whatever's wrong with Blackout. And, finally, I will be consulted on all matters regarding the safety of Dragonfire and the progress of your mission—" she broke off and corrected herself, "—*our* mission."

Fallon opened her mouth to speak but Nevitt cut her off. "Don't give me a bunch of scrap about top secret protocols or giving me plausible deniability. If you want to operate on my station, I'm going to be part of the team. That's not negotiable."

Fallon met her captain's narrowed eyes. "Agreed."

Nevitt's brow furrowed in puzzlement. Or surprise, perhaps. Fallon had never seen such an uncertain expression on Nevitt, so she wasn't entirely sure.

Nevitt's brow smoothed, and her lips curved into a smirk. "I can't believe you agreed to that."

The absurdity of it all struck Fallon, and she laughed. To her even-greater surprise, Nevitt chuckled.

"Considering that my team has stolen data, broken into a PAC base, and taken down an illegal research lab manufacturing treaty-prohibited items, I'd say your lack of proper security clearance is a minor offense. And it makes sense that you should be informed."

Nevitt's amusement faded to seriousness. "It sounds like you need to fill me in on some things before we proceed."

For the next two hours, Fallon did her best to bring Nevitt into the loop on all of Avian Unit's activities and intentions. Nevitt's expression grew increasingly grave.

When Fallon finished, Nevitt said, "There's one more condition I want to add."

"If it's one I can't agree to, it would put me in a very tricky position, given all that you now know."

Nevitt ignored her. "When you've taken control of Blackout and gotten things sorted, I will be part of the new administration."

Fallon wouldn't have had it any other way. "Agreed."

Getting things hammered out with Nevitt left Fallon feeling energized. She decided that while she was riding high on that success, she'd handle something she'd already put off for too long. She'd made excuses for herself, mainly that she was supposed to avoid excessive stress while her head healed or that she was too busy, but the truth was that she just didn't know how to approach such a dicey situation that involved...feelings. Ugh. Not her forte.

When she walked into the maintenance bay—or the "shop," as the mechanics called it—she saw Wren sliding beneath a propulsion chamber, which must have been removed from some ship. That would be one heck of a repair. Fallon felt a slight chill. The shop was always just a couple degrees below comfortable, for the benefit of all the expensive technology within.

Fallon imagined polymechrine filling her spine. She'd avoided Wren since returning to the station, not knowing how to deal with the mountains that stood between them. But now that she was about to become deeply entrenched in everyday life aboard Dragonfire, she needed to deal with the issue.

She'd rather face a deep-space pirate attack.

She picked up an axial microtuner from a tool tray and squatted next to Wren's feet, which protruded from beneath the hulking propulsion system.

"Here." She extended the tool beneath it, toward Wren.

Her former wife glided out from under the machinery on an anti-grav creeper, her expression guarded. She lay there, wordless.

"Thought I'd give you the one you asked for this time. Better late than never, right?"

Fallon and Wren had first met in this very spot. Wren had called out to her colleague for an axial tuner, but Fallon had mistakenly given her a radial one instead.

Wren's face stayed unnaturally still as she sat up, then pulled herself to her feet. "You remember that?"

"I remember everything. Want to have lunch?"

Fallon sat across from her not-wife at the Bennite restaurant as they sized each other up.

"You remember everything?" Wren's pale cheeks had an attractive pink glow, but otherwise, she kept her expression carefully guarded. Fallon was glad for that.

"Yes," Fallon confirmed. "I imagine that you have a lot of questions for me."

"You could say that. I'll come back to the 'how' part of regaining your memory later. What I really want to know is why you married me. Was it some tactic, from your...employers?"

Fallon appreciated Wren's caution. Privacy or no, there was no good reason to mention Blackout in public. Most people still thought the organization was a myth.

"No. I married you for all the normal reasons that people get married."

"Why?" Wren's fingers drummed on the otherwise-forgotten menuboard. "You made it clear that getting married is just not done in your profession."

"Believe me, I've gotten a lot of shit about it from my teammates. But you pursued me, remember. Relentlessly. And when we started dating, I found that our relationship was something I'd never had before. Nurturing. Caring." Fallon fought the urge to squirm at saying such touchy-feely stuff. "I never thought I'd be interested in a domestic situation, but with you it felt...right." Fallon shrugged, fighting down a swell of remembered feeling. She had no room for that in her life.

"You loved me," Wren translated.

"Yes." Fallon didn't care to put so fine a point on it, but she knew it was the answer Wren needed. And Wren wouldn't stop asking until she got it.

"And no other reason? No ulterior motive?"

"I was sent to investigate you for smuggling, but it was a bogus assignment. I knew that before I even came to Dragonfire. I knew something was wrong in—" she caught herself and adjusted her words, "—the upper levels. That's probably why my team was split up on different assignments, to get us out of the way while they decided what to do with us. Or it might also have had something to do with this." She tapped her temple.

"Right." Wren's mouth squinched up as if she'd eaten a lemon. "I won't ask about your team, or any of that. Clearly, it's not for my ears."

Fallon must have let a hint of surprise escape because Wren smiled wryly. "I was a security chief's wife for six months. I'd gotten quite used to knowing there were things you couldn't discuss with me."

"Makes sense. Do you have any other questions?"

Wren's eyes lit with the irreverent gleam that Fallon knew so well. "Sure. I'd love to know where you've been for the last six months and your history with those four you brought back with you. And yeah, I know it's four. I hear things. But," she continued, "like I said, I'm not going to ask about all that. I guess my only question now is, where does all this leave us? You and me?"

"Where do you want it to leave us?"

Wren tucked a stray pink tendril of hair behind her ear. "I'm not sure. I still have feelings. But I don't know about dealing with all the baggage you bring. And, knowing you, you have some strong feelings about how I reacted to the things that happened."

The reminder sent a streak of resentment through Fallon, though it faded as quickly as it came. "Yeah, you could say that. That was some pretty poor shit."

Rather than being stricken, Wren smiled. Fallon had always liked how resilient Wren was. She had a way of finding the humor in things that would shock or crush other people. It was one of the things about Wren that Fallon had fallen for.

"You swear a lot more now," Wren observed.

Fallon hadn't thought about it, but she suspected Wren was right. She blamed Hawk and Peregrine's influence for that. "Things change."

Wistfulness filled Wren's eyes. "Yeah. They do." She studied Fallon. "But what does it all mean for us? What are we to each other?"

"I don't know. Some sort of friends?"

"The kind of friends that used to be lovers? Or the kind that sometimes still are?"

She should have been able to answer that question, but she could only shrug.

"Sarkavians are good with letting relationships be whatever they are at the moment, but would that kind of ambiguity work for you?" Wren didn't look doubtful, merely curious.

"I guess we'll see."

Wren studied Fallon. "I guess so. Does it make any difference that I've started seeing someone? Just a casual thing. I wouldn't even mention it, but since you wanted monogamy before…" She trailed off.

That had been before Raptor returned to her life, and their relationship had changed. He hadn't mentioned exclusivity, but Fallon had grown up in a very traditional Japanese family, with a strong foundation in loyalty, devotion, honor, and yes, monogamy. She always thought others should do whatever worked for them, but could she feel honorable in that situation herself?

She wasn't prepared to discuss Raptor with Wren, so she only said, "I don't know."

Wren gave a tiny nod, her expression full of understanding. She checked the time on the menuboard. "We should order. I'll need to get back to the shop. I'm on a deadline to get that chamber ready."

"Right. So we'll have lunch. Like friends."

Wren gave her a sunny smile. "Let's give it a go."

As Fallon punched in her order for Bennite stew and bread, she wondered if she could actually manage a friendship with her former wife. Platonic or otherwise.

Some missions were harder than others.

AFTER LUNCH, Wren went back to work and Fallon lingered on the boardwalk. This had always been her favorite part of the station. The boardwalk teemed with life like no other place on Dragonfire, serving as a mixing bowl of everything the station had to offer. She could observe the commotion of travelers coming and going through the docking bays, and people doing their shopping. Fashion choices ranged from the flamboyantly eccentric to the deeply conservative. Yet all of these elements meshed and interacted in this space, forming a community of variety that Fallon found deeply satisfying.

She loved the smells as much as the sights. A deep breath drew in aromas from the delicious foods belonging to a wide variety of cultures. As she enjoyed it, she wandered from one storefront to the next, admiring the array of offerings.

More than anything else, it was the feeling of vibrancy and activity that brought Fallon back to the boardwalk day after day. Here, she had the opportunity to watch the people she protected. They shared meals with friends and colleagues, laughed with the shopkeeps, and created a sense of community that she'd found herself unable to resist. Despite her crazy life, she'd found a home here on Dragonfire. Being a part of a community had changed her. Opened her up to the idea of belonging somewhere.

The window-shopping and people watching recharged her for her next meeting. Fortunately, this one would not be fraught with emotional landmines.

She joined Arin Triss in the security office, where he had been the acting chief of security up to this point. Captain Nevitt had commanded that Fallon continue as the chief, so now Fallon had to reassert herself.

"Let me guess," he said, smiling, as they settled on the two facing couches. "You're here to return me to my life of leisure as your legate."

They both knew that Arin worked hard every day, regardless of his title. He'd always been an above-and-beyond kind of guy. "Yes and no."

"Oh?" He tilted his head slightly to the side.

"The captain does want me to remain chief. But I'm involved with other issues at the moment, and I'll need you to continue to handle more of the day-to-day operations than you did in the past as my legate. So you'll get a lot of the chief's work, but not the title. How do you feel about that?"

He shrugged. "Great. It'll be less than I've been doing, and it'll be a heck of a boost to my duty record for my next evaluation. Besides, I'm glad you're back."

"You've done a great job in my absence."

"Your security system and protocols made it almost easy." He waved his hands in an all-encompassing gesture.

She knew that wasn't true. It took more than protocols to handle altercations, smuggling attempts, potentially hazardous cargo, and unsavory traders. She'd already reviewed the records and knew that Arin had done tremendously well. If she were a normal officer, she'd have recommended him for a promotion and his own duty post right away, without waiting for his next evaluation. But she was far from a normal officer, and she needed his help.

He knew that she was involved in some variety of intrigue, but he didn't know about Blackout. If all went as planned, she'd want to bring him in, but for the moment, it was safer for him to be on the outside.

"Well, for now, we can split the duty schedule between us, as before. I'll want you to continue handling the security personnel and reports to PAC command. But I'll be prone to missing shifts unexpectedly, or even being away from the station for days at a time. So I'll need you to be ready to take over at any given moment."

He nodded. "No problem. I've tapped Jenson as my unofficial second, and he's really stepped into the role."

Lieutenant Mat Jenson. Zerellian male, stationed on Dragonfire for the past two years. The information popped into Fallon's brain along with an image of his face. "Glad to hear it. I've always liked him."

An awkward pause formed between them. Arin looked uncertain. "What about you and Wren?"

Ah. Well, naturally, he'd want to know about that. Both as a friend, and as the legate of security. "We've agreed to give friendship a whirl. See how it goes."

Sadness and sympathy showed clearly on his face, but he only said, "I hope that works out."

"Me too." She snapped back to business. "I'd like you to get to know my teammates. They'll be on the station indefinitely. How about dinner this evening on the boardwalk?"

"I have a date, but I'll cancel. I'd love to meet these people you've been working with."

"A date?" She shouldn't have been surprised. Arin was gorgeous in a way that only Atalans could be, and Dragonfire had relatively few eligible men.

"Nothing serious. You're probably thinking about Kellis. I thought that might go somewhere, but before she left last week, she was pretty clear that she isn't interested in more than friendship right now."

Since the *Onari*'s mech engineer seemed to have an interest in joining a certain clandestine spy establishment, Fallon could see why Kellis had put Arin in the friend zone.

"They're due back in a couple days. If that's going to be awkward for you, let me know. You don't have to greet the ship with me."

"No. It's fine, but thanks."

"Good. Would you rather take day shift, or night?"

Arin shrugged. "Doesn't matter, really. Whichever you'd rather not have, I guess."

"I'll take day. My team likes to have their nights free."

"Why's that?" he asked.

"You'll see when you meet them."

FALLON KEPT an eye on Arin throughout the evening, gauging his reaction to Avian Unit. Though her teammates wore casual clothes on Dragonfire, Fallon couldn't help noticing a certain stealth in their movements, or the way they always remained aware of their surroundings. Fallon saw an edge to them that she didn't see in other people, and wondered if outsiders like Arin could see it too.

After dinner, they all went for a walk in the arboretum. She trailed behind so she could observe.

"Do you visit Sarkan often? It's got to be great being stationed so close to such a beautiful planet," Hawk asked Arin as they led the group along a path that took them deeper into the carefully cultivated greenery. Fallon paused a moment to admire a purple leaf with almost iridescent veins in it. Or whatever those were called. Botany was not her strong suit.

"I take most of my leave time there." To his credit, Arin didn't seem overwhelmed by Hawk's attentions. "The beaches are beautiful, and I love boating."

"Doesn't hurt that Sarkavians are particularly *friendly*, does it?" The wicked gleam in Hawk's eye was evident even from where Fallon stood.

Hawk had not disappointed Fallon by toning down his big personality for Arin's benefit. If anything, Hawk had been more suggestive than usual. He also always ended up next to Arin. Fallon was fairly certain that her legate had no interest in dating men, but it was fun to watch Hawk try.

Raptor and Peregrine seemed to like Arin well enough. Fallon had a harder time interpreting Ross' sentiments. He was friendly, but gave little away regarding his thoughts. He walked next to Peregrine, appearing to enjoy the stroll.

The path curved gently around a copse of trees. The group

halted when they encountered Dr. Brannin Brash coming the other direction.

"Oh, hello." The Bennite doctor smiled and engaged in pleasantries with everyone, saving Fallon for last. "And how are you feeling?" He had good reason for asking, given the brain surgery he'd recently assisted with, which had returned her memories to her.

"Great. No apparent side effects."

"Glad to hear it. You'll be at your appointment tomorrow?" He watched her expectantly.

"Of course. And Brak will also check me out when she returns."

Brak had been the one to pioneer the surgery. She also knew about Fallon's struggle with Blackout, while Brannin remained in the dark about it.

"Excellent." He included the others in his smiling glance. "Well, I won't keep you. Have a good evening." He gave them a quick bow, indicating the proper level of respect, but with an air of casualness.

Fallon and her companions also bowed, then continued on their way. Raptor and Peregrine joined the conversation, probably to relieve Arin of Hawk's unwavering attention. Fallon and Ross were content to listen, responding only when spoken to directly.

Fallon wanted to observe Arin with her team, but she didn't know Ross' reason for being quiet. Maybe he was just tired.

Overall, she was pleased with the evening. Arin got along well with her team and they seemed to like him. She'd talk to him in private later to see what he thought of them. If he had the right instincts, she might recruit him into her rebellion. Assuming she could trust him not to go running to Jamestown Station, also known as PAC headquarters.

In the meantime, she had a station to protect and an insurgency to plan.

2

The next morning, Fallon gathered Avian Unit in her security office on Deck Four to discuss their next mission: making contact with Admiral Colb. As soon as Brak gave her the medical green light for business as usual, Fallon wanted to start sticking it to Blackout. That meant finding all the allies they could, and Colb would be a powerful one. They'd located him, and he seemed to be isolated and on the run, just as Avian Unit was.

"What he's doing is smart," Raptor said. "He's made his presence on Zerellus publicly known. With his high profile, people would immediately notice if he disappeared, and they'd start asking the kind of questions that Blackout doesn't want people asking."

"The kind that might just lead back to them," Peregrine mused, chewing on her thumb thoughtfully. "But it means he'll be difficult to reach. He'll have a fortress of security to make sure he doesn't suffer any unfortunate 'accidents.'"

"Difficult, but not impossible," Raptor countered. "I'm finding out as much about the situation as I can."

Hawk shifted to face Raptor. "We don't have much to prove he's an ally, other than the fact that he seems to be flying solo. No offense to Fallon, but I'm not taking her parents' faith in the guy as proof that he's on our side."

"Neither am I." Old family friend or not, Fallon wouldn't trust him blindly. "Until we're sure he's not working with Krazinski, we treat him as a potential threat."

From the corner of her eye, she saw Ross' frown deepen. He'd said little all morning and his withdrawal had begun to concern her.

Raptor leaned forward, his elbows on his knees. "I'd like to do a scouting mission. Check out the situation in person. That will give me a lot more to work with."

It was the right move, and Fallon's team could use something to do. They weren't tasked with running Dragonfire as she was. The timing would sync nicely.

Travel between the station and Zerellus would take more than a day each way. By the time the rest of Avian Unit returned, Brak would have arrived and given Fallon the medical all clear. At least, she hoped she'd get the clean bill of health she needed. If not, she might have to defy doctor's orders, even if it strained her relationship with Brak.

"Who would you take?" she asked Raptor. As their hacker and infiltration specialist, his expertise would be paramount.

"Hawk, I guess." Raptor looked to Peregrine, as if apologizing for not choosing her. "His tactical assessment would be helpful in making our plan."

"Take Peregrine too. She'll make sure no one recognizes you."

Hawk frowned at her. "That would leave you here alone, and we agreed we'd stay in pairs."

"Ross will stay here." She'd have liked him to serve as their pilot. The others would do fine with a basic flight, but Ross was better qualified to deal with anything out of the ordinary.

Ross met her gaze, then nodded. She wasn't sure how he felt deferring to her, given that technically speaking, he was her superior officer. While the rest of her team did their scouting, she'd have a talk with their former instructor. She needed to know what was going on inside his head lately.

Hawk, Raptor, and Peregrine exchanged glances, then nodded. She sensed their reluctance, and she appreciated it. Those three were her family, and she was theirs. Even though she'd recovered her memories of her parents and brother, her bond with her team was the most significant one she had, and she liked it that way. Her world would make a lot less sense if it were any other way.

"Good. You can work out the details and let me know when you plan to depart." She leaned back against the couch. "That brings us to the last issue. Nevitt will be in the loop on our planning, and may attend meetings. Especially if anything pertains to Dragonfire. She'll be an active member of our team."

Hawk looked like he wanted to argue, so she cut in before he could get started. "That's one of her terms for letting us use Dragonfire as a base of operations."

Hawk grimaced, but said nothing. Raptor met her gaze, while Per frowned her usual frown.

"All right. We're done here. I need to get to Deck Two to check out a faulty sensor."

Peregrine said, "Nevitt's terms are steep. Are you really going to be able to balance your job as security chief with what we need to do?"

"I've wondered the same thing," Fallon admitted. "It depends on how difficult each of those jobs gets."

"So no." Hawk's eyes were full of humor.

She smiled at him. "We're going to find out."

AFTER HER TEAM LEFT, Fallon sat in the chair behind her desk. With one foot, she sent both it and herself spiraling in a slow spin. She'd developed the habit as a child to help her blow off steam and center her thoughts.

She had a lot threatening to pull her off-center. Her loyalty to her team and her duty to Nevitt. Her concern about Ross and most of all, her need to figure out what was happening with Blackout and why her brain had been experimented on.

She knew now that she'd never consented to have illegal, experimental technology installed in her brain. She'd never been asked, either. She wanted to know how long it had been in there, and what had happened in that shuttle before the accident and her memory loss.

She remembered piloting the shuttle outside Dragonfire, then waking up in Dragonfire's infirmary with Brannin and Wren standing over her. Clearly, some serious shit had gone down in that brief interim.

The way she figured it, there were three possibilities. Someone might have removed a device from her brain, causing brain damage in the process. There could have been some altercation that caused accidental damage to the implant. Or perhaps it was a botched attempt to install the device without her knowing.

The details weren't important, in the grand scheme of figuring out who was to blame for subverting Blackout and developing illegal tech that violated the treaties at the heart of the PAC. Fallon's experience was a speck of space dust compared to avoiding intergalactic war.

But it mattered to her and she hoped she'd get at least some of the answers.

For now, she had a malfunctioning sensor to see to.

BY THE TIME she recalibrated the sensor, she was due for her rounds on the boardwalk. She smoothed her hands over her uniform as she rode the lift down to Deck One. She hadn't done this in an official capacity for over seven months now. And the last time she'd done it, she'd been operating with only a couple weeks' worth of memories.

Her amnesia seemed surreal in hindsight, but she was proud of herself for managing as well as she had. With her two realities now meshed, her identity in check, and her team on the station, she felt complete for the first time in over two years.

She watched for her young friends Nix and Robert, but they didn't seem to be down here today. They must be having lunch at school.

She wasn't surprised when Cabot Layne stepped out of his shop as she walked by.

"Chief," he said warmly, bowing. "It's so good to see you back on the job."

"It's good to be back," she answered as she returned the bow, surprised by how much she meant what she said.

She expected him to refer to the covert work he had at least some inkling of, or to the favor he'd done her in securing a ship for her and her teammates. But he merely smiled and fell into step beside her as he'd done many times before.

"Has everything gone well on the boardwalk in my absence? Is there anything that needs my attention?" she asked.

"We've been well taken care of. Young Arin has done an excellent job."

"That's good to hear."

"And you?" he asked. "You're well?"

She searched his face for some hidden meaning, but saw none. "Yes. Very well, thank you."

"I'm glad." He halted and stood in place, causing her to do the same. "I'd love to walk the rest of the way with you, but I'm afraid I have an appointment with a customer. Perhaps tomorrow?"

His geniality made her smile. "That would be nice."

"If you think of anything you or your friends need, let me know."

Again, she suspected a double meaning, but his face gave nothing away. Either he was being straightforward or he was damn good. Given what he'd managed to do for her previously, she'd put cubics on him being damn good. "I will."

"Good."

He bowed and she returned the courtesy.

The rest of her tour of the boardwalk was unremarkable. She received friendly greetings from people glad to see her back on the job, but she had no questions about their backgrounds or motivations.

Cabot Layne was another matter altogether. The man did a perfect imitation of a simple trader, but she knew him to be more. How much more, she had yet to discover.

FALLON'S TEAM left for Zerellus that evening, which made her uneasy. Not going with them felt wrong. She'd make her lemons into lemonade, though, and use the time to have a talk with Ross.

The doors to his quarters opened just seconds after she touched the chime. "Took you five whole minutes to get here. I'm disappointed." His expression didn't match the teasing words, but she gave him points for trying.

She followed him in and they settled in the living area. "You know why I'm here. Tell me what's going on."

He propped an ankle across his opposite knee, looking conflicted. "Here's my problem. I've seen the evidence against Krazinski. Raptor verified the data and his guilt is clear. His attempt to extort Brak only adds more evidence of his corruption." His voice sharpened. "But it doesn't make sense to me. I've known John for two decades, and I'd have staked my life on him being devoted to peace and promoting solidarity among the PAC allies." His fingers slowly curled into a tense fist.

She didn't know Ross well enough to understand his inner workings. "So what do you make of it?"

His hand uncurled and he smoothed it over his pant leg. "I don't know. That's the problem. I can't argue with the evidence, but it doesn't add up against what I know of the man. That bothers me."

Silence stretched between them. Finally, she said, "I wish I had answers for you, but I don't understand his motivations either. I can't imagine what would be worth violating multiple treaties and potentially throwing this sector of the universe into chaos. But we're going to take care of it, regardless of his reasons."

"It's what you do, right?" His voice was flat as he stared into space.

"No," she answered honestly. "I've always been the tip of the arrow, not the bow." His eyes shifted to her and she decided to be brutally honest. They needed to understand each other the way she and her team did. "Look, I'm an adrenaline junkie with a hero complex and a certain amount of moral flexibility. I've always been perfectly happy to throw myself at whatever target I was pointed toward, because I had faith in the people doing the pointing." She could see she had his full attention, so she continued, "But the person who's been directing me has become corrupt, and now I'm pointed right at him. My team never wanted to become administrators, but if that's the job that needs doing, we'll do it."

"Yeah." Ross didn't look less troubled.

She leaned forward and rested a hand on his propped knee. "We'll figure out what happened to Krazinski. That *is* what my team and I do."

He sighed and patted her hand. "I know. And there's no one

else I'd want on the job. That's why I came looking for you. I guess I'm just weary. I thought the universe would be a better, more solid place when I was middle-aged. That my colleagues and I would have spent our lives on the betterment of the PAC. Instead, I'm finding that my cohorts are destabilizing everything we, and previous generations, have created."

He smiled at her, with a touch of sadness. "It's disheartening to look toward my advancing years and feel less hopeful about the future than I did when I was a fresh young officer."

"Would it make you feel better if I promised you could smack Krazinski once we have him? A really good one, right across the face." She demonstrated by smacking one palm against the other.

He laughed. "Maybe."

"Don't lose your sense of humor," she advised. "I found out a long time ago that sometimes it's all we have."

"Yeah. I guess you're right. I'll try harder at not letting myself get dragged down."

She nodded. "It's a requirement of the job. Focus on what's ahead of you. Don't get bogged down in dwelling on the rest."

"I'll stay on track. Thanks."

She understood where he was coming from. He'd lost his sense of community, and he needed a new one.

"How about you come down to the boardwalk with me? We can get some dinner and I'll introduce you around." Thus far, he'd spent most of his time alone. Brooding. It wasn't good for him.

"Is it smart to be so open about my presence here?" he asked.

"There's no hiding the fact that I'm here, and the assumption will be that my team is too. Blackout will have already concluded that you're on our side."

"All right," he agreed. "Show me the boardwalk."

She'd been mildly hungry, but now that she'd entered the haven of delicious aromas, her stomach started growling. Fallon and Ross had only just sat down at the Bennite restaurant and picked up their menuboards when Captain Nevitt appeared.

Fallon was so surprised that she forgot her stomach and simply stared at her captain. She'd only ever seen Nevitt on the boardwalk when she needed to greet an important guest to the station upon arrival. Fallon couldn't recall ever having seen Nevitt eat.

"May I join you?" the captain asked.

Fallon found her voice. "Of course."

"I had a craving for some stew," Nevitt said, quickly keying her order into a menuboard. She glanced up and noted Fallon's expression. "Fine. I've decided that if things around here are changing, then I need to change with them. Assuming things go the way we think they will, a closer relationship with the people on my station will be necessary for everyone's well-being."

"That's very forward-thinking." Fallon keyed in her order for stew, bread, and cold tea.

"Not at all. Just pragmatic." She focused her attention on Ross. "So what's your story? You've been on my station for weeks and I know almost nothing about you."

He smiled amiably. "Oh, you know. Former academy instructor, recently retired. Bumming around the PAC zone while I decide what to do next."

Nevitt smirked. "Right." In such a public place, Ross could hardly be more forthcoming, but Nevitt didn't seem put out. "I hope your stay on my station proves to be productive."

That earned her a grin from Ross. "So do I, Captain."

"Call me Hesta. I'm not on duty."

Fallon somehow managed to keep her jaw from dropping. She'd never heard Nevitt suggest anyone call her by her first name.

The captain eyed Fallon. "You too, when we aren't discussing official business."

"Is a captain ever not on duty?" Ross asked.

"I'm going to start. Just did, in fact, a minute ago. It looks like this." She sat watching them.

Prelin's ass. The captain could be funny. Fallon didn't know what to make of this unexpected turn of events. "I might have to work my way up to calling you by your first name."

Nevitt lifted a challenging eyebrow, which somehow ignited all of Fallon's competitive tendencies. Damn, that woman had skills.

"Fine. Hesta."

To her credit, the captain—*Hesta*—didn't gloat. She simply nodded in acknowledgement.

"So what's *your* story?" Ross asked.

Nevitt folded her hands together on the table. "Oh, you know. A typical space station captain, bumming my way through this assignment until I can move up in the hierarchy."

Ross laughed. "Fair enough."

The two bantered throughout the meal, with Fallon commenting in the appropriate places, but mostly observing. She needed to work harder at adjusting her perception of Nevitt.

As time wore on, fatigue settled over Fallon. She and the others had long since finished eating and simply remained, talking. She wanted some time to herself to think and realized that she needn't stay. Ross was making a new friend, as she'd hoped. So she excused herself and returned to her quarters. The space seemed quiet without Peregrine, even though her partner wasn't talkative in general. Her absence left a big hole, as did Hawk's and Raptor's. Without her team, Fallon felt incomplete.

She sat in front of the voicecom, thinking of Wren. Had Fallon's isolation from her team played a part in her relationship with her?

Of course it had.

She sat looking at the voicecom, wondering where Wren might be at that moment. But rather than call to find out, she opted to shower and get ready for bed. She couldn't let Wren be a fallback for when her team wasn't around. Fallon was too self-aware for that, and Wren deserved better.

So she went to bed with her better judgment rather than with a soft, warm partner who understood her.

3

When Fallon woke up the next day, her sense of isolation remained. She brushed it aside as she went through her daily routine as chief of security. Her morning check-in with Captain Nevitt now felt a little different, thanks to her shifting impressions of the woman. Otherwise, there was a coziness to her routine. Checking the security systems, looking over the night shift's report, and noting the day's arrivals and departures all felt comfortable and productive.

Doing her afternoon rounds on the boardwalk particularly pleased her. Citizens of the station and familiar visitors greeted her warmly as she walked along. She enjoyed looking after the people of Dragonfire, and the station itself. She just plain liked the place. The bustle of activity, the variety of people. The sense of community made her feel more rooted than she ever had.

Not that she'd ever minded being rootless. Her main focus had always been her job. She'd never needed or wanted roots.

Bah. It was all much more introspective than she cared to be. She just wanted to get shit done, not waste time worrying about feelings.

She quickened her step, only to notice Wren step out from

behind a Rescan. She flashed Fallon a smile as she angled toward her. Wren had a nice walk. Smooth and rolling, with even steps that, if measured, would be the exact same distance every time. But with a slight side-to-side sway that caught the eye of several passersby.

"Hi." Wren smiled, her eyes sparkling with her particular brand of humor.

"Hi."

"Are you avoiding me?" Wren gave her a teasing look.

"No." Fallon hadn't sought Wren out, but she hadn't avoided her either. "Why would I?"

"Your team is gone and you haven't looked me up. I thought you might, since we talked about it and decided to just see what happens."

Fallon didn't know whether to be amused or disconcerted by Wren's understanding of her quirks. "It seemed too complicated."

"It couldn't be simpler, really," Wren argued. She glanced around to see if their conversation might be overheard. She hitched her head toward the concourse and they began walking.

Once they'd put some distance between them and the busiest part of Deck One, Wren continued, "You and I clearly aren't over, though we're no longer exclusive. There's no reason we can't see each other. Unless you've decided you're uninterested, or that partner of yours would have a problem with it."

Did Wren know about her and Raptor? "Which partner?"

Wren gave her a sidelong look of amusement. "I've seen you two together. I could practically see the sparks."

Fallon decided not to argue the point. She had nothing to hide about her relationship with Raptor. It predated her relationship with Wren by more than a decade. "When have you seen us together?"

Wren shrugged. "A glimpse in the gym. A peek on the boardwalk. It doesn't matter. The question is, have you two become an exclusive thing? I didn't get that impression from you the last time we talked."

"No."

Another person would have asked for more details. A non-Sarkavian person would, anyway. But Wren nodded and pressed on. "So second question. Are you uninterested in me?"

Wren stepped in front of Fallon, forcing her to stop and return her gaze.

Wren was hard for Fallon to ignore on the best of days. Her willingness to face off and demand point-blank answers only made her more appealing. "No."

Wren smiled, and the distance between them decreased until it verged on the inappropriate-for-being-on-duty. Then she spun around and resumed walking. "Would you like to have dinner tonight?"

Why was it that Fallon had no qualms about flying a ship right into a firefight, yet the thought of a meal with this woman made all of her mental alarms go off?

No, she decided. *No.* "Yes."

Prelin's ass. Fallon cursed herself for her habit of jumping off whatever cliff she happened to be standing on.

"Good." Wren smiled. "Pick me up at my quarters after your shift ends."

There were plenty of reasons to say no. But she didn't want to.

THE DOORS to Wren's quarters swished open. Fallon entered, refusing to be affected by the fact that this had been her home for six months. She didn't look at the wall she'd thrown knives into, or the couch where they'd snuggled and watched holo-vids. The important thing to remember was that this place belonged only to Wren now.

Wren led her to the living area. She wore a simple dress and Fallon hoped it indicated a casual evening with no expectations.

Fallon had gone casual as well, hoping to send her own message. Cargo pants and a short-sleeved knit shirt seemed to her to be an entirely unromantic choice of clothing.

"Have a seat wherever you like." Wren gestured at the couch and chairs. "Would you like a drink?"

"Zerellian ale, if you have it." She didn't sit. She stood behind the couch, running a hand over the synthetic suede fabric.

Wren laughed lightly. "Of course I do." She returned in less than a minute, offering a tall glass with a light froth on top.

Fallon wasn't sure how to feel about Wren's ability to read and anticipate her so well. It made her feel unarmed.

She noticed an enticing smell coming from the kitchenette. "Are we eating here?" She'd assumed they were going out.

"Yes. I hope that's okay. I figured we'd be talking about some things that we'd prefer other people not overhear."

"Must we? I was kind of hoping we could keep edging around each other, unsure of where we stand. So we could really prolong our awkwardness."

Wren laughed. "As fun as that is, I think the time has come to really talk, Em." She sobered and corrected herself. "Fallon. I know you prefer Fallon now."

Fallon took a long drink before responding. "I do, but I don't mind when people forget. I think of it as a nickname."

Wren stood behind the armchair, playing with the stem of her wine glass. "I guess names don't much matter in what you do?"

"So we're jumping right in, then?" Fallon had expected a good deal of idle chitchat while the two tested waters before wading into deeper subjects.

"Yeah, seems like it. I've been waiting around for months, and there are things I need to know."

"You haven't exactly been waiting around."

Wren's lips parted in surprise. "Wow. I'm guessing that means you have a problem with me dating? I thought you might." She took a breath. "Okay. I get it. And I'd rather be just a friend to you than nothing at all."

"I didn't say that. I'm still trying to figure all this out. It doesn't feel backward to you to go from being married and exclusive to being in an open relationship?" Fallon felt her fighting instincts kick in and wasn't sorry for it. She was better at combat than she was with relationships. "And if you're seeing someone else you don't want to stop seeing, why are you still interested in me?"

But Wren wasn't a fighter. She'd never engaged with Fallon in that way. She merely tipped her head to the side thoughtfully. "Exclusivity was your thing, not mine. I tried it and it was fine because I've never cared about someone so much, but it isn't natural for a Sarkavian. This is just part of who I am, like your inability to live a normal life is part of you."

"Normal is entirely relative."

"That's exactly what I'm saying." Wren took a sip of her wine. "Having a short-term relationship with someone else doesn't make me any less invested in a long-term relationship with you. The real question is, why did you get involved with me to begin with?"

Fallon had been asking herself the same question for some time now. "I always knew the kind of life I wanted, even as a kid." She let out a slow breath. "But you were different than anyone I'd ever met. You made me think about my life in a new way."

Wren ran her hand over the back of the chair. It was a nonchalant gesture, but Fallon knew Wren didn't feel the least bit indifferent. "I wondered if I was part of some plan. If I was being used."

Fallon looked directly into Wren's pale eyes. "No. You weren't."

"I realize that now." Wren made a helpless gesture. "But everything came down so hard, so fast. Your memory loss, this guy who showed up, saying you were part of some team. I wanted to stick it out, even though you might never remember me. Because you were still *you*, and we were still *us*."

"What changed your mind?"

Wren moved around the chair and sat heavily. "I found out you were a BlackOp. That you'd married me with that massive secret between us. Even then I wanted to stay. Marriage isn't something I take lightly. But if I stayed, only to realize I was being used, I'd never have trusted my own judgment again. I couldn't do that."

To Wren's credit, she had no tears in her eyes, no waver in her voice. She owned up to her choices, and Fallon had to respect that.

Fallon eased around the couch and sat. "I get it, and I don't blame you for your choices. I might have done the same. Probably would have. When I think it through rationally, I totally get it."

"And when you aren't being rational?"

Fallon set her glass on the narrow table between them. She gave Wren a long look, not sure how well she'd handle her answer. But she wasn't going to lie. "I deserved better from my wife. If I'm going to be with someone, I deserve a person whose gut instinct is to cover me, no matter what. Someone who would watch the whole world burn rather than lose me."

Wren sat frozen, her eyes flickering with a half-dozen discarded replies. She wasn't the only one of them who could read the other. Fallon saw everything she felt.

Finally, Wren asked, "Does he feel that way about you?"

Fallon didn't have to think about who she meant, or how Raptor felt. "Yes. But it's different with him. He and I are...raw. Visceral. Like a chemical reaction. A bond that never breaks. But it's not..." Her eyes trailed over the quarters, remembering them again as a place of comfort and warmth. She and Raptor had never walked hand-in-hand on the beach, or had breakfast in bed together.

Wren looked at her wine glass and blinked as if surprised that she still held it. She took a long time setting it on the table before meeting Fallon's eyes again. "It sounds like, between him and me, you have everything you need."

"Maybe. But I married you. You were supposed to be everything all by yourself." Fallon couldn't keep a touch of bitterness out of her voice.

"And you were supposed to be the person you said you were when I married you." Wren's words held no accusation.

Whose wound was worse? Fallon couldn't measure hurt against hurt, and she was tired of trying. "For what it's worth, I'm sorry."

"I'm sorry too. And I'm glad you have him. Someone who'll have your back when you're out there, doing who knows what." Wren was quiet for a long moment, then she bounced to her feet. "I think dinner's ready. Shall we eat?"

"Seriously? You still want to have dinner after all this?"

Wren shrugged as she placed a basket of bread on the table. "The only way through life is by forging through it. Let's just move forward and let whatever happens, happen."

If it meant she could avoid having more talks like this, Fallon was on board.

WHEN FALLON RETURNED to her quarters and climbed into bed, she was as alone as she'd been the previous night. But thinking of Wren and Raptor and how complicated relationships were, she was much more content to be that way.

She'd become a PAC officer because she wanted to serve and to fight. She needed to shake off the other stuff and focus on that.

FALLON WOKE up ready to attack her full schedule. She ran through her normal morning routine, then went down to Docking Bay Five to meet a new arrival. The *Onari* had returned.

Jerin and Brak arrived through the airlock first, followed by Demitri, Kellis, and Trin. After a moment, more friendly faces spilled forth. Dr. Yomalu, Corla and her baby, Ben Brooks, and Endra. And they kept coming. Fallon felt a spark of pleasure at seeing each face that emerged. Most didn't even bother with the bows that protocol indicated. They stepped right in and gave Fallon a hug instead. She found it all overwhelming, but in a good way.

As usual, the boardwalk teemed with activity. The residents of Dragonfire held the crew of the *Onari* in high regard and delighted in their visits.

"How was your trip?" Fallon asked Brak and Jerin as she escorted them down the concourse to their respective quarters.

"Elective procedures on Dineb are always a pleasant experience," Jerin answered. "Not only do we earn a good deal, but some of the crew also get to enjoy some shore leave." As the captain and chief medical officer of the hospi-ship, Jerin took great care in seeing to the needs of her crew.

"Were you working, or living it up on Dineb?" Fallon asked Brak, knowing perfectly well her friend was not likely to pass her leisure time on the party planet.

Brak chuckled, a soft growl of a sound. Fallon smelled the sweet musk of Briveen amusement. "No cybernetics were needed, so I spent the time in my lab. I wouldn't exactly fit in at the Dinebian dance clubs."

The three chuckled. No, a tall, scaled woman would definitely stand out. Not that Dinebians would mind that. Brak would probably have found herself a short-term celebrity. But Fallon couldn't quite imagine Brak breaking out some dance moves among a crowd of strangers.

"So long as you had a good time," she said.

"I did."

Fallon stopped at a door. "These are your quarters, Jerin. Let us know if you need anything."

"I'm sure I won't, but thank you. I'm eager to put on my pajamas and have a good, long sleep."

It was barely midday. The doctor must have been exhausted. She disappeared inside, while Fallon and Brak stopped at the next door.

"And these are yours," Fallon said.

"Thank you for walking with us. You didn't have to."

"I wanted to. It's a pleasure to have you all back."

"It's nice to be back," Brak said. "I'd like to take a brief rest and eat, but I know you're eager for me to give you the medical all clear. Do you want to meet me in the infirmary at the end of your shift? We'll get that examination out of the way."

"I'd love to. I'll let Brannin know to expect us."

"I'm sure he's anticipated our arrival already," Brak said, amused.

"I bet you're right."

The good Dr. Brash was a highly astute fellow. He would know Fallon was eager to get back to pushing her physical limits in the gym.

"I'll see you this evening." Brak entered her quarters and the door closed behind her.

With renewed enthusiasm, Fallon went back to the security office for an afternoon of work.

"JUST RELAX," Brak advised.

There wasn't much else Fallon could do, lying on a techbed. She tried not to fidget, wondering if Brak would give her brain a clean bill of health. Fallon needed to know if her head had healed enough for her to go with her team to make contact with Colb.

She stared up at the ceiling, counting the tiles and making spatial-relations patterns out of them. The great thing about having a fantastic memory was that she had a lot inside her head to keep her entertained during times of boredom, such as this. That didn't keep her from feeling itchy with anticipation though. She was far better at action than being still.

"One more thing," Brak said, sounding distracted. After a couple more minutes she said, "There we go. You can sit up."

Brannin stood alongside Fallon in case she needed assistance, but she didn't. He smiled at her encouragingly, clearly knowing that waiting for Brak's pronouncement had her on edge.

"By every measure I can conjure, you are in perfect health." Brak pulled her lips into a smile.

"No issues you foresee with the inducer?"

"It's doing everything I'd hoped it would. You'll still need to get regular checks—monthly, ideally—and let me know immediately if you have any confusion or issues with your memory. But otherwise, you're cleared for duty, as well as all physical activity. Though I'd recommend against blows to the head, of course. But that's pretty standard advice for all my patients."

Fallon and Brannin smiled.

"I'll do my best," she promised.

"I think this calls for a celebration," Brannin said. "Would you two care to join me for dinner? I'm technically off shift."

"That would be great," Brak said, "but I have plans with Kellis, Jerin, and Trin already. Why don't you two join us?"

"That sounds perfect," Brannin said. He looked to Fallon, questioningly.

"Absolutely. When are you supposed to meet them?"

"Now. They'll be having drinks already."

A drink sounded good to her. "Great. I'll buy the first round."

"I've never been much of a drinker," Brannin admitted.

"Oh, well that's perfect. This is absolutely the right night to start."

They laughed as they left the infirmary.

"WHAT A LOVELY SURPRISE," Jerin said as Brannin sat next to her. Fortunately, they'd chosen a large table in the back of the room that easily accommodated two extras.

Brak and Fallon sat, with Fallon next to Kellis and Brak on Jerin's other side.

Fallon enjoyed the meal. Not only did she have good news for her team when they returned, she also had an opportunity to catch up with her friends.

She'd never seen Brannin so relaxed and engaged in a social setting. She recalled him hovering around the edges of such gatherings, cordial, but slightly formal. He seemed more confident, more animated. Happier. He and Jerin talked most of the evening, often quietly having side conversations while the rest of the group discussed something else.

All in all, it was a lovely evening.

But Fallon couldn't wait for her team to return so they could move their plan forward.

BRAK JOINED Fallon for a run the next morning. Despite not being able to exercise for the past two weeks, Fallon kept up with Brak as they ran around the track above the gym. Brak made her work for it though. As always.

"So your team will be back in a day or two?" Brak wasn't even winded. She simply looked fantastic, with her strong body and her iridescent scales.

Fallon was sure she did not look fantastic. She was soaked with sweat and probably red-faced. "Yes."

"Can I assume that whenever they get done with whatever they're doing, you have plans to do things I shouldn't know about?"

"Fair assessment," Fallon agreed.

"Ah." Brak said no more, and Fallon appreciated her discretion.

"I do have plans that involve the *Onari*, though. I'd like to talk to you, Jerin, and Kellis privately at some point today." It took some effort to spare enough of her lung power to get such a long sentence out.

"Ahhh." This time, Brak sounded satisfied. "I can coordinate that, if you like."

"That'd be great."

"Okay. Are you ready to get serious about this run?"

Fallon wondered how much more serious they could get, but she wasn't one to pass up a challenge. "Let's go."

FALLON INVITED her friends from the *Onari* to her quarters. Once they'd settled in the sitting area, she launched right in. She looked from Jerin to Brak to Kellis as she talked.

"You know that I'm working an off-the-books mission. I'm also pretty sure you know that I'm working directly against all official and unofficial PAC departments."

She saw no flickers of surprise. She continued, "Anyone who wants to know nothing more of this should say so now."

Silence.

"Okay." She forged ahead. "Anyone who doesn't want to get involved with espionage and, possibly, treason, should say so now."

Still not a peep.

"Really? I'm talking about some bad shit here, and once you know about it, there's no not knowing it. You'll be in, whether you like it or not."

Kellis spoke up. "Could you move on? We didn't have you on our ship for months because we thought you were selling muffins." She glanced at Jerin and her cheeks grew pink.

Jerin waved a hand at Kellis. "You said what we're all thinking."

Fallon took a breath, preparing to say words that no BlackOp ever did. "My team and I, as you may have suspected, are part of Blackout. Someone corrupt has taken it over, and we're trying to take control. If we don't, every treaty the PAC has ever signed will be publicly broken, and we'll be embroiled in war for decades to come."

She gave them a moment to process that, then dropped another bomb on them. "We're setting up a rebellion, right here on Dragonfire. And we want the *Onari* to be part of it. I want you to make Dragonfire your home port. I'll ensure that you're properly funded, and in return, you'll be our allies and, perhaps, run missions for us."

"What could we do to help? You already have a top-notch infirmary and CMO here on the station," Jerin said.

"We do," Fallon acknowledged. "But we need Brak. Whatever Krazinski is planning, it involves the kind of dangerous technology that blew a chunk out of my brain. I need her, ready and able to analyze any data, or any medical technology I discover. Possibly to look after other test subjects, if we find them." She shifted her gaze to Kellis. "Kellis has already expressed a strong desire to be of help, because of her abhorrence for corruption and the suffering it causes. She brings technological and mechanical expertise that could be invaluable to us."

Kellis nodded.

"And me?" asked Jerin. "What do I have to offer?"

Fallon smiled. "To be honest, I'm not sure. Yet. The *Onari* is a heck of a ship though, with a heck of a crew, and I need all the allies I can get."

"Fair enough." Jerin looked satisfied. "Who all is in on this?"

"My team, including Ross. Nevitt. Arin and Endra know something's up, but none of what I've told you here. Wren knows I'm a BlackOp, but little else."

"That's it?" Jerin's eyebrows arched high. "That's a pretty small rebellion."

"I guess I'm conservative when it comes to gambling with people's lives," Fallon returned dryly. "I'd like to bring Arin in, but I'm not certain he'd want to be involved, and once I reveal the situation, I can't just let him say 'no, thank you,' and go on about his life."

"What if we'd declined?" Jerin asked.

"I didn't think you would. But if you had, I'd have had to kill you," Fallon deadpanned. When no one laughed, she added, "I'm kidding."

Kellis and Jerin looked unimpressed with her humor, while Brak remained unaffected.

"Tough room." Fallon shrugged. "My team would have found that hilarious."

"I guess I'll have to work on finding death threats amusing, given the people I'll be working with," Jerin noted.

"You'll get the hang of it," Fallon assured her. This time, Jerin and Kellis both looked mildly amused. It wasn't the reaction she'd have gotten from Peregrine, Hawk, and Raptor, but she had hope for these three.

FALLON RELATED the conversation she'd had with Jerin, Kellis, and Brak to Nevitt, then returned to her quarters. Once her team made it back from Zerellus, she'd arrange a meeting with all her allies. Her entire rebellion, together in one room. She couldn't wait.

She enjoyed a long, steamy hydro-shower, standing under the water for far longer than necessary. As she dried off, she traced the tattoo on her stomach, hoping her teammates would return soon.

With her brain officially certified as ready for service, she finally felt like she had what she needed to take over Blackout. She still required the intel to make it all happen, but she'd get that. She was no longer the pawn in Krazinski's game. She wasn't even a mere king. She owned the entire chessboard.

It was hubris to think that way. She knew that. But people like her needed an excessive ego to be able to do their jobs. Fallon wasn't too good to let some healthy self-aggrandizement ease her way.

As she got into bed she smiled, thinking about how much ass Avian Unit would soon kick.

Fallon leaped to her feet almost as fast as her eyes opened, then froze, listening for whatever had woken her.

She touched the back of her waistband, making sure her knife was in place. Creeping toward the doorway, she stayed right outside its sensor range. Waiting.

The door opened and she raised her fists, prepared to take down her opponent by any means necessary.

"Relax," a familiar voice said. "How about you don't attack me this time?"

"Lights!" she called, even as Raptor snaked an arm around her waist and pressed against her. "How about you don't sneak up on me when I'm sleeping?"

"But it's fun," he argued.

He was right. She loved the feeling of the adrenaline zinging through her. And she was glad to see him. But she scowled at him anyway.

He grinned. "Miss me?"

"No."

"Good. I didn't miss you, either." His other arm came around her and they leaned into each other. She let his warmth soak into her.

"Where are Peregrine and Hawk?"

His arms rubbed against her sides as he shrugged. "Off to the pub, I think."

"What about the mission debriefing?"

"It's the middle of the night. They thought they'd let you sleep."

"I guess you didn't tell them you were planning to wake me up anyway."

His smile was wicked. "Nope."

"Can you at least tell me if the mission was successful? You're back awfully fast."

"Completely successful."

"Good." She studied his expression, part playful, part intense. He seemed happy. "So this is an ongoing thing between us?" She hadn't been certain of their relationship protocol when they boarded Dragonfire, and they hadn't discussed it in the meantime.

He looked down at her, suddenly serious. "You were the one who decided to change the parameters of our relationship when we were on the *Nefarious*." He dropped his arms, stepping back. "I guess you've changed your mind, now that you have your memories back?"

Without giving her a chance to answer, he launched into a stream of profanity that would have made Hawk proud, then spun on his heel and strode out the door of her bedroom. "I should have expected that. You've always run away from me," he called back as he walked through the common area to the exit. "You know what? Fuck you. I'm done."

The doors to her bedroom closed in her face.

"Security override," Fallon barked, then gave her code to the computer.

The doors whisked open and she charged in. Electricity streaked down her spine and through her limbs. She was more than ready to fight.

Two surprised faces turned toward her.

"Fuck *me*?" she hissed at Raptor as she stepped in close to him. "Fuck *you*. I ask one question and you storm out on me? Bullshit."

She glanced at Ross, who looked surprised but entertained. "Excuse us." She skewered Raptor with a look and stalked to the nearest bedroom.

"That's Hawk's." Raptor didn't earn himself any points with his dry observation.

"Fine!" She stomped to the second bedroom and went in. She stood, arms crossed, waiting for him to follow.

When the doors closed behind him, she launched her assault. "You—"

"I'm sorry."

"What?" She searched his face, but his expression was as soft as his voice.

"I thought you were going to blow me off again," he explained. "I guess I was more worried about that than I realized. I'm sorry."

She'd been ready for a fight, and now he wasn't cooperating. The man was impossible. "How do you know I'm *not* blowing you off?"

His whole face lit with amusement. "You didn't chase me

down and misuse your security override to tell me you want to be just friends."

"Prelin's ass! Stop being right."

He laughed. "I really pissed you off, didn't I?" He stepped closer.

She scowled at him.

"Good."

"How is that good?" she snapped.

"It means that I finally matter to you."

"You've always—"

"Kind of. As long as it didn't get in the way of our job."

Her irritation burned off. He wasn't wrong. "I thought you felt the same about it."

"I did. I mean, not at the very first. But then we were together, as partners and sometimes more, and that worked. I was good with it being that way."

"Then I went and changed things on the *Nefarious*, after I got burned."

"Yeah," he agreed. "You started it. Changed us." He rubbed his ear and stared past her to the wall. "When you lost your memory, it was like a reset. You didn't remember us. I figured maybe that was better, so I told you as little as possible. But there was still a spark between us. And you wanted to actually be with me—for real, not as stress relief after a near miss. I started thinking about it as a real possibility."

"It was never just stress relief," she told him. "It was more like, when the chips were down, all the stuff about not being together didn't matter."

His expression softened. "I know."

She sat on his bed. "In my quarters a minute ago, I was only trying to clarify. We'd never talked—"

"Like I said, I jumped to a conclusion. I was wrong. But I've already said 'I'm sorry' twice now, and I'm not doing it again." He sat next to her with a teasing smile.

"Okay. So where does this leave us?"

He leaned in and kissed her neck, right over her carotid artery. "No idea." His hair brushed against her ear and she could smell its familiar scent—unchanged after all these years.

She ignored it. She had to be entirely clear with him. "I'm still involved with Wren. I think. I mean, since we've been back she and I haven't..." Yeah, there was no good way to finish that sentence. "But she and I aren't finished. There's still something there."

"I know. But would you be here right now if you'd never married her?"

She had to think about that for a minute. Being with Wren had opened her up to possibilities she'd never considered. "No."

He moved closer and kissed the corner of her mouth. "Exactly. So I don't care."

"Maybe you don't care tonight. But maybe you will tomorrow."

He covered her hands with his. "I've had plenty of time to think this through. There will never be anyone but you for me. And I know you'll never share what you and I have with anyone else either. So if she's the adapter that makes the two of us fit, I'm good with that."

"What about monogamy?" she asked. "I was raised to think it matters."

He curled his fingers around her hands. "So don't pick up any stray lovers and you can be monogamous with both of us."

She laughed. "That's not how it works."

He slid his hands up her forearms. "It does if it works for us."

She sighed. "This love stuff is foolish and messy. There's a reason I wanted to keep it professional."

"Yes, I know." He leaned in close to whisper in her ear. "Also, ha ha. You said 'love.'"

Dammit. He was right. But she felt strange about the idea. She didn't want to be less than loyal to Raptor or Wren. "What if you change your mind?"

"I won't. So shut up." He shifted so his lips were a breath from hers.

She shut up.

SHE WOKE up alone in Raptor's room. After a quick shower she put her clothes back on so she didn't have to run them through the processor. They were lounge clothes, but she'd dash back to her own quarters and get dressed. Nobody would see.

But when she stepped out of the room, her team had already assembled in the sitting area. Hawk, Peregrine, and Ross glanced at her from seated positions without pausing their conversation.

Fallon turned her back on them to look toward Raptor in the kitchenette. She tried to send him a message with her eyes. *No one is surprised by this?*

He arched an eyebrow at her.

Of course they'd figured it out. They were intelligence operatives, for Prelin's sake. They'd simply been minding their own business all these months.

She saw Raptor silently laughing at her as he approached and handed her a cup of hot tea. "Here."

"Thanks." She sat with the others. "It's good to have you back."

Hawk winked at her. "We missed you too, kid. Wasn't the same without you."

"What did you find?" She sipped her tea.

"Everything we needed," Peregrine answered. "It was almost too easy."

"'Too easy' as in 'it must be a trap'?"

"I don't think so." Raptor had taken a seat on the couch. "It's just that Colb is staying in plain sight, behind several layers of security. It wasn't hard for us to get a good look at it all to see exactly what we were dealing with. I mean, it would have been impossible for your average Joe, but we knew what we were looking for."

"Right." Colb had such a high profile that if anything happened to him, it would immediately be noticed and featured on every news cycle. He probably had some provisions in place as well, as security against being kidnapped by Blackout. Certain documents and statements, probably, that would be released in the event of his capture. It was what Fallon would have done, and what Blackout would expect.

"So we can get in to see him?" Fallon asked. "Without Blackout seeing us do it?"

"I'm still working out a few details," Raptor said. "But yes."

"Anything happen on Dragonfire while we were gone?" Hawk asked.

"Yes. Brak approved me for physical activity and I've recruited the *Onari*. Jerin, Brak, and Kellis are with us."

"Wow," Hawk said. "That's quite a development."

Peregrine nodded. "That's great."

Raptor only smiled. Was he smiling at her more than usual, or the regular amount? She frowned at him, but that only made him grin outright.

"So when do we go see Colb?" she asked.

"I should know later today," Raptor answered.

"Good." She sipped her tea. "Anything else to report?"

They shook their heads.

"In that case..." She set her cup on the table and stood. "I'm going to get dressed and start my day. Some of us have to work for a living." She smiled at their pretend outrage before slipping out the door. "Keep me posted."

4

She did her job, and her team did theirs. By the time her duty shift ended, Avian Unit had a plan to acquire Admiral Colb. It was about damn time.

"Will we need any additional gear?" she asked after they'd outlined their plan in her quarters.

"No. We're set," Hawk said.

"Okay. I'll update the captain on our plans and let Arin know that he's in charge of security while I'm gone. Anything else?" When no one spoke up, she said, "Good. I'll see you all at the docking bay in the morning."

Peregrine said goodnight and made her escape. She probably had a date.

Ross and Raptor left together, but invited her along for some dinner.

"No, but thanks." She appreciated the offer.

Hawk was last to leave. "Meet me at the pub in an hour," he said as he stood.

"What? Why waste an evening on me when there's a whole station full of people you haven't seen naked?"

He gave her knee a light slap as he went by on his way to the door. "Hardly wasted on my favorite drinking buddy. It's been too long since we had a drink together."

He was right. It had been a couple months, at least. "Okay, but you're buying."

"Sure."

"And I haven't had dinner, so you can buy me that too."

He rubbed his beard. "So long as you eat it at the bar, fine by me."

"See you in an hour, then."

FALLON WAS HALFWAY through her ale when Hawk finally said, "Sooo..."

"Nope. Uh-uh."

"What?" He feigned innocence so well that she could almost believe it.

She fixed him with a frosty look. "I know what you're after. I already had to have a 'feelings' conversation with Wren, and then another with Raptor. I am not doing it again with you."

"Didn't say you had to."

"Good. Because I won't." She tipped the rim of her glass at him to make her point.

"Good. I hate that stuff." Hawk finished his drink and punched in an order for another, since they were at a table rather than sitting at the bar. He'd made only a token complaint about that because the bar had been full. "Feelings. Bleh." He wore a look of disgust, which made her smile.

He waited a full minute until he said, "Although..."

She pointed at him in warning.

He chuckled. "You told each of them about the other, right?"

"Of course. They're both *fine* with it."

"Sounds like you aren't fine with them being fine. Are you mad they aren't jealous, or something? That each of them knows what they want, and it doesn't involve the need to be your one and only?"

"No!" She bristled. He made her sound childish when she was only trying to be ethical.

His drink arrived and he began pouring it down his throat. He banged the glass down and wiped his mouth with the back of his hand. "I don't see your problem. You can relax and have a good time."

"It's not about a good time."

"Maybe it should be. You've been way too serious the whole time I've known you. Probably before I knew you, too. Why shouldn't you just enjoy yourself, for once in your life? Especially when we're talking about two people who love you, and aren't making demands on you? You're one lucky asshole, and you don't know it."

She frowned at him. "I'm ordering food now." She requested a variety of finger foods, then on second thought, doubled the order. Otherwise, Hawk would end up eating all her food.

"Give it some thought, will you?"

"Fine. I'll think." She added a dessert to her order. A big chocolate cake-pudding-pie thing that sounded both awful and awesome.

"That's all I'm saying."

She studied him. "Okay. You're right about me being driven, at least. I was always that way, even as a kid. Fortunately I had a good family—still have a good family. They helped me channel my energy into something positive." He had met her parents when they raided the Tokyo PAC base.

"But what about you? You grew up hard, didn't you?" she asked, shifting the attention to him. She was sick of talking about herself.

He heaved a huge sigh, followed by a long pause that made her think he wouldn't answer. Finally he said, "Yeah. Very hard.

Tell you what. If we live through this thing we're doing now, I'll fill you in. But not tonight. Deal?"

"Deal. But if you want dessert, you need to order your own."

"I don't need any sweets."

"Fine, but I'm serious. You're not eating mine." She gave him a threatening look.

He smiled.

Their food arrived as they finished their drinks, chatting about pleasantly impersonal things. As much as she preferred that, she felt she needed to be sure that Avian Unit wouldn't change, in light of recent events.

"So," she ventured, "you don't have a problem with Raptor and me?"

"No. Never did. It was you two who were up your own asses about it."

She laughed in surprise. "What about the whole complicating-the-team thing?"

"That's the company line, but how's it any different, really? We all look out for each other. Blood and bone. Whether you and Raptor bury your feelings for each other or not."

She had no answer for that. "What does Peregrine think about it?"

He squinted at her. "If Per thought she had a shot at Raptor, she'd damn near throw you out an airlock. Since she knows she doesn't, then yeah. Pretty much the same as what I think."

Fallon laughed again, relieved.

The food arrived and they dug in while enjoying their drinks. When her dessert finally was set in front of her, Fallon gazed at it in amazement. The thing was a good thirty centimeters high.

"Guess you won't mind if I have a bite after all." Hawk's fork began a trajectory toward her plate.

"Back off, lumberjack. Get your own."

"You're kidding. You can't eat that whole thing on top of what you've already had." He looked from her to the dessert and back again, as if calculating which one would win in a fight.

"Bet me."

"You're on. Loser has to moon the Briveen restaurant."

"No. Those poor people are eating mandren. They don't need to be forced to look at your hairy ass, too. Besides, I work here. Try again," she ordered.

"They'd be lucky to see my ass," he grumbled. "Not that I'm going to lose. But fine. Loser has to go to that trader's shop and buy the worst thing the winner can find, then present it to Captain Nevitt as a gift."

She laughed long and loud. "It's a bet."

In the end, she ate the dessert, no one had to see Hawk's ass, and she'd get a good laugh at some future date.

It was a good night.

WHEN FALLON WOKE, there was a face centimeters from hers. Since she had gone to bed alone, she immediately tried to punch it.

Raptor caught her fist. "Easy, Chief."

"You seriously have to stop sneaking into my room."

"But it's fun." He flopped back onto the bed and tried to snuggle up to her, but she was already sitting up and hitting the light panel.

"For you."

"That's why I do it. Besides, the Ghost has to keep his skills shiny, right?" When she glared at him, he added, "Fine. I just wanted to see you for a few minutes, privately, before we left. Once we have Colb, shit is going to come at us fast and hard. I wanted a chance to exist in the same space together before all that happens."

That was actually kind of sweet, but she wasn't sure how she felt about sweetness from Raptor. It was...different.

They stared at each other.

"So this is weird." His eyes crinkled at the corners, but she saw uncharacteristic uncertainty in him.

"Very." She smoothed nonexistent wrinkles out of the blanket.

He bumped her shoulder gently with his fist. "We'll figure it out."

"Yeah?"

"Sure." His humor was back full force. "Assuming we don't die in the coming days. But then, if we do die, we don't *have* to figure it out. So, you know. Silver linings."

She snorted and got up, headed for the necessary. "Thanks for the pep talk."

"Anytime, Chief."

She paused. "You seem to have switched to calling me that rather than Fury. I noticed the others have too."

"Have I?"

"Yes," she affirmed.

"I guess I like it better. It fits you."

"I think so too."

She stepped toward the necessary, but paused again. "Do you need to shower?" She lifted a provocative eyebrow.

He was on his feet immediately. *"Yes."*

The awkwardness between them disappeared. This was the part they did well.

IT WAS GO TIME. Fallon sat in the pilot's chair of the *Nefarious*, pointed toward Zerellus and glad to be alive. The thrill of flight and the mission ahead made her feel like a supernova. She'd been waiting so long for this. The first real step in taking over Blackout.

"She's got that look again." Next to her, Hawk wore a long-suffering expression.

"What look?" Fallon demanded.

"Like you're going to eat planets and shoot laserbeams out of your eyeballs." He added, "Freaks me out."

She grinned at him. The idea of freaking out that mountain of a man was laughable.

"What freaks you out?" Ross stepped onto the bridge.

"Spiders. Soap. Very small rocks." She pinched her index finger and thumb together.

"Well, who isn't afraid of spiders?" Ross stood between her and Hawk.

She smiled. Ross fit in well with her team. He seemed much more relaxed now. Maybe he appreciated the chance to get the job done as much as she did.

"What can we do for you?" she asked. She'd expected him to be in the ship's mess hall, playing card games with Raptor and Peregrine.

"Thought I'd take a shift up here. No need for you to be glued to the bridge. It'll take us almost two days to get there."

"That's thoughtful. I'll pull up a shift schedule. You can start the next shift in two hours, but I'm fine for now. Glad for the chance to fly, actually."

"Gotcha. I guess I'll go take a nap so I can be fresh for my shift."

"You're not too keyed up to sleep?" Fallon was, at the moment.

Ross grinned, reminding her of the roguish instructor she'd once known. "It's the benefit of age. I've had a lot of experience taking things one step at a time."

"I'll see you in two hours, then."

After he left, Hawk stood, stretching his arms. "I'm going to give his wisdom thing a try and see if I can sleep for a while."

"I've always said you could use some wisdom."

He lightly bopped her on the head on his way out. That left her staring out into space, flying them toward their goal.

Which was how she liked it.

A DAY AND A HALF LATER, they made it to Zerellus.

As soon as the airlock to the docking station opened, Avian Unit pushed through it. They rode the orbital elevator down to the planet's surface, primed and eager.

All five wore a backpack, carefully filled with the items they'd need. Raptor had planned this maneuver in intricate detail. Since Ross had no transmitter tattoo, he'd stick with another team member at all times.

Wearing casual clothes, they followed Peregrine's lead. Since she was a native Zerellian, it made perfect sense for her to bring a group of friends to her home planet. They chatted casually through the transport station and during their taxi ride, with Peregrine telling them about the planet as if none of them had ever been there.

As they neared their destination, Peregrine promised, "You're going to love this restaurant. Best rastor dumplings in the quadrant."

"Ugh," Fallon said. "Maybe I should wait outside." The stench of them seemed to fill the air already.

"In the dark?" Peregrine teased. "No way. Seriously though, don't worry. They make plenty of other things."

"If you say so."

Peregrine paid their driver, and they stepped out in front of the Blue Elephant restaurant. "Ready?" she asked. When the rest of them nodded, she said, "You're on, Raptor."

Their jovial façade faded as he led them into the restaurant. They nodded to the hostess and walked past the main dining area, toward the wing where VIPs entertained private parties. They followed the hallway, turned left, followed another long hallway, and entered the last room.

Fallon's attention went to a long table, already laden with food. Mashed root vegetables covered in heavy sauce, glistening cuts of juicy meat, and thick slabs of bread beckoned. The mix of aromas almost made her hungry, even filled as she was with anticipation for the job they were here to do.

She had to give the Zerellians credit. They knew how to cater a private party with a lot of money to spend. Raptor had indicated their impending arrival, and the meal had been laid out in style. Most importantly, no staff would return to the room until summoned.

"Sure we can't take a few minutes to eat first?" Hawk joked.

"Later," Raptor snapped, all business. "Any questions?" When there were none, he touched a microcomputer on his wrist. "I've deactivated the door sensor. Let's go."

They stripped off their outer clothes, revealing the sleek black jumpsuits beneath. Raptor then led them out the back of the room, where they dashed across the barren courtyard behind the building. There, they scaled a three-meter-high wall and dropped behind an outbuilding at the rear of a personal estate.

Raptor glanced at his wrist, then nodded at Fallon.

Under the cover of the outbuilding, Fallon lowered her backpack to the ground and sat next to it. In seconds, she'd extracted a hand-sized dark-gray drone, its controls, and two VR headsets. She handed one to Raptor and put the other on her own head.

With the tiniest movement of her fingers, she launched the drone and it immediately became invisible. Even in daylight it would have been hard to spot.

Via the headset, the drone's perspective filled her vision as she flew it around the estate. She saw the outbuilding and her team, as well as the top of her own head, then zoomed off to canvas the entire area. She noted two guards and a security camera at every entrance. Every window also had a camera. Seated next to her, Raptor saw everything she did through the second pair of goggles.

She took him on a tour of every feature of the place. She kept her altitude low, to avoid tripping any passive detection. Most planets had such systems, but an able pilot with the latest technology would always be ahead of them.

She felt a hand press her thigh. Raptor had what he needed. She brought the drone back, landed it, and removed her VR gear.

Raptor had already taken his off. He made a series of gestures, instructing Hawk to follow him and Peregrine to lead Ross and Fallon two minutes behind.

By the time the second group arrived, Raptor and Hawk had taken out the two guards, opened the door, and dragged the pair inside. Ross and Peregrine stripped the guards of their uniforms and put them on over their jumpsuits. They took special care of the guards' comports, which would no doubt send an alarm if they were out of position for much longer. Then they took the guards' places at the door.

Fallon trailed Raptor while Hawk followed on her heels as they rushed down the hallway, careful not to make noise on the black-and-white tiled floor.

From here, Raptor would be working from blueprints of the building that had been filed with the housing commission when it was built. If any unreported restructuring had happened since, Avian Unit could be in trouble. But Raptor led them decisively down one hall, took a left, then stopped at a security breakstop—a solid metal wall that was vacuum sealed and locked. To get to Colb, Raptor had to find a way past it. He gestured for Fallon and Hawk to cover him while he worked at the electronic mechanism.

The moment Fallon started to worry, she heard a soft beep and a *woomph* as the seal broke. The wall retracted to the side.

"Here we go." Raptor opened the door behind the breakstop.

They rushed in, ready to take on however many dozens of

guards Colb had, only to stop short when they saw the man himself, standing in the middle of the room. Smiling.

"Greetings, my young friends," Colb said, bowing to them as a teacher would to a student. Or a parent to a child. "I'm glad you've finally made it."

THEY SEARCHED the place to be sure it wasn't a trap. But there was no one there pulling Colb's strings. A message to Peregrine and Hawk had them arriving a few minutes later, looking wary. Fallon felt the same.

"Ah." Colb bowed to them, and they returned the bow. "Now we can begin. Shall we sit?" He indicated a traditional tea table.

The members of Avian Unit exchanged uneasy looks.

"You're wondering why I didn't simply summon you, right?" He looked from one face to another. "Well, I'll be honest. I didn't know exactly who I was waiting for. I'd hoped that *someone* would figure out what Krazinski was up to. But until someone came looking for me, I couldn't know who was in his pocket and who wasn't." He looked directly at Fallon. "I'm glad it was you."

"How do you know we're not here to capture you for him?" Peregrine asked.

"Because he wouldn't want you to, if you were working for him. He'd want to keep me right here, frozen in a prison of my own making, unsure of who I can trust."

Fallon searched his elderly, familiar face as he talked. He was only a little older than her father, but time and the loss of Colb's wife had taken a great toll on him. She saw nothing that indicated insincerity though. He looked just as he had when he'd read her stories when she was a little girl.

"Is that why your security was so easy to break?" Raptor asked.

"Well, it was enough to keep out the looky loos," Colb answered. "But I needed you to be able to get in."

"Hell of a risk," Hawk noted. Clearly, he'd dispensed with proper protocol for addressing a senior officer.

Colb smiled, ignoring the breach. "Not really. You were my last hope. If it turned out I truly had no allies, then I might as well meet the wrong end of a stinger. At least that would raise questions."

Fallon exchanged a look with her team. His story made sense. But could they trust him?

"I understand that you're skeptical. But I have data. Proof. I can show that Krazinski's been involved in treasonous deals for over two years now. He squeezed me out because I tried to stop him. I wasn't fast enough to maneuver him out before he did it to me." He slapped the edge of the table, his cheeks red.

"We have data too," Fallon said. If Colb couldn't give them more than that, he wouldn't be very useful to them. "The trouble is that we don't know who we can trust at PAC command. We don't know how many people he controls. Jamestown Station might be teeming with people loyal to him."

Colb nodded. "I have some suggestions. So let's talk about how we're going to get this done."

Fallon sent a questioning glance at her team members, but saw agreement in their eyes. They'd needed an ally of his stature, someone who still had ties within the bureaucracy, and now they had one.

"Okay," she said. "What's next?"

THEY TABLED the discussion until they could get Colb up to the *Nefarious*.

They covertly returned to the restaurant. After putting street clothes over their jumpsuits, they ate enough of the rapidly cooling food to make it appear as if a dinner party had taken place. Hawk did the majority of the eating, while Peregrine disguised Colb for the trip back to the *Nefarious*.

Once on board the ship, they spent the next three hours talking, first suggesting tactics, then hacking them all apart. Finally, exhausted, Hawk suggested they get some sleep. They'd start on their way back to Dragonfire after they rested.

In her quarters, Fallon got dressed for bed, but only stood staring at her bunk. It didn't look inviting.

Instead she went next door to Raptor's berth and touched the chime.

"Thought you were tired." He looked like she might have woken him, but he moved back so she could enter.

"I'm practically asleep right now." She eyed his narrow bunk. "Mind if I sleep here?" She willed him not to make a big deal about it.

"Sure. But I get the wall side. If someone's falling out, it'll be you."

She smiled. "It's happened before."

"That's why I want the wall side."

He sat on the bed, and she waited for him to lie down before she hit the light panel and squeezed in next to him. "Goodnight."

"Night," he answered, his voice rough with fatigue.

Despite her own tiredness, she listened to his slow, even breathing for several minutes before closing her eyes.

FALLON TOOK the first flight shift, to be sure they got properly under way and because she was somewhat domineering about the pilot's chair. Afterward, she was glad for a chance to sit down with Colb in his quarters and get reacquainted.

"You've been well?" she asked, seated across from him. He

looked healthy enough, albeit weathered, for a man of his age. Andra's death three years earlier had taken such a toll on him.

"So they tell me." His smile brought back images of her childhood. He and Andra had shared many meals at the Kato household. Her mother had enjoyed hosting them, and afterward, Colb was always happy to play whatever game Fallon suggested. His own children had been a good deal older, and he'd seemed to have a particular fondness for young Kiyoko, as he'd known her then. He'd been so close to the family that he'd called her Kiyoko-chan, just as her mother and father did.

His fondness for her hadn't changed as she'd aged. He'd been the one to sponsor her application to the PAC academy. Perhaps he'd even put her name in front of the people who ran Blackout, though he'd never hinted at such.

He and Andra had been like family—a favorite aunt and uncle. Even now, seeing him without her honorary aunt seemed strange to her.

"How are Rolly and Jenna?"

He smiled ruefully. "Oh, you know how it is with grown children. They go off to this galaxy or that and you end up hearing from them only on odd occasions. But last I talked to them, they were both busy and happy. Jenna had a second baby and Rolly still hasn't settled down."

Fallon nodded. She'd never known his children well. They'd been adults by the time it had occurred to her to wonder about them.

"I imagine it's hard to have your kids so far away," she said.

"Yes, but they're happy, and that's what matters." He gave her a knowing look. "No doubt your parents were thrilled to see you."

She chuckled. "That hardly describes it, but yes. I hadn't been home for a long time." When she'd visited a few months ago, her parents had been strangers to her. Now that she'd recovered her memories, she wanted a real visit with them. She knew that her near future had no trip to Earth in it, but maybe her parents could come visit her.

"I imagine they were beside themselves." Colb folded his hands over his knee. "I've never seen parents as proud of their child as they've always been of you. And your brother, of course," he added quickly.

"Kano was always the more easygoing of the two of us," she admitted.

"Still quite the achiever, though."

She gave him a small, seated bow in acknowledgement of the compliment to her brother.

He waved his hand. "No need to be formal with me. I knew you when your mother still put your hair in pigtails."

She let out a long sigh. "How did it all come to this? Fighting the very thing we've always wanted to be a part of."

Sadness washed over his face. "I've spent a lot of time wondering that, myself. Some people don't recognize what they have. It makes them blind to the tiny changes that lead to disaster. When they finally realize what's coming, it's too late."

"What did Krazinski miss?" Fallon leaned forward, watching him intently.

"The fact that the galaxies are always changing. Power is always shifting. We have to keep ourselves informed, so that we have time to adapt. I think John was complacent for too long, and when he realized the PAC was losing its authority, he panicked. Turned to illegal methods."

"How were we losing authority? I never heard anything about that."

Colb frowned. "Of course not. The only thing worse than losing a political advantage is advertising that the advantage has been lost. The entire power dynamic would shift. Planets would reconsider their allegiances."

"So what was happening?"

"Neighboring galaxies were infringing on our sovereignty.

Nothing major, but they were pushing at their limits. Seeing how close they could get to breaking a treaty. They knew we would tolerate more than we should, for fear of touching off a war. And that put us on the defensive. In the weaker position."

"How do we put a stop to that?"

Colb's face hardened. "We have to draw a harder line. Punish infractions. Even push back if we must. Being tolerant of incursions on our sovereignty makes rivals think we're an easy mark."

"Sounds like that will be our first order of business once we get Krazinski out," Fallon agreed.

"It's imperative, if we don't want the PAC to fall."

"So how do you suggest we get him out?"

Colb tilted his head. "Shouldn't we bring your team in to discuss this together?"

"I'll fill them in. I'm the team leader. They'll follow my lead."

Colb smiled at her. "That's my girl." He rubbed his palms together gently. "You know, in some ways, you are more like a daughter to me than my own Jenna. I love her dearly, don't get me wrong, but I don't understand her art. You, though, were always what I imagined my child would be like."

"I'm flattered. You've always been family, as far as I'm concerned. So let's talk strategy."

For the next hour, she picked Colb's brain on the inner workings of Blackout bureaucracy and how they could take control.

She wished she could call a team meeting as soon as she left his quarters, but she'd have to wait.

Finally, after Colb retired for the night, she called Avian Unit, including Ross, up to the bridge. As they gathered around, she studied their faces.

She regretted what she had to tell them. "We have a problem."

"I'VE KNOWN Masumi Colb all my life. He's practically family to me. But he's lying." Fallon paused for a moment to let her team digest that fact. "I've come to the conclusion that he's working with Krazinski to bring us in."

A heavy silence fell as her team worked that idea through.

"How do you know?" Hawk's mouth set in a grim line.

"He knew that I've been to see my parents. I didn't mention that, and my parents wouldn't either. He thinks that I assume they would, but I know better."

"So Blackout knows we saw your parents when we were on Earth." Peregrine's typical frown had deepened into something much more grave.

"Apparently. And Krazinski and Colb set up a plan to make Colb look like a potential ally because they assumed I'd trust Uncle Masumi."

Raptor scowled. "We took that bait, and now here we are, being led into the dragon's mouth."

"Pretty much," Fallon agreed.

"So what do we do?" Hawk shifted restlessly. "Confront him now and force the truth out of him?"

Ross spoke up. "We have the splitter I brought in Fallon's vault on Dragonfire. We could take the answers if he doesn't offer them."

Fallon had thought of that. She'd been forced to decide whether to commit an atrocity for the safety of her galaxy. As a Blackout operative, if she'd been ordered to use illegal tech that amounted to torture, she'd have done her job like a good little soldier. But she no longer had the luxury of relying on others to determine what lines must be crossed for the greater good.

"No. We will not."

Her teammates' faces registered relief.

"What, then?" Hawk asked.

"Krazinski and Colb have a plan for us. Let's find out what it is. We'll play the part that they would have us play."

A shadow of a smile flitted over Peregrine's mouth. "They'll think they have us where they want us, and we'll flip it all right around on them."

"Exactly," agreed Fallon.

"We'll have to lock him down pretty hard," Raptor mused. "Here, and especially on Dragonfire. Without him realizing we're doing it. Monitor his transmissions, make sure he isn't calling an attack on us or transmitting information about our activities or access to the station's systems."

She'd had time to think about that, too. "We'll dummy up the station's records and status. Anything he accesses will be what we want him to see. The real details will be under such tight security even the rest of the Dragonfire crew won't have it."

Hawk whistled. "Think Nevitt will agree to that? That's going to impact her ability to do her job. And if there's an attack on Dragonfire while we're providing false data, there will be major chaos."

"She'll have to agree. We can't give Colb access to the station's real data, and we can't let him know he's locked out, either."

Hawk grinned. "Sounds fun. We've definitely never run an op like it."

"We'll have to create the program over the next day, so it's ready when we dock. Then we'll have to keep Colb occupied and away from any voicecom access long enough to install it." Her eyes went to Raptor. As their hacker extraordinaire, a lot of this would fall on him.

He straightened. "No problem."

"Good. In the meantime, we have to be very careful not to let on to Colb that we know his game. No slip-ups," she ordered. She glared at her team. "This is serious. Quit looking so happy."

Each of her teammates, Ross included, wore a kid-in-a-candy-store smile.

Hawk stood and moved to put his arm around her. "Aw, lighten up, Chief. Think of how epic it'll be when we pull it off. We'll be legends."

She'd thought of that too, and the legend part didn't matter to her. But the intricacy of the job appealed. "Among ourselves, and to the scant few people who know about it—if they don't end up incarcerated for the rest of their lives."

"Exactly!" Hawk thumped her on the back.

She couldn't resist. She grinned back at her team. "Fine. It's going to be awesome. But only if we win."

"Of course we'll win." Hawk lifted a fist into the air. "We're Avian Unit. Blood and bone!"

The others raised their fists.

"Blood and bone!" Fallon said with them.

5

Fallon wasn't surprised when Raptor came to her quarters that night.

"You doing okay?" His face showed a caring concern that she hadn't yet gotten entirely accustomed to.

"Yeah. Other than being a little concerned about my parents and brother, I'm good."

He made a hum of understanding and sat next to her on her bunk. "Your parents have been in the game longer than you have. I'm sure they've seen a lot and know how to take care of themselves."

"They've always done on-the-books work. They don't have experience with the kind of stuff we're doing. Colb knows that I've been to see them. Under normal circumstances, they'd mention that to a close family friend. Since they didn't, he must suspect they know something."

Raptor made another sound of agreement. He put a chummy arm around her. "But," he said, "what if they know that he knows we know he knows they know?"

She laughed. "They probably don't. But maybe they suspect."

"Whew. Glad you followed that. I'm not sure I did." He gave

her a playful jiggle. "Don't get too far inside your own head. Just do the job. Work the problems as they come."

"That's pretty much been my whole approach to life, until recently."

"And now?" He sounded genuinely curious, no longer teasing.

"I find myself caught up in feelings and relationships. Why do you suppose that is?"

He turned his head at an awkward angle so he could look at her. "Are you looking for platitudes, or truth?"

"Let's try platitudes," she decided.

"It's a temporary thing because of your situation. Once we get past this threat to the PAC, things will sort themselves out and you'll get back to normal."

She mulled that over. It was possible. If life went back to normal and she threw herself back into her job, the rest of it all might recede. But she didn't think so. "Okay, let's try truth."

"We've all been changed by what's happened to us. Being split up. Having to fight to get back together, and to stay together. Having to battle our own handlers. We've had to become more than we ever intended to be."

Unfortunately, that had the ring of truth. "How do you feel about that?" she asked. "About how it affects your life, I mean."

"It is what it is. I've never given much thought to what-ifs. I mean, think about it. We're tiny specks in the cosmos. Not even that. When you compare us to all the galaxies and planets and stars, we don't even register. There's an infinite amount of everything my life is *not*. There's only a tiny bit of what my life actually is. So I choose to focus on that."

Somehow that was what she'd needed to hear. She didn't want to spend her time reflecting and philosophizing about her life. She wanted to live it. "That was kind of wise. Maybe you should teach at the academy when all this is over."

The humor returned to his voice. "Me, a teacher? Nah. I need a job where I get up each day never knowing if I'm going to have to jump out of a plane or hide in a swamp."

She smiled. "The Obafuran mission."

"Yeah," he said wistfully. "Good times."

"If you call a thousand mosquito bites and the rotten stench of swamp good."

"Well, not at the time. Damn bugs chewed my face up. But it was a good mission."

"It was," she agreed. She had to admit that she liked diving out of planes, too. She glanced at the chronometer and stood, causing Raptor's arm to fall to his side. "I have to get to the bridge and relieve Ross. My shift starts in five minutes."

"I'll walk you up there."

It was a silly thing for him to do, but she decided to live in the moment. "Let's go."

Upon docking at Dragonfire Station, the *Nefarious* was treated to a grand welcome, including a personal visit from Captain Nevitt.

"Admiral Colb." The captain bowed. "Welcome to Dragonfire. We're pleased to have you."

Fallon stepped through the airlock as the pair exchanged pleasantries. As far as Colb was concerned, Nevitt was only a station captain.

Fallon smiled, outwardly as a greeting, but secretly in pleasure at imagining the noose tightening around Colb's neck. She could feel herself getting closer to her goal. Maybe one day, she'd reflect on the betrayal of someone who'd been like one of her family. At present, she cared only about her job—protecting the PAC and its citizens.

"Please allow me to give you a tour of the station before

showing you to your quarters," Nevitt said to Colb as they stepped out of the docking bay.

To refuse would be terribly rude, so Colb was forced to smile and say, "It's my pleasure, thank you."

And away they went, providing Avian Unit with the time they needed to dummy up the station's computers. At least, Fallon hoped they'd have enough time. Even with Raptor's skills, it would be tight.

In her security office, they worked. Ross monitored Nevitt and Colb progressing through the station while the rest of the team installed and implemented the program Raptor had written while on the *Nefarious*.

The last step was to run the software and test it. They tried accessing the station's specs, the security protocols and codes. Every time, they received either the appropriately wrong information or a security lockout. Perfect.

By the time Nevitt joined the team, they were floating on a cloud of success. As soon as she stepped in and cast a keen eye around the room, she nodded.

"I gather you accomplished your mission."

"Yes, Captain," Fallon said. Nevitt arched an eyebrow at her and Fallon corrected herself. "Hesta. Colb won't be able to gather any intelligence that could potentially hurt us."

"Good. The idea of that man on my station makes me itch," Nevitt said.

"Thank you for keeping him busy," Raptor said. "You did an excellent job."

"Of course I did. I'm fantastic at my job." Her dry tone made Fallon smile. "Now what?"

"Now we wait for him to lay his trap for us, and we figure out how to walk into it and make it snap closed on him and Krazinski instead." Fallon had no doubt they'd succeed.

"I'm not sure whether to be excited or terrified," Nevitt admitted.

"Be excited," Hawk advised. "When we get the job done, you can brag about how you knew all along it would work."

"And if it doesn't?"

He shrugged. "We'll all be dead and having been terrified won't have helped any."

Nevitt narrowed her eyes at him, and then her lips curled into a small smile. "Hawk, I'm beginning to like you."

FALLON AND RAPTOR monitored every outgoing and incoming signal with excruciating diligence. Colb wasn't foolish enough to attempt any communication with Krazinski. But it sure would have been helpful to Fallon if he had. Where was a little arrogance from the admiralty when she needed it?

She'd expected Colb to launch right into whatever he had planned for them, but he seemed to be in no rush. Was he doing reconnaissance, or was he stalling? The idea of him stalling made Fallon wonder if her team should hit Blackout at Jamestown immediately, hoping Krazinski wouldn't be ready for them. But the logistics were far less than ideal, and she'd be walking her team into an unknown situation when she had an alternative. She just had to wait for Colb to set them up.

While she waited for the chance to double-cross Colb's double-cross, she still had her job to do as the station's chief of security. So she did it.

She made her midday rounds as usual. The boardwalk was extra lively, which was the norm when the *Onari* was visiting. Fallon suspected that enthusiasm would fade, now that Dragonfire served as its home base.

Thinking of that reminded her that she hadn't talked to Brannin yet about the *Onari*'s presence at Dragonfire. Hesta had said that she'd need to be the one to deliver the news. They didn't want to step on his toes, or make him think his skills were inadequate. But she couldn't tell him about her real reason for wanting her allies close at hand. So the situation would require finesse.

She put that thought away for later when she saw Nix and her friend Robert come trotting out of Cabot Layne's shop, beaming at her.

"Hi, Chief!"

"Hey, Chief!"

Their ringing greetings made her smile. "Hey, you two. What do you have there?" She peered at the bundle in Nix's arms.

"Art supplies," Nix answered. "We're supposed to create something in the neo-industrial style."

"Huh," Fallon said. Neo-industrial always seemed to her less like art and more like mechanics that did nothing. But far be it from her to second-guess the academic instruction on Dragonfire. "Well, good luck with it. I've never been very artistic, myself. I can barely draw a straight line."

The young teens laughed. "I'm sure you do fine," Robert assured her.

"I promise you, I'm really bad at it. But that's okay. We all have things we're good at."

A sly expression slid onto Nix's face. "Speaking of which. You said that if I did well in my classes, you'd arrange a security internship for me. The year's about up, and I'll be taking my final exams next week."

Fallon groaned inwardly. She wanted to see Nix flourish, but this was not a good time. "Do your best and we'll see what we can arrange," she promised.

"I'm going to get all firsts, like you said." The spark of determination in Nix's eyes reminded Fallon of herself at a younger age. She had to smile.

"I believe you."

Robert tugged on Nix's upper arm. "We'd better get back. Lunch period is almost over. Want me to carry that?"

"Nope. I got it. Bye, Chief!"

The two disappeared as fast as they'd popped up. Fallon stood looking after them, thinking how nice it would be to have such simple goals.

"Bundle of energy, aren't they?" Cabot stepped out of his shop.

"Oh, yes. I'm always glad to see them."

"They make me smile, too." He gave her a proper bow, in accordance with her status on the station.

"You don't have to bow," she told him. "I think we're friends enough that we can dispense with it."

"Is that right?" He seemed surprised. "I'll have to think about that. I don't know that I'd feel right not bowing to you." Cabot gestured to the door of his shop. "Would you like to come in for a minute?"

"Thank you. That would be nice."

He followed her in and closed the door behind them. This was not unusual behavior in his shop, since he always offered complete discretion. No one would take it amiss.

"You okay, Chief?" He guided her to a chair and materialized a cup of hot tea from somewhere, then pressed it into her hand.

"Yes. Of course. I just have a lot of people depending on me."

He nodded slowly as he sat across from her. "I'm sure that's a great deal of pressure."

"No," she denied. "I actually like doing security. I like making sure people are okay."

"But..." he prodded.

"No, there's no but. I've been working hard lately. That's all."

"Would it help if I told you I'm glad you're the one doing... whatever thing you're doing?"

She had to chuckle. "A little." He probably knew, or at least suspected, a lot more than he let on.

"If there's anything I can do to help, let me know." He stared at her hard. "I mean it. Anything."

Okay, he definitely knew more than he let on.

"Understood. Thanks." She took a deep breath and let it out slowly, as her father had taught her to do as a child when she needed to focus. "I should get back to work."

"One second." He rose. "I want to give you something." He disappeared into the back of his store, behind the counter. He returned only a moment later, grasping something.

He placed it on the table in front of her. It was a small silver rectangle.

"What is it?" she asked.

"It's a good-luck piece. Davitrian. Ancient. The legends say that it has so much luck in it, it could suck up all the power within a nine-meter radius." He laughed. "Perhaps its luck will rub off on you."

She stared at the thing. It was no more ancient than she was. It was cutting-edge technology. And from what he was saying, it would temporarily knock out all electrical systems within ten meters. She wanted to ask him where he'd gotten it, but she couldn't. If he knew what he was giving her and she knew what she was receiving, it would make them both criminals. Not that she wasn't already one, technically, but there was no reason to bring him along for the ride.

"Thank you. I could use some luck."

He smiled, and the light in his eyes showed amusement at their subterfuge. "And you deserve it." He started to bow, but caught himself. "I'll work on the bowing thing."

She gave him a deep bow, far more than a PAC officer would ever give a shopkeep. "It's my honor, Cabot. You're a good friend."

He looked surprised, then pleased, and finally he reverted to his benign, pleasant expression. "Whatever I can do."

"One of these days, we're going to have a very long talk."

He laughed as he showed her out.

She finished her rounds with a sense of contentment. The exchange with Cabot probably shouldn't have mattered to her, in the grand scheme of everything she was trying to do, but it did. It was nice to have a friend.

WHEN FALLON FINISHED her duty shift, she still struggled under the burden of not having discovered Colb's plans. Rather than brood over events she couldn't control, she allowed herself to feel a moment of serenity in the eye of the storm. The next phase would happen when it happened, and when it did, she'd be ready.

Since her last task of the day had taken her to Deck One, Fallon stopped by the Bennite restaurant. She cradled a warm bundle of stew and bread as she walked to the lift, looking forward to a quiet evening in her quarters.

Until she saw Wren waiting for her.

"Hi," Fallon said, not knowing what to expect.

"Hi." Wren twinkled with playfulness.

Since Wren just stood there smiling at her, Fallon asked, "What's up?"

"I thought I'd catch you at the lift to see if we could have dinner, but you already have that covered." Wren's gaze bounced down to the package Fallon held and back up.

"Sorry. Maybe tomorrow?"

"How about I grab some takeout of my own and meet you at your quarters?"

Peregrine might be there, but Fallon didn't mind that. She tried to think of some other reason to decline, but couldn't. "All right," she finally agreed.

"Great! I'll meet you there in a few minutes." Wren turned to go.

"Actually, I'll wait here for you. That way you won't need a temporary passcode for Deck Four."

"Great. I'll be right back."

Fallon's food would stay plenty warm, so she didn't mind waiting. But she wondered what Wren wanted. Not that she had to want something. Fallon still had no handle on where they stood with each other. She leaned against a bulkhead with her dinner warming her chest and her arms, trying to figure out how to approach the evening. Like a date? Like a get-together with a pal? She had no tactical plan.

Within minutes Wren was back, holding her own bundle of food. "Let's go! I'm starved."

"Busy day?" Fallon asked as they rode the lift up.

"Oh, that doesn't even begin to cover it. I had to interview mechanics via the voicecom. I talked to eight people and though they all seemed decent enough, none of them is half as good as Josef. He and I work so well together. He's one of those coworkers that you can't replace, you know?"

Fallon shifted the food she carried and leaned against the lift wall. "I saw the report that he was leaving. Where's he headed?"

"He's got a job as a private mechanic on Caravon, working on the personal vehicles of a super-rich person. He'll be on call at all times, but for the most part, he'll just be keeping the newest models shiny. A huge salary for not much work. Living on Caravon will be no hardship, either."

The lift doors opened to Deck Four. "You could get a job like that," Fallon said as she led the way to her quarters.

"And be bored out of my mind? No thanks. I like the tough cases. Like the assembly block I was working on after the interviews."

Fallon keyed in her credentials to unlock the door. "Taking out your frustration on an innocent engine?"

Wren laughed as she followed Fallon in. "Absolutely." She glanced around, saw the table on the far side of the room, and sent Fallon a questioning look.

Fallon nodded, moving toward it. She noticed Wren taking

stock of her new digs, but trying to be subtle about it. "I hope you're feeling better now that the interviews are done."

"Some." Wren pushed her package onto the table and took a seat. "I thought having dinner with you would take the remaining edge off."

Fallon unwrapped her bread and opened the container for her stew. "I wasn't aware that my presence was particularly soothing."

Wren smiled. "It's not. But you always manage to make me forget about work stuff."

"Do I?"

"It's one of the things that's always attracted me to you." Wren opened her lightweight recyclable container and speared a vegetable from her sauté with her fork. "You fill a room with your presence and make it entirely impossible to ignore you. You give everything weight. Like this dinner. Just having this meal feels like something significant."

"I never knew you felt that way." Fallon put a spoonful of stew in her mouth and sighed as the rich flavors spread across her taste buds.

"I didn't think of it that way until we were apart." Wren shrugged, downplaying her words. "Sometimes you don't think too hard about things when you're happy. You take things as they are, you know?"

Fallon took her time chewing, then finally answered, "Yeah. Makes sense."

A companionable silence fell between them for a few minutes.

"Tell me about that assembly block you were working on," Fallon said.

Wren brightened and launched into a speech full of technobabble that Fallon could only somewhat follow. She'd known what she was getting herself into when she asked, though. Wren loved her work, and it made her happy to talk about it.

Fallon's mild unease with Wren wore off. They knew each other well. They had history. Fallon still enjoyed her company and had nothing to be uptight about.

Wren paused in her description of phase transducers, tilting her head to one side. "What?"

"Nothing. I'm just having a nice time."

A smile lit Wren's face. "Me too." Then she launched right back into her mechanic-speak.

At the end of the evening, Wren suggested it was time for her to go and there was a pause where Fallon could have suggested she stay. She didn't. She wanted the evening to be only what it was, completely at face value. She didn't feel like she and Wren were in the right place for there to be more.

At the door, Wren leaned in, cupped Fallon's face, and gave her a light kiss. Fallon rested a hand on Wren's waist.

Then Wren stepped back. "Good night," she said softly, her cheeks pink.

The doors opened.

"Good night. Thanks for...this," Fallon finished lamely.

Wren only smiled, turned, and disappeared from view.

FALLON WALKED BACK across the living room she shared with Peregrine, her steps slow and ponderous. She didn't feel like sleeping. Or working, either.

She half perched on the arm of the couch, wondering what to do. A sound at the door drew her attention, and a moment later Peregrine entered.

The doors closed behind her and she sent Fallon a questioning look.

Fallon shrugged. "Trying to figure out what to do. I'm used to having clear-cut goals and the means to achieve them, and there are just too many shades of gray in my life right now."

Peregrine bounced farther into the room on the balls of her feet, looking like a prizefighter. "Sounds like you need to go a few rounds to clear your head."

Fallon touched her head in the general area where Brak had implanted the inducer that allowed her to access her memories. "I'm cleared for normal activity, but that nasty jab of yours probably isn't a good idea until we're sure this thing will stand up to a beating."

Peregrine dropped her fighting stance. "Too bad. I could use a good bout, myself."

"Why? Something wrong?"

"Nah. Not really. I just miss the old days. Taking out assassins before they could ice their targets, rappelling down the side of the building for a hasty retreat, taking important things from important people."

"Getting shot at," Fallon pointed out. Their typical work came with a drawback here and there.

"Yeah." Peregrine sighed wistfully. Apparently she had fonder memories of dodging stinger blasts than Fallon did. "I don't mind being stationed in one place. I just miss the action. We could use something to break up the monotony."

"I know. Sometimes it feels like we're stuck in a revolving door, spinning in circles."

Peregrine sat on the other couch arm. "I don't want to sound like I'm complaining, but yes. There have been plenty of jobs where we had to sit tight, waiting for an event to occur, and I don't mind that because we know what we're waiting for. In this case, I feel like we're operating in a void. Wasting time with so much meeting and talking." She hurried her next words. "Not that we don't need the meetings. I just..."

"Hate them," Fallon finished for her.

Peregrine's lips twitched upward. "I wouldn't say that. But yeah. I'd rather do less meeting and talking and more doing."

"Me too. We'll get there. We just need to persevere through

this part. Krazinski knows we can do the action stuff. But he doesn't know we're more than highly trained beasts. He doesn't know how much we're capable of as a team."

Peregrine ran her hand over her long ponytail. "We're playing the long game. I know. But maybe your time as security chief here has prepared you for it better than the rest of us."

"If I can adjust, so can you."

"Maybe. I'm not counting on it, though." When Fallon started to talk, Peregrine cut her off. "It's fine. I'm fine. I'll be here for whatever you need, giving it my best. I just don't think I'm cut out for bureaucracy is all I'm saying."

"None of us planned on being administrators. We're just working the op in the only way we can." If Fallon could have left all these meetings and planning sessions to someone else, she surely would have. And while she was wishing, she'd wish away her memory loss, too. But wishes were for children and fairy tales. All Fallon had was cold, hard reality.

Peregrine stood. "I'm not railing against my circumstances. I'm just wondering what it means for the future." She sighed. "I know I have too much time on my hands when I'm thinking about the future."

"How about we go to the training rooms and work on some target practice?"

"Stingers or knives?" Peregrine asked.

"Either. Both."

The crinkle between Peregrine's eyes finally smoothed. "Go grab your knives."

FALLON FELL INTO BED TIRED, but satisfied. Target practice always made her happy, and Peregrine's spirits seemed to have lifted, as well.

She half expected Raptor to pull his nighttime commando

routine as she drifted to sleep, but it was a call from Colb that woke her two hours before her usual time.

"What is it?" she asked the voicecom display in her room, using an audio-only feed. Colb didn't need to see what she looked like first thing in the morning.

"I've figured it out. How we can get in. Meet me in my quarters in ten minutes."

The channel closed. Admirals were accustomed to giving an order and having everyone scramble to obey.

If she hurried, she'd have time to take a quick shower and smooth out her hair.

Eight and a half minutes later, she settled herself in Colb's quarters, which were a mirror of her own, but unshared by a roommate. Another privilege of the admiralty.

Peregrine and Ross were already there, and Hawk and Raptor followed within moments of each other.

"I'll get right to it." Colb paced the quarters in a leisurely fashion. "I've been trying to work out how to get into Jamestown, given that Krazinski will be watching for us, and will have changed everything specifically to keep us out."

They waited, letting the admiral have his moment.

"I've worked through every scenario, and I kept coming to the same conclusion: it can't be done. There's no way for us to break in."

Fallon exchanged a look with her team. She wondered where Colb was going with this. She'd been working scenarios as well and had come up with two plans that had a chance of success. Not that she would share that information with Colb.

"So what are we going to do?" she asked.

"We have to get them to let us in. So I'm going to tell Krazinski that a taste of life on the outside has convinced me to rejoin him. You five will be my supposed peace offering, led here under the guise of attacking him."

It sounded awfully thin to Fallon. She was supposed to

believe that Colb thought Krazinski would actually take him back into the organization under those circumstances. Once trust was broken in intel, there was no mending fences.

But Colb wasn't a field operative. He saw things from a more top-down perspective, where everything he said was law, and it was the job of people like her to accept it.

Agreeing too easily might make him suspicious, so she said, "How do you know Krazinski won't kill you anyway?"

He paused in his pacing and drew himself up. "I don't. He might. But the doors will have been opened, so to speak, and the rest of you will have your chance."

Ah, so he was pretending to be willing to sacrifice himself for the greater good. That was clever, actually. A group of BlackOps would buy into heroism and martyrdom, right?

But she said, "We won't be able to plan the assault. We have no idea what we'll be dealing with in there."

"It's the chance we have. We'll have to find a way," Colb said.

Fallon had to give the man credit—he looked sincere. Stalwart. Prepared to fight the good fight.

"When do we get under way?" she asked.

As Fallon prepared to leave Dragonfire, she had to deal with reality. Colb's plan was a lie, but the danger was real. There was a reasonable possibility she wouldn't return.

She felt the need to make a few visits before she left. Fortunately, she had two hours before departure time. That would allow her to get done what she needed to, without allowing her to drag it out.

Captain Nevitt's office was her first stop. Naturally, Hesta had some opinions on the matter.

"Your doubt is duly noted," Fallon said. "It *is* risky. But I'm accustomed to calculated risk, and this course of action gives us the best chance of success."

Nevitt wore her patented look of dubious disdain. "I shudder to think what your second and third choice plans were."

Fallon smiled. "We'll not speak of them. Anyway, I've left you some files in case I don't return. Things that will help you know who you can or can't trust, and details about station security. There's also a program to return the station's systems to normal once Colb has disembarked."

"I appreciate all that. I can only hope you're successful. For the good of the PAC, but also because I want to see you back here."

"Thank you, Cap—Hesta. I plan to come back."

"See that you do." Hesta's words were crisp, but her expression showed concern.

FALLON'S VISIT with Brak and Jerin was brief and to the point. She filled them in on her upcoming mission and instructed them on what to watch for and how best to protect the *Onari* from the war that would come if Fallon didn't return.

Both gave her hugs and well wishes. Fallon was glad they had each other to talk to. She knew firsthand how lonely it could be to keep a secret to herself.

Her next stop would be a trickier one. On the way down to Cabot's shop, she tried to decide what to say. With the others it had been easier, since the relationships were defined. With Cabot, she had more questions than answers, but in her gut she trusted him to be a man of good character, although of sketchy means.

He gave her a knowing look when she entered his shop, and he closed the door to give them privacy.

"What can I do for you today, Chief?"

"To be honest, I'm not sure. But I'm leaving the station and felt like I should say goodbye."

He gave a slight nod. "Are you thinking of not returning?"

"Not on purpose. But you never know. If I don't come back..."

"I'll look after your friends and the station."

She smiled. "And yourself. Things could get bad if this goes wrong. Very bad."

"I understand. But I'm expecting to see you back, so I won't stress too much just yet."

"If I do return, a lot of things will change. I might even have a job for you."

He raised a sardonic eyebrow. "I already have a job."

"So you wouldn't be interested?"

He leaned in closer, as if preparing to tell her a secret. "Oh, I very much *would* be interested."

"Good."

"Good." His demeanor never changed from pleasant and obliging. She could only wonder what all lay beneath his shopkeep persona—and she did believe it to be a persona.

"I'll be on my way."

"Best wishes, Chief. And don't forget that charm I gave you." He looked at her meaningfully.

"Got it in my pocket," she assured him.

"Ah, good."

She caught a hint of fierceness in his eyes before turning to leave.

IN AN UNCHARACTERISTIC BURST OF UNCERTAINTY, Fallon waffled back and forth about the last goodbye on her list. In the end, she decided she'd been a bad enough wife to Wren as it was. She didn't want to disappear forever without saying goodbye. Not that she was going to. But just in case. A BlackOp never knew which mission would be her last.

She found Wren in the mechanics' shop. When Wren turned to see Fallon, her eyes widened with fear. Clearly, she had some inkling about what was to come.

"Here we are, where we first met," Fallon said as she approached her former wife.

"Why? What's happening?" Wren's voice was a whisper, even though no one else was close enough to overhear.

"I have something I need to do."

"No. Don't go."

"It's not optional. But I wanted to tell you goodbye in person."

Wren rubbed a hand over her forehead, smearing a thin streak of grease across her skin. It made Fallon smile. "Don't say goodbye. That makes it sound permanent. Just say you love me and you'll see me soon."

Could she say that? With the messy past between them, and her not really knowing what they were to each other? The feeling was there, but saying it would be skipping way ahead of where their relationship currently was.

But whether they ever worked as a couple or not, she'd always feel deeply for Wren. So she hedged. "I do feel for you. It isn't perfect and it isn't easy, but I do."

Wren smiled. "I'll let you get away with not actually saying it."

Fallon laughed. Wren was the most resilient person she'd ever known. She would always find her way forward, no matter what. "I'll see you soon."

With her goodbyes said and her just-in-case messages created, Fallon narrowed her focus on what she had to do. She had no idea what would unfold, but it would be big. After these months waiting to go toe-to-toe with Blackout, she was more than ready to go back to where it had all started.

IT WOULD TAKE the *Nefarious* four days to reach Jamestown. They could get to headquarters sooner if they were willing to burn out some of the ship's components, but the team had agreed that doing so would be a risk that outweighed its benefits. Colb had pushed for greater speed, but quickly backed down when he saw that the consensus was against him.

They had a few hidden assets that Colb didn't know about, and she hoped that would be enough to keep them a step ahead of him. She carried the electricity suppressor Cabot had given her. Kellis had installed the sensor blocker Hawk had acquired for them after the pirate attack. It would make it a lot harder to see the *Nefarious* coming. Such a device was illegal to have within the PAC zone, but being brought to trial for owning contraband was the least of Fallon's worries. The fact that she seemed to be developing a habit of acquiring illegal items struck her as ironically amusing.

Hopefully, their surprises and their awareness of Colb's duplicity would keep them alive. Some well-placed vainglory didn't hurt either, and Fallon had faith in her team. This would be their biggest adventure yet. If it all worked out, Hawk would have some fantastic stories to tell at the bar.

The closer they got to PAC command, the higher her adrenaline soared. By the final day, she couldn't sleep. Her senses clanged with awareness. She was ready to work.

She was reluctant to relinquish the bridge of the *Nefarious* to Peregrine at the end of her shift. She wanted to see everything, be on top of every detail. But they were surrounded only by empty space, so she rose from the pilot's chair.

"We'll be there soon," Peregrine observed. "Are you ready?"

"I've been ready for months."

Peregrine smoothed her long ponytail as she sat. "Ever wonder what life looks like for us once we're done with all this?"

"Right now I'm just taking things as they come. But I'm sure restructuring will require creating more oversight and accountability, even in the clandestine divisions."

"I'm not made to be a bureaucrat." Peregrine's customary frown was firmly in place.

Fallon paused. Peregrine wouldn't be mentioning that again right now without a reason. "Are you saying you wouldn't take part in reorganizing Blackout?" It hadn't occurred to her that Avian Unit wouldn't do whatever came next as a team.

"I'm saying that I'll never be someone who sits in an office every day, giving orders. You and Raptor could do that. Hawk and I aren't made that way." Peregrine fixed Fallon with a steady gaze.

"You've been worried about this." Fallon wished she'd realized this was weighing on Per so much. Fallon hadn't been thinking far enough ahead to worry about what came next. Per clearly had.

"Yes. I'm not sure what my place would be in the new order of Blackout."

Fallon put a hand on her partner's shoulder. "We'll figure it out when we get there. No matter what, we're a team, as always."

"Right."

Fallon wasn't sure Peregrine sounded entirely convinced. Maybe more like eighty percent. But what else could Fallon say? She could only keep pushing forward.

"I mean it. We've gotten through everything else. We'll figure that out too. Blood and bone," she reminded Peregrine.

Peregrine nodded. "Blood and bone." At least in that, she sounded one hundred percent confident.

FALLON PAUSED at the door to her quarters, then went past it to Raptor's. He might still be sleeping, but he was due to be up soon anyway.

The door opened immediately, and she was surprised to see Ross inside. Raptor waved her in.

"Hey. Anything up?" She hoped she didn't have more existential crises on her hands. Their team needed to be focused on the mission ahead, and nothing else.

Ross looked up at her and smiled, but the hand he raked through his shaggy hair belied his attempt at reassurance. "Would you believe we were talking about the Terran pegball championships?"

"No."

"Well, scrap. The truth is, I'm nervous about this mission. I don't like going into a situation with so many unknowns."

"It's not my favorite either." She leaned against the wall. "But we work with what we've got. This is our best shot."

"I know. But I haven't seen as much of this kind of op as the rest of you. Until recently, I'd spent the last decade teaching teenagers at the academy. It's not exactly high-stakes stuff."

She glanced at Raptor, but he didn't seem concerned. Ross was simply having some nerves, then. Fortunately, he'd gone to the right person to talk him through it. That let Fallon off the hook, though as the team leader she still had an obligation to be sure that they could count on Ross.

"You'll be staying on board the *Nefarious*, anyway. Someone needs to, and you're the next-best pilot. If we're lucky, you'll only be minding the store while we're gone." And if they weren't, he might have to engage in some tricky maneuvers to keep the ship safe. But she didn't think saying so would do much to calm his nerves.

"It's too bad we couldn't bring that engineer friend of yours. The one you want to recruit. Would have been comforting to know that if we take damage, someone could repair it." Ross had relaxed some, so she judged that he was only thinking out loud.

"Kellis. Yeah, I'd have liked to have her along for this one too. But she's too green for something this intense. Just our quick pop into the Tokyo base had her white-faced and edgy. She needs training before she can be useful in high-stress situations."

"Hopefully in the future," Raptor added.

"I hope so." She suspected that Raptor and Ross needed to do more talking, so she pulled away from the wall. "Well, I'm going to go check in on our dear admiral."

"Better you than me." Raptor didn't smile. "One of the perks of being our fearless leader."

"It's not a bad job, all in all. I think I'll keep it."

FALLON GAVE Colb the proper bow, not that he deserved it. She'd be glad when she could drop the charade. Showing respect to a man who might cause the PAC's destruction made her grind her teeth. Never mind what she'd gone through when she'd lost her memory. But she was good at her job and let none of this show.

"I hope you're well, Admiral." She didn't ask to enter his room and he didn't invite her.

"As well as can be expected. I have to admit, the stress of all this has taken its toll, and I'm spending a good deal of time resting, so I can be ready for what's ahead."

"That's good. We'll need you."

"You'll be able to count on me." He smiled at her. "I never missed a single one of your competitions, did I?"

She remembered him sitting with her parents, quietly cheering her on at the various combat tournaments she'd competed in as a youth. His face communicated only fondness and pride.

"Never." She smiled warmly. "Uncle Masumi was always there."

He chuckled, looking nostalgic. "I haven't heard you call me that in many years. Funny what this uniform does to us." He smoothed his hands down the front of his admiral's uniform.

"Yes. It is." At least that statement she wholeheartedly meant. She stepped back. "I'll leave you to rest."

"Thank you for checking in on me. I hope you know I've always been as proud of you as if you were my own daughter."

She bowed. "Thank you. I can't tell you what that means to me."

As she returned to her own quarters, she burned with anger. She didn't soothe it away. Anger wasn't always a bad thing. She wanted it. She'd use it for what was to come.

SHE TRIED to lie down and sleep, but her body wasn't having it. Sighing, she sat up and began studying the schematics of Jamestown she had on her voicecom display. Not that the schematics were likely to help, because Krazinski would have altered things. And not that she didn't already have every detail committed to memory. But she had nothing else to do with her time. She could think of only the job ahead, and she couldn't afford to work out until exhaustion. She needed her body to be strong and ready.

So she waited out the final hours alone. Ironic, maybe, for someone with two love interests, and one of them sleeping next door. But she would always be herself before she was someone's lover. She was a soldier. A warrior. A person who got shit done.

She rolled out of her bunk before it was time to relieve Hawk on the bridge. After putting on a clean jumpsuit, she took the long way through the ship.

Long tradition held that a captain toured her ship before a major battle. Fallon was far from a traditional captain, but she felt like the *Nefarious* belonged to her. She'd crawled through every conduit and memorized every system. She always felt the bridge was hers, and only on loan to anyone else.

She was proud of her ship and her team. Of her service

record. Of her attempt to save the PAC. If this was the mission she didn't come back from, she had no regrets, so long as they saved the PAC.

When she arrived on the bridge, Hawk squinted at her. "Prelin's ass, you look like you're ready to chew straight through the hull of Jamestown."

She grinned. "I am."

He scowled at her, but she knew it was fake. "You've always been the scariest asshole I've ever known."

"And you've always been the biggest one I've ever known."

They glared at each other, then broke into laughter.

"Ready?" he asked.

"So ready." She slid into the pilot's chair, feeling instantly more powerful.

"Mind if I keep you company?" He gestured toward the chair beside her.

"Not at all. You don't want to sleep?"

"Who can sleep?" He leaned against the seat and she saw the mania in his eyes that she understood so well.

An hour later, Peregrine arrived. An hour after that, Raptor sauntered onto the bridge. They sat together, telling old stories, insulting one another, and watching the distance between them and their target shrink.

Fallon got her first glimpse of Jamestown on long-range sensors. "Here we go," she intoned. "Hawk, call up Ross and Colb."

"Will do." But before bringing up the others, he stepped forward and extended his fist. "Blood and bone, my friends. It's been a pleasure serving with you."

Fallon smiled and touched her fist to his. Raptor and Peregrine followed. For one moment, they were together, united, and everything they'd ever intended to be.

"Blood and bone."

FALLON'S first close-range look at Jamestown made her heart leap. Sure, it was a cold gray monster of a flying saucer with barely any stem section. It didn't have Dragonfire's elegance. It didn't need it. Jamestown was strong, imposing, and huge—about four times the size of Dragonfire. Fallon always viewed it with a smidge of childish awe.

"Do they see us?" Raptor edged closer, looking at the display.

"If they do, they're not letting on, but it's entirely possible they have the technology to see through our disguise."

"Proceed as planned," Colb ordered, as if he had an actual say in how events would unfold from here on out.

But Fallon played along. "Aye, sir. Establishing a brute docking attitude."

Ahh, brute force. It was her favorite kind.

She came in faster than a ship normally would, but any jarring she caused only worked in her favor. So she hit Jamestown with as much force as the *Nefarious* could tolerate without structural damage.

She interfaced with the dock, ignoring the usual safety protocols. She latched onto it, then blasted Jamestown with a program Raptor had devised to keep it from rejecting them. In seconds, they'd rewritten the docking system's protocols. Raptor's subroutines would keep the mainframe computer from overriding his code. The man was a genius. She shot him a grin.

He grinned back, and she returned her attention to the controls. "Pressurizing the airlock."

The people inside would now scramble a security team, then send them to the breached dock. Fallon was ready for the fight.

"Go!" she ordered.

Avian Unit bolted, with Ross escorting Admiral Colb. Fallon was the last to leave the bridge. She patted her chair.

She ran through the airlock with a stinger in each hand. Then she stopped. No security team had come. Emergency lighting dimly lit the airlock, but beyond it, she saw no light at all.

"Did you already kill everyone?" she joked in confusion.

"No one came." Peregrine's frown seemed etched into her face.

"What does that mean?" Colb asked, sounding baffled.

Like you don't know, Fallon thought grimly at him. But she wasn't ready to show her hand. "I don't know. Maybe they've set up an ambush somewhere?"

It didn't make sense, because no security protocol would fail to respond to a breached dock and an incursion. But she had no other suggestions.

"No," Raptor said, frowning at a voicecom terminal. "Most of the station's been depressurized. Something is very, very wrong here."

Depressurized? She sensed that everything was about to take a big left turn. "Put on pressure suits and continue as planned," she ordered. Though "as planned" meant one thing to Colb, and another to the rest of them.

Once suited up, Hawk and Peregrine edged forward, leading them into the depressurized corridor. They all turned on the light sources in their suits to provide adequate illumination in what would otherwise be pitch black. Raptor assisted Colb, and Fallon brought up the rear. She was poised for the slightest sound, for the sense of a presence.

But they made their way through the corridor unimpeded.

"I'm getting a bad feeling about this," Hawk's voice transmitted to the receiver in her helmet. His light, like hers, penetrated several feet into the gloom, creating a small zone of bright light surrounded by utter darkness. It was creepy as hell.

Finally, they made it to ops control. The immensity of it didn't fail to impress Fallon, even as she and Raptor rushed to consoles. She refused to think about how eerie it felt to see it abandoned. The others covered the entrances, just in case.

She quickly assessed the situation, which sucked the recirculated air from her lungs and the feeling from her gloved fingertips. But she rechecked. And examined all auxiliary systems that might prove that the other systems were lying.

But it was true. The camera feeds were genuine.

"We're alone here," Raptor said.

Dead silence filled the channel.

Finally, Hawk turned away from the door. "What do you mean, 'alone'?"

Fallon answered, "He means that the only people on the station are dead ones. About three hundred of them, from the look of it."

She felt sick. Hollow. This was the headquarters of the entire PAC, not just Blackout. The identities of the dead became a critical concern.

"Split up and begin identifying the dead." Scanning their IDs wouldn't take long. She added, "I'll escort Admiral Colb." She had to fight to keep bitterness from twisting her mouth as she spoke the words. He knew what had happened here, though it clearly wasn't what he'd expected.

If what she suspected was true...their situation was even worse than she'd thought. So much worse.

6

"About half of the department heads are dead, along with a variety of other officers and enlisted. A few civilians." Hawk's expression was blank as he relayed the information to Fallon. She was aware of Colb's presence, even as she processed her own horror.

"How did they die?" she asked, toneless. Professional.

"Close-range energy weapons for some. Stingers, most likely. Others appear to have suffocated under depressurization."

"What happened here?" Raptor wondered.

"I don't know," Peregrine said. "But it's messy. Not a precision strike."

Fallon had a lot to take in and little time to do it. She kept Colb in her peripheral vision. He'd proven entirely useless on this trip. He hadn't led them into a trap, whether he'd intended to or not.

"You seem surprised, Admiral." She turned her full attention on him.

"Of course I am. This violence, all these people...my friends. Aren't you surprised?"

She frowned, watching him closely. "Very. But still not nearly as much as you."

His brow furrowed. "I guess I'm not as accustomed to bloodshed and death as you are."

"Bullshit. Enough lies." She stared at him hard.

His mouth gaped. "What?"

"You heard me. You were expecting something specific, and this wasn't it. I think you need to explain yourself."

His eyes widened and he struggled to compose himself. "I don't have to explain myself to anyone," he declared. "Not even you, regardless of how fond I am of you. I'm an admiral. You five are by far my subordinates."

"And yet, since you seem to have outlived your usefulness, you're the one faced with a first-person view of the cosmos as you fly out of an airlock," she observed calmly.

"How can you—" He swallowed and began again. "How can you say that? You're like a daughter to me."

"Maybe I was, once. But you led me here, along with my team, to see us killed. We knew that all along." And that was everything there was to say.

Colb only stared at her. She could see in his eyes that he wouldn't tell them anything. They'd have to figure it out on their own. She dropped into the chair at a science station. "Take him to the brig on the *Nefarious*. Search him thoroughly."

Hawk clamped a meaty hand on the back of Colb's neck. "Do me a favor and resist, will ya?" he snarled. "I've always wanted to see how fast I could rip a pressure suit off."

Colb's face twisted. Transformed. One second he was a befuddled, kindly uncle, and the next he was a dragon. "Fine, lock me up. But there are things in play you haven't even begun to guess at." He gave Fallon a sly look. "You think it was happenstance that you met that wife of yours?"

Fallon was on her feet and across ops control without even

being aware of it. "You do not want to talk about her." She kept her voice calm, but with an icy razor edge.

"Kill me and you'll never know the truth." He smiled smugly and pressed his lips closed.

As much as she wanted to tear his lungs out through his nose, she refrained. Sat. Turned her attention back to the science station. "Take him," she ordered. She didn't look as they went.

Raptor put a hand on her shoulder. "You okay?" he murmured.

"No. We need to find out what happened here. That means you're on point." She gestured to another science station. "First of all, some lights would really help."

"I'm on it." And he got to work without another word, thank Prelin.

THEY FOUND the databanks wiped and destroyed. The station lacked life support to all areas but the docking bays and the parts of the station that ran on a separate system. Even Raptor couldn't retrieve any data. The man had a nearly magical talent but even he couldn't combat what he called an "Armageddon wipe."

What had happened here? Why kill some people and evacuate the rest? Were the survivors her allies or her enemies, and why had they crippled Jamestown, then locked it up tight?

"I want to do one more thing before we go. Ten minutes," Raptor said. His instinct, like hers, must have been telling him this was not a good place to be.

Fallon had no reason to think their presence on the station had gone undetected. Ships should be on the way. Patrolling ships needn't be more than a few hours away. If that was the case, she wanted to be long gone by the time they arrived.

"Fine. Peregrine, stay with him. I'm going to go to my storage compartment and get some things."

"Actually, there are a few things in my compartment we could use, too," Raptor said.

"Same here," Peregrine said.

Not surprising that they'd all put some things away for a rainy day. And it was raining like hell now.

"I imagine Hawk does as well. Okay. We'll take the time to grab our stuff. But let's be quick. Change of plans. Peregrine, you can come with me, then relieve Hawk in the brig so he can get his stuff. Raptor, finish up here, get your stuff, and get to the ship as soon as possible. Twenty minutes with regular check-ins. No longer."

As she and Peregrine made their way to the lift, she felt empty. Their pivotal moment hadn't gone like she'd expected. She had no resolution. No answers. Just another crisis and a lot more questions that made her worry for the people of the PAC.

At least the lifts still worked. They ran on self-contained power with backups. Knocking them out would have required an EMP.

She and Peregrine didn't talk as they descended into the lower decks of Jamestown. When the lift doors opened, Fallon ignored how eerie it felt to walk through corridors that should have been bustling with activity. The light source from the pressure suits centered them in an illuminated bubble, surrounded by a massive, shadowy ghost station. She ignored the four bodies that appeared in the sphere of light, and disappeared again once she and Per walked past.

At least the open voicecom link in her helmet distracted her from the silence. Stations weren't supposed to be silent. Panels on the walls should have been lit and ready for access. The whole place should have been bursting with life. She was walking in a tin can full of dead bodies.

She focused on the task at hand—getting to the storage bays. She and Peregrine shared space in the same one, as did Raptor and Hawk. They found their units and as soon as Fallon used her code and retina scan for access, she grabbed a large rucksack inside, dumped out the survival supplies, and loaded it with the items that would be of use. Ammunition. Weapons. Covert operations gadgets.

Finally she put the rucksack on and hauled out the cases with her heavy artillery as well as an anti-grav cart. She loaded it with three personal laser cannons. One RPG launcher. One anti-aircraft weapon for use within planetary atmospheres. She debated bringing that last item, but figured better safe than sorry and stacked it with the rest.

She secured her storage space and turned to see Peregrine weighed down with various bags and cases. She hadn't even bothered with a cart. Show-off.

"I like that we've all stockpiled for doomsday." Peregrine almost smiled.

"We've got to have hobbies, right? Let's go."

Back on the *Nefarious* they stored the heavy gear in weapons lockers, then Fallon headed to the bridge. Peregrine went to keep an eye on Colb while Hawk returned to Jamestown to grab his own belongings.

Fallon dropped into the pilot's chair and stabbed the initialization sequence. Ross had scooted over to the adjacent seat when he'd seen her, without saying a word. She wondered what it had been like for him, listening to events unfold while he remained here. She wouldn't have handled it well.

As soon as everyone returned, Fallon launched the ship. She burned the engines hard just long enough to get a good distance from the station, then continued at a more reasonable pace.

Raptor and Peregrine joined her and Ross on the bridge. Hawk had returned to keeping an eye on Colb. She wished she could turn Colb in to PAC command, but even if she could have trusted them, she didn't know where the remaining members and support staff of PAC command were now.

And where was the noise about that? The datastreams should

have been alive with the story of Jamestown going dark. So it must have happened very recently.

She wanted to bury her face in her hands and wallow in frustration for a minute or two, but had no time for that. She had a team to lead.

"Here." Raptor held something out to her and she extended her palm. He dropped a tiny chip into it.

"What is it?" She turned it over with her fingertip, but it revealed no distinguishing characteristics.

"I was doing an encryption algorithm search. It didn't yield any data, but it told me that PAC files had been downloaded and encrypted. That means they took with them the data that they wiped. I also found what's on that chip."

"What is it?"

"A message, I think. I didn't take the time to look at it. I almost didn't find it, but I noticed an odd pattern in the sequence of the systems had been deleted. It was a code."

"What was the message?"

"Not really a message. It was the date of our first day at the academy. Not a series of numbers that would be significant to anyone else. When I followed it back, I found this little file tucked away in a location that matched our graduation year."

"Wow. Nice work, Raptor." Fallon was already sliding the chip into a slot, but she paused. "And you're sure it's not a virus or something that's going to blow up in our faces."

"Positive."

She inserted the chip and an image of Krazinski appeared on her panel, apparently seated at a voicecom and staring into it. He looked rough. He had dark circles under his eyes, and his uniform had a small tear in the fabric at his shoulder. He began speaking gibberish.

She looked to Raptor, who rushed forward and leaned over her to fiddle with the display. She opened a channel to Hawk. "Hawk, we need you up here for a minute."

After a few minutes Raptor said, "There. The admiral sure didn't want this being seen by the wrong person."

"Just play it."

"Fallon," Krazinski said. "By now you know that Blackout has been corrupted. I realized too late, and wasn't able to protect you and the rest of Avian Unit. I'm sorry for that, and for your headache. I can only hope we can reverse what's been done to you. And now I'm forced to leave my own station." His gaze tracked to the left, away from the voicecom, then flicked back. "I don't have time to tell you everything I need to, and I couldn't risk that information falling into the wrong hands, anyway. What I can tell you right now is that Masumi Colb is the one behind all this. I've known this for over a year, and have been working to quietly take care of the problem. I don't have to tell you that if certain facts become publicly known, the entire Planetary Alliance Cooperative will be at risk."

His eyes flicked to the side and back again. "Colb was bringing you here to get you to attack the command. He intended to take over Jamestown in order to complete his plans. I had no choice but to make the place useless to him and to purge the people who were about to stage an uprising to assist him. Unfortunately Jamestown is now also useless to us, without months' worth of repairs. I can't tell you where we are now, as this file could become compromised. But if you put your head to the ground, you'll figure it out." His gaze jerked to the left.

"I have to go. I hope to see you soon. Whatever you do, don't trust Colb."

The image disappeared, but Fallon kept staring at the screen.

Hawk arrived, and they replayed the message. Fallon didn't get anything more the second time around, but it gave her time to think.

"Hang on," Hawk said. "Krazinski isn't the bad guy here?"

Fallon weighed the facts in her head. Losing Jamestown was devastating, even if they'd managed to take the databanks with them. Krazinski wouldn't have leveraged the entire station as an attempt to convince her team he wasn't guilty. He'd only do so in response to a much greater threat.

She rubbed her hand over the short, bristly side of her hair. "Per, is 'put your head to the ground' one of your odd Zerellian phrases?"

Peregrine shook her head. "No. Never heard it. I wondered what he meant by that."

"It's an odd thing to say." Fallon kept rubbing her hair. The sensation against her fingers helped her think.

"I could research the language circuits. See if it's a translation of something," Peregrine offered.

"It's worth a try." She suppressed a sigh. "Do you all think it's worthwhile to talk to Colb?"

"You could try," Raptor said, sounding doubtful. "He didn't seem inclined to do anything but bait you."

"No." Hawk's voice rang with authority. "He's too much like us. He'll lie, he'll weave stories, and you'd never know what was true and what wasn't."

"Yeah. You're probably right. But he mentioned Wren."

Raptor frowned. "Tactics 101. Keep your opponent off-balance, and make them think you have something they want."

She straightened. "Agreed. He'll stay in the brig. With a guard, whenever possible."

"Standard brig security not enough for you?" Ross asked. "If he tries to tamper with the system, he'll get thirty milliamps and find himself not breathing. He knows that."

"Call it paranoia," she answered.

"I'm good with paranoia," Hawk said.

"Okay. So we need a new plan. I'm open to suggestions."

"Dragonfire?" Hawk suggested after a moment of silence.

"Yeah. That's what I'm thinking too. We'll have the best defensive capability in case some friend of Colb's comes looking for him. The brig there is first-rate. It's the best option until we have more to go on."

"By the time we get to Dragonfire, there may be a panic about Jamestown. The first shouts will go up when someone goes to dock there, or communications don't get returned." Peregrine chewed on the pad of her thumb.

"Nothing we can do about that," Raptor said. "We can hope it happens later rather than sooner, but that's it."

"PAC allies will get very nervous once they know, and those who are not our allies will sense an opportunity."

"No pressure," muttered Hawk.

Fallon took a deep breath. "Fun time's over. Back to work."

"Where was I for fun time?" wondered Peregrine, but a hint of humor glinted in her eyes.

"Fun time was when we were going to storm the castle. Had my ass-kicking pants on and everything." Hawk ran his hands down his thighs.

"We all wear the same style of jumpsuit," Raptor pointed out.

"We were all wearing ass-kicking pants," Hawk explained.

"Still are," Peregrine reminded him.

"There will be no ass-kicking today," Fallon decreed. "Unless something unexpected comes up. But we will kick ass another day. Guaranteed."

FALLON SPENT her off shifts pacing her quarters end to end. She needed a new angle, a new strategy. A way to discover where the command staff from Jamestown had gone. They had answers she needed.

If Colb had been the one working against the PAC all along, did that mean that Krazinski was necessarily innocent? All the data pointing at Krazinski had been verified as genuine. But Colb could have created genuine documents that contained falsified information.

What about Krazinski's attempt to blackmail Brak into creating neural implants that were in violation of the PAC's treaties? The only way that added up was if Krazinski had been testing Brak—either to see if she'd do such a thing, or if she had already been asked to. Which could make sense, if Krazinski were trying to shut Colb down from the inside.

But why did Colb want treaty-breaking technology? And why install it in her head? He'd had many people to choose from, so why her? Maybe because he'd known her for so long. Or maybe he'd perceived her as a threat to his long-term plans.

She had all the questions, but none of the answers. And though she doubted he'd give her any real information, she wanted to look at Colb's face while she asked him the questions. Even if he told her only lies, she might come up with some useful tidbit. Besides, she had nothing more productive to do.

"Kiyoko-chan. It's so good to see you." Colb looked tired, but well enough. The brig wasn't big on privacy, but it provided adequate comfort.

"You can call me Fallon." She sat opposite the force field that kept him contained and exposed to scrutiny.

"Fallon. I've been hoping you'd come see me. I feel awful about what I said before. I was angry at being accused, but I can see how you'd suspect me. It's the hazard of what we do. When things go wrong, we're paranoid enough to suspect everyone."

What he said was true. But he'd had three days to think about his approach. She had to admit it was a good one, and he seemed utterly sincere.

"You mentioned Wren." Her tone was as hard as her gaze.

"Yes. Again, I apologize. I was just trying to keep myself out of the brig long enough to explain things to you. I knew your wife would be a tender spot that would get your attention."

"So you're no longer saying that there was some additional significance to my meeting her."

"Well there was," Colb said. "But only in that your assignment on the station was to investigate her."

"To keep me busy? Out of the way? With the rest of my team scattered in various places on equally bogus assignments?"

"I didn't think your assignment was bogus." Colb sat still, hands folded in his lap. "There was a legitimate concern of smuggling on Dragonfire, involving an insider."

"So you're maintaining your innocence. You're the good guy, fighting against the corruption."

"Of course. I still don't understand what caused you to suspect me. Clearly, I'm not the one who attacked Jamestown. I had to leave there months ago." His forehead furrowed with puzzlement.

He didn't know that she'd suspected him before they even arrived at PAC command. And he wasn't aware that Krazinski had left her a message. She could almost believe she'd made a mistake. That she'd misjudged Colb and reframed everything assuming his guilt. It all hinged on her belief that her parents wouldn't tell him that she'd visited them on the run from Blackout. If she was wrong about that, all of this could be upside down.

But she was sure she wasn't wrong.

She let doubt flicker briefly on her face as she thought. Any more than that and he'd be on to her. Maybe he already was. They were two trained liars, lying their best. She'd played the game plenty of times, but the stakes had never been this high.

"So tell me your story," she said. "Convince me."

SHE LEFT COLB AN HOUR LATER, feeling indecisive. She'd promised to go talk to him the next day, after they returned to Dragonfire. He'd made a convincing argument for himself while spinning a story that fit with Krazinski's supposed guilt. But she wasn't buying it.

She usually loved head games, but not this time. Losing meant a lot more than a failed mission or her own death.

She wedged herself into her bunk and closed her eyes. She'd be taking the last shift on the bridge before their arrival at Dragonfire, so she'd need the few hours of sleep she could squeeze in.

BEFORE THEY EVEN ARRIVED AT the station, Fallon had instructed her security staff there to prepare for a protected guest. She told them nothing of who the guest was, or why that person needed protected status. She simply ensured that when Colb arrived, the team could usher him to a private holding cell with no witnesses or security feeds.

She had Peregrine and Hawk handle that transfer while she went to update Hesta on what had occurred. She didn't resent the necessity of reporting to someone who was technically lower than her in the hierarchy, despite possessing a higher officer rank. Covert officers had elevated security ratings and didn't typically take orders from anyone less than an admiral, unless maintaining a cover identity. But Fallon had always reported to someone, and this was Nevitt's station.

Fallon hadn't been on Dragonfire long when her comport alerted her to a message from Wren. Fallon would have to wait until after her shift to answer it. She didn't have time for a personal call.

She went from one thing directly to the next, making sure Colb was secure, talking to her team, telling Raptor to search for clues about where they might find Krazinski and the rest of the PAC command. Then she attended to her job as security chief on the station. She got a status report from Arin, checked the station's systems, and looked at the reports that had been filed during her absence.

All the while, she kept thinking about what Krazinski had said about putting her head to the ground. So far they hadn't turned up any phrase matching, except for the colloquialism "keep your ear to the ground," which meant to pay attention to everything around her, particularly what people were saying. Did he mean that things happening at Dragonfire had greater meaning than they seemed to? That she might be missing some clue? Or maybe that she should be paying more attention to the datastreams because something of significance was happening there? It was just too vague a clue.

In her security office, she did a thorough search of all trending topics on the public voicecom channels, but nothing seemed relevant to her situation. So far, no one had raised the alarm about Jamestown, which was a relief. She was sure PAC command had done all they could to reroute signals and discourage ships from the area, but it was only a matter of time before someone noticed things were not as they should be.

She pushed back from her desk and sent her chair into a slow spin. Closing her eyes to accommodate an epiphany did not cause one to arrive. A shame.

She checked the time. Already well past the end of her shift. Wren would probably be asleep by now. She sent a text-only message for Wren to find when she woke, apologizing for not getting back to her sooner and telling her to get in contact the next day.

Finally, she locked up her office and went to get some sleep. Her rest schedule had been inconsistent because of her shift rotation on the *Nefarious*, and she'd need a good long slumber to get herself recalibrated.

Maybe she'd come up with an answer in her dreams. But then she thought of the strange memory dreams she'd had during her amnesia, and she hoped any big revelations waited until she woke up.

As she was about to get into bed, her door chime sounded. She expected to see Raptor or Hawk, but the door opened to reveal Wren's sparkling eyes and impish smile.

"Hi," Fallon said, stepping back so Wren could enter.

"Aha, I surprised you. I like that."

"Something wrong?"

"No. I just wanted to see you. You've been gone more than a week. But it looks like I might have woken you up. I can go."

Wren had seen her in her lounge clothes before, so that didn't bother Fallon. "It's fine. Come in, have a seat."

Once settled, Wren asked, "Did your trip go well?"

"I can't talk about that."

"Right. Then...are you well?"

Fallon wasn't sure how to answer that. "All systems functioning."

Wren smiled. "That's good to hear. Actually, that's probably the ideal answer to that question, when the person doing the asking is a mechanic."

"Fix anything fun while I was gone?"

"No, only the usual. Scheduled maintenance, a burned-out coil pack here and there from reckless use. Nothing interesting."

Fallon racked her brain for something else to say. "At least Endra's on board for you to hang out with."

"Yes. She told me they were making this their home port, which works great for me. They're preparing to leave for a distress call, though."

Fallon frowned. "Yes. Captain Nevitt told me about that."

A small cruiser had encountered some trouble, and the hospiship was the best-equipped vessel in the area to make sure the occupants got the care they needed. They'd also be able to tow the ship back, if needed. Such emergencies were common out in the void of space. The cruiser was lucky to have a hospi-ship in such proximity.

"I hope the crew's okay."

"Me too."

Wren stood. "I should let you get to sleep. You must be tired."

Fallon's goodbye before her departure to PAC command went unmentioned, but she knew Wren had to be wondering about it.

"I'm glad you came by." Fallon followed her to the door.

Wren smiled and kissed her cheek. "Goodnight."

"Goodnight. I'll see you tomorrow."

Wren's playfulness ignited. She gave Fallon a jaunty grin. "Count on it." She retreated down the concourse with a spring in her step.

Fallon watched her until she was out of sight.

IN THE MORNING, Fallon got up early for her regular workout. She'd arranged to meet Brak for a run.

When she stepped out of her quarters, though, she saw Raptor leaning against the wall of the concourse, waiting.

"Good morning." He wore workout attire.

"Morning. What's up?"

"Thought I'd run with you today."

"Sure. Brak's going to be there too, so I hope you're ready to work." She set off toward the lift.

"She didn't go with the *Onari*?"

"No. Said she'd serve no purpose and she might as well remain here. She's set up a small lab in her quarters. I need to find her a better space for it. She can always use her lab on the ship when it's docked, but it would be nice if she could work independently of the ship's flight schedule."

"Think that'll happen a lot? I somehow think of her and the ship as a package deal." He sounded surprised.

"Yeah, me too. But it would be an advantage to her to have a larger space for her work. She could even take on some interns, which would allow her to create more prosthetics in a shorter amount of time."

"Well, that's great. I'm glad things are working out for her. And glad she'll be there this morning. I've always wanted to find out how I measure up to her at a run."

"Have you been avoiding me?" She hadn't intended to ask that, but his sudden appearance had her wondering.

"No. Not exactly."

"What then?" she asked.

"Nothing. Just giving us space. Time."

"Hm," she said. "The space-time solution. How's it working?"

"Fine for me. How's it working for you?"

"Fine." Good, actually. Despite the escalation of their relationship, she didn't feel cornered. "You're a smart man," she admitted.

"Why, thank you. I've been waiting years for you to notice."

She snorted and bumped him with her elbow. He returned the bump, harder, causing her to sway to the opposite side. She shoved back with her shoulder to do the same to him.

"You'd better quit before we start fighting right here on the concourse," he warned her.

"*You'd* better quit," she argued, grinning.

"I hope you're ready to run hard today."

"Hah. I've been running with Brak for a while now. If you're looking for a competition, be prepared to lose."

They continued their trash talk all the way to the gym.

BY THE END of their run, they were both sweaty and bruised. Fallon considered it the best date of her life. Even if it hadn't really been a date.

She smelled the sweet musk of Brak's amusement.

"Are you two always like this?" she asked.

"Always," Raptor affirmed.

"Pretty much," Fallon admitted. "I don't think two humans ever reminded me so much of my own people."

Fallon pursed her lips as she thought about that. "Considering that you left home, I'm trying to decide if that's a compliment or not."

Brak tilted her head in a very Briveen gesture of humor. "Partly. Partly not. But pleasantly nostalgic, nonetheless."

"I'll be proud of that, then." Raptor winked before entering the men's locker room.

Brak and Fallon went into the women's room together and began to strip down for showers.

"May I ask a personal question?" Brak asked.

"Sure."

"Why do PAC facilities divide locker rooms and restrooms based on gender?"

That was not at all what Fallon had expected. "I take it Briveen facilities are all unisex?"

"Yes. We don't segregate normal functions like eating or bathing."

"Well, most species eat together because they consider it a social thing. Some people feel like personal care is a private thing, though. It's long been PAC tradition to have a male, a female, and a neither facility. It's the best shot at providing comfort for the biggest variety of people."

"It's always seemed inefficient to me," Brak said as she wrapped a towel around herself.

"Modesty certainly can be, but it's a social convention, and they can be extremely ungainly."

Brak nodded with understanding. "Ah. Yes, like the Briveen's penchant for rituals. It's a wonder my people get anything done."

"I've wondered about that," Fallon admitted. "Do people ever dodge one another just to avoid the rituals involved?"

Brak looked nostalgic, even as Fallon smelled a hint of sweet, musky amusement. "Sometimes."

Fallon didn't press further, since Brak said no more. She knew Brak was very private about her life on Briv and didn't want to pry.

After they had their showers and dressed, Brak closed her locker and paused. "You and Raptor have an unusual relationship. For humans."

"Neither one of us is a typical human. I guess it makes sense that we'd be as odd together as we are separately. Maybe even more so." Fallon zipped up her tote bag and slung it over her shoulder. Brak looked like she wanted to say something else, but she didn't. Fallon knew that Brak must smell how she and Raptor felt about each other, and it might raise a lot of questions.

But Brak didn't pry either. And Fallon had an idea to tuck away for later use.

FALLON WAS DOING her daily rounds on the boardwalk when all hell broke loose. When an emergency alert came through on her comport, she turned and ran. Fortunately, the brig was part of the Deck One security office, so she didn't have far to go. She flew through the door and bolted past the security checkpoints, which all hung open and unstaffed.

She came to a skidding stop in front of the highest-security brig cell. The one she'd assigned to Colb. It stood empty, other than three of her security lieutenants staring upward in shock, where a neat hole had been surgically cut out of the ceiling.

"Report!" she ordered.

Lieutenant Mat Jenson pulled himself together. "We had him

on continuous video monitoring and ten-minute physical checks, as ordered. Between one check and the next he disappeared."

"Halt all departures and arrivals. Lock down all decks. No one without alpha-one clearance leaves their deck. Advise all personnel to remain where they are."

Arin burst in. "Brief the legate," she continued. "Arin, report to the captain when you're up to speed. I'll keep you posted."

She ran for the lift. On the way, she used her comport to reach her team and bark out terse orders.

By the time she arrived at her office, her team was already inside. Peregrine sat, straight-backed, on the couch while Ross and Hawk paced. Any other time, she'd have complained about Raptor breaking through her security, but in this case she was glad he was already working on the problem.

"What do you see?"

"I'm isolating the Deck One office and brig's electrical systems and all components leading to that area," Raptor reported, his words clipped.

She wished she had a second hardlined voicecom display so she could work too. This was her station, and she didn't want to stand around. But Raptor was the best, and she had to leave it to him.

"There," Raptor muttered.

She waited for him to say more, but he only feverishly entered commands. Each time he swore, her anxiety rose.

Finally his fingers stopped their frantic activity and he pressed a hand to his temple, staring at the screen.

"What?" she demanded, moving to stand behind him.

"Two hours ago, someone wired the feed of a different cell to the circuit that was being monitored for Colb, which kept it from alerting anyone. Then they programmed a recurring loop of video, showing him sleeping. Someone cut through the bulkhead above his cell, bored a hole into the force field, and pulled him out."

Precious few people would have the tools and the skills to do such a thing.

The room went still. Quietly, Fallon asked, "How many ships have departed in the past fifteen minutes?"

Raptor's voice was equally quiet. "Two."

"Was either of them fast enough that we won't be able to find it?"

"One of them was."

"Then that was his ship." Her words fell like rocks.

They all stood frozen. Even Hawk was stunned silent. It was impossible. They'd put every security precaution into place.

Finally, Peregrine spoke the words they were all thinking. There was no other conclusion, since Fallon and Raptor had locked Dragonfire down so tightly that even the Ghost himself couldn't sneak in. They'd also been vigilant about investigating every person they allowed on the station.

"We lost him. And it was an inside job."

They searched every floor, scanned every conduit. Then they crawled through the triple-reinforced conduit above the brig's holding cell. Fallon peered through the hole, down to the empty cell below. The tools it would have taken to do that and to create an opening in the force field could be nothing but Blackout issue.

Which begged the question: Who was helping Colb? Maybe someone backed by a rival government? Was the traitor a member of the other half of Blackout? A double agent? Fallon had no answers. Everyone on Dragonfire had been accounted for. As far as they could tell, no one had left with Colb. Which meant Colb's ally was still on the station.

Once they'd done everything they could, her team, along with the captain, gathered in her office and sat in silence. Fallon knew exactly why no one spoke. Once they did, they'd have to start pointing fingers.

This job had required access, skills, and Blackout tech. That meant the only people on the station who could have pulled off this jailbreak were the five members of Blackout.

AFTER AN EXHAUSTING CONVERSATION, Fallon dismissed everyone, including Hesta, from her office. They'd somehow managed to avoid speaking of the thing they all knew but didn't want to discuss. They'd focused instead on managing this situation for the citizens of Dragonfire.

Fallon had appearances to keep up and upset people to soothe. As the chief of security, most of this job landed squarely on her shoulders.

She made a station-wide announcement about a fictitious training drill and praised the security team as well as the residents of the station. She extolled the virtues of such a well-protected station and assured them of her continued confidence in its safety.

Her security staff knew it was bullshit. They'd done plenty of drills in the past but never anything like this. And though she'd ordered the staff aware of Colb's escape to say nothing to anyone, she knew they had many, many questions. But they followed her orders, and several of her more senior officers made themselves conspicuous in public, smiling and making people feel safe.

She would have done the same, but it would have been too much. Too obvious. So she remained in her office until the end of her shift, which was what she'd do on a normal day. But inside, she seethed.

Logic and her training both demanded that she consider Hawk, Peregrine, and Raptor as suspects. But to do so would break something in her she'd never get back. She couldn't doubt them any more than she could doubt her own innocence.

Outside of her team, who could she trust? Brak? If Brak wanted Fallon dead, she would have died during her brain surgery, and no one would have been suspicious. So Brak was unlikely to be an adversary. Still, Brak had been in contact with Krazinski early on, and those interactions had been part of what had made her believe Krazinski was the one behind it all. And she had the skill to manufacture the things that had been in development at that secret lab.

Nevitt's treatment of Fallon had changed drastically several months ago. Cold resentment had turned into eager participation in a rebellion. What if Nevitt hadn't been helping her, but setting her up by letting her think she'd created a safe hideout?

What about Ross? He'd been in on Avian Unit's inner workings. Had he taken incredible risks to gain their trust?

Fallon didn't want to pace her quarters, so she walked the station instead. She took a slow, ponderous tour of each deck while she played devil's advocate to every instinct she had. When she found herself passing Wren's quarters, she paused. Maybe the one person she could trust was the one person she'd trusted before, when she'd had no memory.

All roads led to Wren.

So she rang the chime and before she could change her mind, Wren answered the door.

"This is a nice surprise. Come in."

She followed Wren in. "You changed the color." The walls were now a bright, sunny yellow.

"I needed something different. Something happy. You know?"

"Yeah." She did.

"You okay?" Wren's face was pinched with concern.

"Fine. Why?"

"I can tell when something's bothering you."

Fallon relaxed her face, her shoulders, and told the rest of her body to do the same. "I'm fine."

Despite her wishes, her instinct told her not to tell Wren the truth. Fallon's instinct had served her well, and though it was contrary to what she wanted, she wasn't about to ignore her gut.

"Okay. Good." Wren brightened. "I was going to watch a holo-vid. Want to join me?"

"You didn't have a date tonight?" Fallon forced humor into her eyes, though she didn't feel the least bit lighthearted.

"Nah, I was tired. Wanted a night in. I was thinking I might put on some classic vid and fall asleep watching it."

"I'm tired too, actually. A holo-vid would be great some other night."

"Did the drill today create a lot of extra work?" Wren looked sympathetic.

"Yeah, it did."

"How about a drink? I can tell you about the engine manifold I worked on today, then you can finish your drink and run away before I even get to the part about the switch gaskets."

Fallon smiled. "That sounds about right, actually."

So she sipped a Zerellian ale, listened to some technobabble, and let it distract her slightly. Afterward she gave Wren a light kiss and returned to her quarters.

Somehow she knew that Raptor wouldn't visit her that night. She wouldn't visit him, either. Each knew that the other should be considering them as a possible traitor. She already knew she couldn't do that, but maybe he was a better BlackOp than she was. She'd give him room, just in case.

"In the end, a spy is always alone." She turned off the lights and pulled the blanket up to her chin.

It was the last line in a book she'd enjoyed as a teen. For the first time, she truly understood it.

WHEN FALLON WOKE up the next morning her situation was the same, and she felt no better about it. But she still had a job to do.

She went for her morning run with Brak. She reported to Nevitt. She worked through security diagnostics and protocols and continued her search for the meaning of "put your head to the ground."

She'd exhausted all linguistic databases and come up with only two matches, but neither seemed applicable to her situation, even in the most abstract sense. So she continued to search for phrases that involved "head" or "ground."

Stomping ground, covering ground, shaky ground, common ground. Head of state, head of security, department head, head of the line, head over heels, kick in the head.

He could have meant *her* head specifically. It had been through a significant experience. If Krazinski had been referencing her injury, though, what did he mean by putting her head to the ground?

She blew out a breath and went back to the beginning. To the message on the chip.

Krazinski *wanted* her to figure out what he'd said. He wanted her to join up with the rest of PAC command. Maybe he was genuine, and maybe it was a trap, but either way, this was a puzzle he intended for her to solve.

That meant she should already have everything she needed to figure it out.

Okay, her head. Putting it to the ground. What if he meant electrical grounding? As in, using what was in her head to complete a circuit, through which current could flow.

So what the hell would that mean? The original implant was gone, leaving behind only the damage it had caused. The new implant Brak had given her worked differently. Did Krazinski know that she no longer had the implant Blackout had given her? If he didn't, his clue was useless.

She could talk to Brak and see if she had any ideas, since she had much more intimate knowledge of the technology. Fallon had no choice, really, if she wanted to pursue this angle. Brak had the data from the research station as well as her own expertise.

What other angles could Fallon work? She sent her chair into a spin and watched her office become a swirl of motion. She closed her eyes.

Without Krazinski, she was left with Colb. As her chair slowed to a stop, she reoriented herself toward the security vaults across the room. Priyanomine made the storage as tamper-proof and durable as possible. And within one compartment lay the splitter Ross had given her.

She could have used it. She could already know everything Colb knew.

If Blackout had ordered her to do that, before all this had happened, she would have. Now she had to weigh morality versus reality. Had she made a mistake in not using what was available to her?

But all this had started because someone had developed technology acknowledged by all PAC members to be wrong. One person's decision could change the outcomes of billions of lives. Could reshape history.

Which left her with only one question: How could she shape it back the way it was supposed to be?

Hoping Brak could help her find some of the answers she needed, Fallon asked her to come up to her office. It was a long shot, but she couldn't afford to overlook any possibilities.

"I'm sorry. There's nothing left of the original implant, and no way to simulate its activity." Brak lifted a shoulder in contrition, though she had nothing to be sorry for. "The implant I gave you is entirely different. If you're supposed to somehow use the device you had, that's just not possible."

Fallon smelled the vinegar scent of Brak's regret. If she'd had any lingering wisps of doubt about Brak's loyalty, that would have ended them. Briveen couldn't fake their emotive aromas. Some with great self-control could suppress them somewhat, but they couldn't manufacture a scent they didn't feel. Just as they were excellent lie detectors, they were terrible liars.

"I thought as much." Fallon reclined into the sofa cushions. "I'll have to hope that isn't the key I need."

"I could manufacture an implant like it, modeled on the research from the lab. Theoretically."

Fallon didn't have to think about it. "No. Bringing more stuff like that into existence is the opposite of what we're trying to do. Besides, I could never ask that of you."

"Good. I'm not sure I could have actually brought myself to do it."

"I'm glad we won't need to find out," Fallon agreed. "Do you have any ideas what else 'put your head to the ground' could mean?"

"There's an old saying on Briv." Brak executed a series of words, growls, and tonal sounds that Fallon could never hope to reproduce. "Roughly translated, it means, 'She who keeps her head near the ground, can best protect her eggs.' It's generally used to caution a young person to be patient."

"Hm." Fallon thought it over. "It's possible that Krazinski was telling me to be patient and wait for my opportunity. Or that I need to stay in place and protect what's in front of me."

"Either would seem to make sense. But which would it be?"

"I don't know. It could be neither. I'll have to keep looking." Fallon rubbed her fingers over the short side of her hair.

"I'll help with whatever I can," Brak said.

Fallon started to thank her, but her voicecom display made a sharp sound that she'd only ever heard during practice drills. But no drills were scheduled. She and Brak locked eyes, then rushed to the display on her desk.

Admiral Sokolov, Commanding General of the PAC, appeared on the screen. He looked like a kindly yet regal grandfather with his steely hair and gentle gaze.

"Citizens of the Planetary Alliance Cooperative, and friends. Today I must inform you that our government has been the recipient of a terrorist threat that we deemed highly credible. Do not be alarmed by this. We are strong, and always prepared to protect every station and every planet within our alliance.

"Once we verified the threat as credible, we immediately instituted the necessary protocols to ensure our collective safety. Jamestown has been vacated and temporarily disabled, so that no combatant may use it for their own purpose." His kindly face showed no worry, and his voice was as warm and smooth as a hundred-year-old Sarkavian brandy.

"Do not be alarmed. This is a protocol that keeps PAC command and the entire cooperative safe and strong. Anyone who attempts to attack us, I can assure you, will not succeed. As always, if you have any personal concerns, please contact your local representative, who is already aware of the situation, and your concerns will be addressed." He paused, smiled, and said, "We are already on the trail of these terrorists, and will bring them to justice. Even a mere threat to the PAC will not go unanswered. Good day, my friends and family."

The message ended. Brak clacked her teeth in agitation. "That guy's so smooth, I could almost believe him."

"Me too." Fallon understood why command had been forced to issue a statement. Any day, someone might notice that something was wrong at Jamestown. She only hoped that Sokolov's statement fended off panic.

"Do you think local representatives were already contacted?" Brak asked.

"No. Maybe leaders of PAC bases. Major installations. Everyone else will be expected to play along and say that yes, of course they're well aware, and there's nothing to worry about."

"Funny government you have," Brak said.

"Hey, your world is a PAC member too, even though you maintain your own planetary government. Most of the time, PAC procedure works. But in times of crisis, a few corners get cut here and there."

Fallon watched as messages for her began to roll in. They started as a trickle, then became a stream. "I see my work is cut out for me for the rest of the day."

Brak chuckled. "I'll let you get started. I have my own work to do."

"What are you working on now?"

"A pair of cybernetic legs. Farming accident."

Fallon cringed. "You're a good person, Brak."

After Brak left, she indulged herself in a sigh of resignation before answering the first message.

Fallon made a station-wide announcement to reassure everyone, and thought she did a damn good job of it. She even tied in the "training drill" that had locked the station down, explaining it as an abundance of caution and preparedness. She continued responding to messages. Mostly, people just wanted to be reassured. Each time she talked to someone, she felt their tension ease.

Not that people weren't still worried. They'd have to be idiots not to be concerned about their government disabling its own headquarters and moving to a secret location. But near-panic ebbed to reasonable levels of worry. No doubt the same scenario was playing out in thousands of locations across the PAC zone.

Those other locations weren't Fallon's problem, though. She squeezed a meeting with Avian Unit, Ross, and Hesta into her schedule.

In her office she told them, "I think we're at the point that we need to let Arin know everything that's going on. I see no benefit in continuing to keep him innocent of our plans."

Unanimous agreement. Good.

"Per PAC protocol, I will increase training drills, both for security staff, officers, and residents of the station. People would find it odd if I didn't."

More agreement.

"Am I missing anything?" She looked from one face to the next.

"Any thoughts on finding Colb?" Hesta asked.

"It's a big universe," Hawk said.

"He won't return to Zerellus," Peregrine added. "He'll be looking for someplace where he can disappear."

"Yeah. He's not going to leave any trail for us." Fallon wished it could be as easy as tracking him down. "We have to talk to Krazinski. He has the bigger picture in all this. That might tell us what Colb needs and where he might go."

Hawk scratched at his beard as he thought. "I'm hoping he doesn't have many allies left, after command cleaned house at Jamestown. That he's on the run, alone."

They agreed that until they found Krazinski, their priorities would be protecting Dragonfire, staying aware of what was going on in the PAC zone, and looking for their traitor.

"I'm glad Krazinski seems to be on our side," Ross said.

"You did have a hard time with the idea of his guilt." Maybe Fallon should have given his doubts more weight. She had to wonder how that might have changed their actions and their current situation.

"Yeah. It never made sense to me. I hope he's for real." Ross kept his hands folded in his lap.

"We all do." Raptor nodded.

The room went quiet. It seemed they had exhausted all of their discussion topics. "Let me know if you notice anything unusual going on. If morale on Dragonfire takes a turn for the worse, I'll deputize the four of you and put you to work." Fallon smiled pleasantly at her team.

And that effectively cleared the room. Except for Hesta, who left at a much more leisurely pace, looking amused.

FALLON TOOK an evening stroll around the station. If people saw her unstressed and going about life as usual, they'd do the same. Command officers always set the tone for those who depended on them.

She didn't return to her quarters until well into the night. She'd missed her chance to check in on Wren. By now, she would be sleeping. Fallon would check on her first thing in the morning.

After a long, steamy shower, she dried off and wrapped a towel around herself, then began drying her hair. Leaning forward, she called out, "You can quit hiding and come in here."

"Aw. How did you know?"

She turned to watch Raptor come into her bedroom. "I suspected you'd show up tonight, so I was listening extra hard."

"And I thought I was being extra quiet," he teased as he pulled her close and mussed her hair.

"Stop that. I just got it all smoothed out."

"It's going to get messed up when you sleep on it anyway. Besides, it's cute when your hair's all wild."

"Are you sleeping over?" she asked.

"Am I invited?"

"Yes." She'd been hoping he'd show up. She'd considered going to his quarters, but she needed to remain in her own, in case someone came looking for her.

"Then yes."

"I'll be asleep as soon as I stop moving, so you should go ahead and shower." She pointed to the necessary, as if he didn't know where it was.

He tugged on her towel. "If you're on a timer, how about we make better use of the minutes you have left and I can shower while you're sleeping?"

His suggestive smile made her grin.

"Deal."

A MINOR EMERGENCY with a hazardous spill in Docking Bay Five messed up Fallon's entire morning schedule. She tried contacting Wren via the voicecom twice, but failed to connect with her.

She spent the entire day playing catch-up. At the end of it, she tracked Wren down in person. She'd put off checking in with her for too long. She checked the mechanics' shop, since she'd finished her shift on Deck One, but when Wren wasn't there, Fallon headed up to general crew quarters.

The doors to Wren's quarters opened before Fallon could touch the chime. She pulled her hand back. "Oh, sorry. I didn't realize you were going out. I won't keep you."

Based on Wren's attire, Fallon guessed Wren had a date.

Wren's cheeks pinkened. She made blushing a very pretty thing. "No, it's okay. I'm early anyway. Do you want to come in for a minute?"

"I won't hold you up. I just wanted to check on you. Make sure you're okay with all that's been going on lately."

Wren laughed, but it was a little high-pitched and uncomfortable sounding. Not at all her usual confident self. "Actually, I've been a little on edge. But I'm sure things will be fine. Of course they will." She smiled gamely.

"I'm sorry all this has rattled you. You're not the only one. Fortunately, most people on the station are trying to take it all in stride."

Wren's smile became more genuine. "People who live on space stations are a sturdy bunch. We'll be fine."

"If you ever need anything, you know you can call me anytime."

"I know. Thank you."

The conversation lagged for a moment too long. "Well, have a good evening. I should get going."

As she strode away, Fallon tried to shake off the awkward encounter. She'd only meant to make sure Wren was doing okay. She hadn't meant to make her uncomfortable. It seemed that Wren wasn't as breezy about seeing Fallon and dating someone else as she'd thought she'd be.

FALLON HAD ALMOST MADE it back to her quarters when her comport alerted her. A call from the captain. Hesta. Whatever.

She hurried through the doors and took the call in private.

"Fallon here."

"Chief, I was wondering if you'd like to join me for a drink."

Fallon stared dumbly at the screen. She shook herself and quickly said, "Yes. Of course. That will be an interesting first."

Hesta smiled wryly. "I know. Work with me here. I'm breaking old habits."

"Difficult and honorable work," Fallon said. "When and where?" She didn't know whether Hesta was thinking of a night out, or a personal tête-à-tête.

"The pub. Twenty minutes?"

"I'll be there." Fallon wondered what a night out with Hesta Nevitt would be like.

She was about to find out.

7

Fallon had to hand it to the people of Dragonfire Station. They faced a terrorist situation unlike anything they'd seen in history, along with an uncertain future. And now their previously antisocial captain sat in the bar, sipping a startlingly dark-green beverage.

And yet people simply carried on with their lives. They'd continued doing their jobs as scheduled, and no major freak-outs had been reported. All things considered, Dragonfire Station's people kept their shit together nicely. Fallon was proud of them.

"Zerellian ale," she said to the bartender as she passed by on her way to Hesta's table. Then she stopped and turned back. "Actually. What's that the captain's drinking?"

"Cordovan whisky," the captain called loudly, causing a few heads to turn.

"Give me a Cordovan whisky," Fallon told him.

"Instead of the ale?" he asked.

"In addition to." She joined Hesta at her table. "Your invitation was a pleasant surprise."

Hesta toasted her with the whisky. "You know what? I'm aiming at being surprising lately."

"I have to admit, I find that deeply intriguing. Say more."

Hesta laughed. Again, heads turned, but people only glanced at the captain before returning to their own conversations, smiling.

Fallon could practically feel the mood of the place lifting. If the captain was in the pub, laughing and having a good time, things couldn't be too bad, right?

Hesta might be a genius.

Fallon's drinks arrived, and she toasted Hesta with her own whisky. "To the most puzzling person I've ever had the pleasure to serve under."

She tossed back the whisky and felt a roar of fire race down her throat, into her chest, and quite possibly begin to burn her alive from the inside out.

"A fan of Cordovan whisky?" Hesta asked as she took a swig of her own.

"First time trying it," Fallon admitted, attempting to seem unaffected by the liquid fire that seemed intent on consuming her.

"First lesson—don't down it." Hesta looked like she was trying not to laugh.

"Lesson learned." Fallon took a drink of her ale. It had its own kick rather than being soothing, but she figured the more alcohol she had, and the sooner she had it, the less she'd care about her burning throat and sinuses.

"To what do I owe the honor?" she asked Hesta. "You could have invited anyone."

"I invited you."

"That's not an answer," Fallon pointed out. "Since I already knew that."

"It's the answer you're getting." Hesta's eyes crinkled in amusement.

"All right."

They watched each other. Challenging. Measuring.

"You've gone quiet." Hesta sipped her whisky.

"Just waiting for you to start the conversation."

"I thought I had."

"No, those were only the preliminary ground rules."

Hesta laughed again. It was a rich, warm sound. "I should know better than to try to go toe-to-toe with someone in your line of work. Fine. Truth is, I want us to get to know one another better. Nothing more. So in the interest of doing so, you can ask me any question. I'll give you a truthful answer."

"Now that's an opening salvo." Fallon folded her napkin in a geometric pattern as she considered. "A lot of pressure though. I need to think of a good one." She took her time, considering her options. Finally she made her decision. "Okay. What kind of name is Hesta?"

"I give you access to any detail, and that's what you ask?"

"Yep."

Hesta shook her head in amused puzzlement. "You're an odd one. But okay. It's a family name. Comes up among the girls every three or four generations. It's a variation of the name Hester, which is an ancient Earth name, and means 'star.'"

"Suits you, being captain of a space station."

"I never thought of that. Funny." She straightened. "So do I get to ask you a question now?"

Suspicious, Fallon asked, "Is that why you offered to answer a question? To get to ask one in return?"

One corner of Hesta's mouth lifted. "No. Sometimes a suggestion is only a suggestion, Fallon. No ulterior motive."

"Really?" Fallon affected a surprised expression. "What's that like?"

Hesta smiled. "Somehow, I think you're being more honest than you are joking. Which would be disturbing if I took time to really think about it."

"So what's your question?"

Hesta's expression grew thoughtful. Finally, she asked, "After you lost your memory and you 'met' me for the first time, what did you think of me?"

"Is this a trick question?"

Hesta arched an eyebrow. "No. I'm curious about your impressions."

"I thought you were regal. Respectable. Beautiful. And I thought you hated me."

"I never hated you. I resented that you were forced on me. But life happens the way it happens, doesn't it?"

"Sometimes." Fallon preferred to shape the way things happened, but that hadn't worked well for her lately.

Hesta drew a swirling pattern on the table. "Funny how when things go wrong, as in really wrong, that you never know if it's a long-term disaster or a greater-good opportunity. Don't you think? It's only when we look back on history that we apply those labels of good and bad. Or barbaric and heroic."

"How do you think people will look back on what's happening right now?"

"That depends on what happens from here. Can we turn it and make it into a chance for improvement, for growth and learning, or does it become something with long-term impact for the worse?"

"It could go either way. But it's probably always like that during pivotal moments. Is it my turn for another question?"

Hesta nodded.

"Do you regret any of your choices, up to this point?"

Hesta's eyes unfocused as she weighed and measured her life. Finally, she fixed her gaze on Fallon and said decisively, "No. I'm not much of a regrets person."

Fallon raised her glass. "Me neither."

They toasted with the remnants of their drinks. Hesta didn't order another, so neither did Fallon.

"My turn for a question." Hesta's expression became sly. "What's Ross' story?"

Fallon had anticipated a number of questions, but not that. "You like Ross."

"I'm not nine years old," Hesta chided. "But he does interest me."

"He's a good guy. I've always liked him. I don't know him especially well from a personal standpoint, given that he was an instructor. He's been a good addition to my team. That says a lot, considering how closely the rest of us have worked together for so long."

Hesta only nodded, so Fallon asked, "Want me to ask him if he likes you?"

"Shut up." Hesta smiled. "If I decide I'm interested, I definitely don't need any help."

Fallon pointed a finger gun at Hesta, who blinked. "What's that?"

"A thing Trin does. No one seems to know why. Do you know him?" Fallon would bet she didn't.

"No. I barely know the *Onari* crew." Her expression darkened.

"Since they're based here for the time being, it's probably time to change that." Fallon supposed she might be overstepping, but didn't give a damn.

"Yeah. Probably."

"I'll introduce you around. Don't worry." Fallon reached across the table and patted Hesta's hand.

"It's not that. I was wondering if people around here think I'm a hardass."

"Well, yeah," Fallon admitted. "But all of my friends are hardasses. If they weren't, I don't think they'd be my friends."

Hesta smiled. "Makes sense. All right." She lifted her glass. "To hardasses."

A familiar voice came from behind Fallon. "Now that is a toast I can get behind." Hawk nudged Fallon over and sat beside her. "I'm not intruding, am I?"

"Yes," Fallon answered.

"But it's fine," Hesta added. "Please join us."

Fallon let Hawk take over the conversation, as he so loved to do, and watched her captain expertly engage with his robust personality.

Seeing Hesta let herself become a part of the crew would be fun.

"I SHOULD HAVE MET with you sooner, but it's been one thing after another." Fallon sat across from Arin in her office the next day.

"Is something wrong?" Arin shifted nervously.

"No. Well, yes. Obviously, things aren't right when PAC command is hiding out. But that's why I want to talk to you."

"Okay."

"You know from what happened after my memory loss that I'm not just a security officer."

He nodded slowly. "Yes."

"Have you ever had any interest in being more than a security officer yourself? Going classified?"

"You mean intelligence? Of course. But intelligence officers start that track right out of the academy. I clearly didn't make that cut."

"You've made the cut now, as far as I'm concerned."

His eyes widened. "You can do that?"

"Well, there are some details I'll need to explain, but first I have to know that you're all in. Because this is one of those choices that means no going back. So be sure."

He pursed his lips. "I don't need time to think about it. I'm in."

"Good. Let's dig right in. First off—have you ever heard of an organization called Blackout?"

THREE HOURS LATER, Arin looked shell-shocked.

"Still glad you opted in?" Fallon asked.

"I think so. Ask me in a week."

She appreciated his attempt at humor. Overall, he'd handled her revelations awfully well. "You'll have questions. You can talk to Avian Unit, Ross, Captain Nevitt, and Captain Jerin Remay. I'll have a meeting for everyone soon, to gel the team. We must take all due precautions when discussing sensitive topics, of course. We're working with classified and off-book intel."

"Right. I will. Of course I knew things were going on, but the reality of it all is something else." He shook his head. "And I thought that once my people escaped Atalus, we'd be living in a free and progressive society."

"We are. We will be. We just have to take out the trash."

"You make it sound easy." He scratched at his ear distractedly.

"It isn't. The goal is clear-cut but the means are anything but. Speaking of which—I have two things I want you working on."

"I'll do whatever I can," he promised.

"Kellis needs training. Security, hand-to-hand combat, weapons. Basically, a crash course in everything you learned in security school."

His voice rose in surprise. "Kellis?"

"She knows about Avian Unit, but we haven't discussed details. Mostly she's aware that we're at odds with the PAC and trying to right what's going wrong. She accompanied us for the attack on the Tokyo base, but it really rattled her. She's not going to be any use to us until she has some training."

"I can start working with her this evening, if she's available," he said.

"Good. I'll talk to her, let her know what's going on. Then you two can work out the schedule on your own." She paused. "Now the second job. I've left a stone unturned, and I need you to help me flip it over and inspect it."

"What do you mean?"

"I need information about events on the station that occurred in the year before I arrived. Maybe even two years. First, we'll search the official records, then we'll need to dig deeper. I'll need your personal recollections so we can search personal logs and communications. I may need you to question people about that time. Do not mention any of this to anyone else."

Arin wore the look of a man who was about to stand in front of a firing squad, but was prepared to meet his fate. "Okay. When should we start?"

"Now."

SOMETIMES YOU GO LOOKING for something you don't want to find, and then you find it. It only took a few hours for Fallon to unravel this particular knot. But now that she had, she needed some time to think about her next steps.

She gave herself the night to mull it over. The next day, she'd have to act on what she'd found. It would have both personal and professional ramifications. She wanted to be alone to give it some deep thought, but she didn't want to be in her quarters or her office. Going to the boardwalk was out of the question. But she knew the perfect place, with no risk of interruption.

Her serious expression and brisk pace kept anyone from sidelining her as she walked through the station, and she avoided areas likely to be well populated. On Deck Five, she bypassed the crew quarters to head straight for the center of the deck. Several layers of security later, she stood alone in crisis ops control. It seemed like a fitting location, and absolutely no one would come here. She'd run training drills in crisis ops, but a situation had never arisen to warrant using it for real. It would have been exciting if one had, but she cared deeply about this community, and was glad one hadn't.

Crisis ops had half the space of the regular ops control and was stocked with emergency medkits and rations of food and water. Weapons too. Stingers, low-grade projectile weapons that weren't a risk for hull puncture, and edged weapons.

She really hoped Dragonfire never saw an event that required the use of this room.

She eased into the command chair. It wasn't as comfortable as the one in regular ops, but she didn't care. She wasn't there for comfort. She needed to think about the decisions she'd made in the past couple of years. She analyzed everything, trying to determine whether her actions had caused her current troubles. Whether she'd missed something that would have changed everything.

She couldn't be sure. Had she been blind? Had she helped create this entire situation?

BY THE TIME she returned to her quarters, Fallon had performed a factory reset on herself. She'd never been a very emotional person. She was logical. Tactical. Someone who didn't get so caught up in her relationships with people that she missed something.

She needed to go back to being *that* person.

To say that Raptor's presence on the couch in her quarters was bad timing would be an understatement. She stopped just inside the doors as they whisked closed behind her, her armor up and her stupid heart silenced.

Raptor's wolfish grin faded. He stared at her, and the light seemed to leak out of him. "Well, fuck."

"I need to focus on what we're doing. No more personal stuff until I get it all sorted."

"We've never been anything but focused on getting the job done." His voice was flat. "What happened?"

"I screwed up. Let myself get distracted. It's not your fault—it's mine."

His mouth pressed into a hard line. "Humans are supposed to have feelings. I thought you'd figured that out." He searched her face. "Damn, Fallon, *what happened?*"

His hurt almost broke her resolve. She stood still, her eyes fixed on a spot on the wall. She had to do it this way if she wanted to trust her own judgment, because if she opened her mouth she'd lose it. And the fact that he could make her lose her willpower was exactly why she needed to keep it. This wasn't about what she wanted. The safety of everyone she cared about depended on her objectivity.

She continued to stare at the wall, standing at attention.

"Right." He stood and strode past her to the door. He paused before triggering the door sensor. "If you decide to tell me what's going on, come talk to me. Otherwise, I won't bother you again. All business, just like you want. Blood and bone." His bitter tone made their motto sound like a curse.

Then he was gone. She should have felt bad, but she didn't. She didn't feel stripped, or hollowed. She didn't ache to call him back. No, she felt nothing.

FALLON SLEPT LITTLE. Her task for the next day pressed down on her too hard. After giving herself the night to think about her situation, she now had to act. To address the betrayal. Finally she got up and went to work early, skipping her usual run.

In her office she completed regular security checks with obsessive precision while waiting for Arin to escort the person behind her current difficulties.

When they arrived, she nodded at them both, remaining seated.

For the first time in her life, she didn't want the answers she was about to demand.

"Thank you, Arin. You're dismissed to your duties."

He covered his puzzlement quickly as he bowed and left.

She steeled herself. She felt only her sense of duty. Only the need to do her job.

She focused on the traitor across from her, trying to decide just how long the deception had been going on. Finally, she asked the question she most needed to have answered. "How long have you been in collusion with Admiral Masumi Colb?"

Wren's eyes widened and she sucked in a noisy breath. "What?"

"Drop the act. You know what I am. You know what I do. It took me longer than it should have to connect you to him, but I've corroborated it with eyewitness reports and surveillance recordings. You started meeting with him eight months before my arrival on Dragonfire. Did you know him before that?"

Wren wrapped her arms around herself and rocked gently back and forth. "Oh no," she whispered.

"I'm glad that you've decided not to play dumb." Fallon watched her fair-skinned former wife grow even paler.

"It's not that." Wren licked her lips. "I just want you to be safe. But now…" Her voice broke. "I don't know what's going to happen."

"Start at the beginning. When did Colb first contact you, and how did he identify himself to you?"

"Like you said, eight months before you arrived on the station. I'd never met him before that. He found me in the shop and said he needed to talk to me about vital security. He showed me his identification as a PAC officer, and I was able to confirm with intelligence that he worked for them as an operative."

"He's a little more than that."

"I found that out. I didn't know anything about Blackout at that point. When I learned he was an admiral, I couldn't imagine what he'd want with me. But he said he needed my help to find a clutch of smugglers that had been operating through this station. Chief Pirlin, who was here before you, wasn't as thorough. Things weren't like they are now. I agreed to hand over packages on three different occasions to smugglers, who acted as the middlemen to get the items where they needed to go."

"What was in the packages?" Fallon asked.

"Medicine. Supplies that were being stolen from PAC aid shipments to planets that were in desperate need. They were being sold on the black market instead of getting delivered. And Colb's operation worked. The smugglers did what Colb needed them to do and I never saw them again. Colb thanked me. I thought that was it."

"But it wasn't."

Wren shook her head. "He contacted me again soon after. Said that since he knew he could trust me, he wanted me to continue helping him get those medical supplies to where they were supposed to go. Legitimate smuggling, more or less. Keeping the goods hidden so they didn't invite theft."

"Right." Fallon had to admit it was a plausible story. The PAC had resorted to such tactics in the past.

"I'd pass on a package every day or so. It was nothing. Took a few minutes out of my day. I felt proud to be helping the PAC and the people who needed those supplies."

"So then what?" Fallon asked. Perhaps the biggest mysteries in life were buried in that midpoint between Point A and Point B.

"Nothing. It continued on that way. I didn't hear from him again until he came to the station a week before you arrived. He said that our new chief of security was like a daughter to him and he hoped I'd look out for her in whatever way I could. He said that there was some power shift in your department and he'd assigned you to Dragonfire to keep you safe from all that. I thought it was normal politics. I didn't know then you were in intelligence." Wren's face was pinched, worried.

So what Colb had said implying that her meeting Wren had not been a coincidence was true. It should have hurt. Should have made her go cold, then flush with anger. But she was hard. She was polymechrine incarnate. And she was ready to cut to the chase. "When exactly did he give you a force-field disruptor and a class-eight plasma torch? I'm guessing you hid those in your shop somewhere?"

Wren's eyes widened with the understanding that Fallon knew everything. "I put them in a restricted-access locker, where only I could get to them. Colb gave the items to me right after you and I got married."

"Strange wedding present."

"It wasn't that. He said that the power shift had become something more, and that if we ever needed to escape the station quickly, we should use these."

Fallon squinted. "That didn't seem strange to you?"

"Of course it did! That was my first clue that I'd gotten in over my head, that all this was more than I'd thought. I'm not…I mean, I'm just a mechanic who wants people to be safe and fed and taken care of." Tears of frustration formed in her eyes. "Especially you."

Fallon searched Wren's face as she talked, looking for any hint that would give her away. Prove she was an enemy. But she didn't find it. She only saw a bewildered and frightened woman.

"How did Colb alert you to break him out of the brig?"

Wren stared down at her hands. "An automated message. It told me that if I received it, he'd been taken into custody. That the situation with the PAC command restructuring had become an all-out coup, and your commanding officer, who was the real enemy, had convinced you that Colb was the one responsible for everything."

"And you just did what he said? What about coming to me? Telling me what you knew? Letting me do what I do best? Instead, you acted appalled that I hadn't told you about being a covert operative!" In spite of herself, Fallon found her voice rising.

"You did keep that from me, and I *was* horrified! That part was true. But if I had revealed myself at that point as a liar in league with your enemy, you wouldn't have believed me. I was in too deep." Wren's eyes were wild. "Colb had told me the best way for me to protect you was to say nothing until he could take on the person who had been after you and finally get everyone on the right side together." She pressed her hand to her eyes. "I just wanted you safe." Her voice was a ragged sob.

Fallon tried to poke holes in Wren's story, but couldn't. Wren had been duped by a master who had put time into grooming her. She'd thought she was protecting Fallon.

"So you know I'm a BlackOp, then?"

Wren laughed—a wet, manic sound. "I'm naïve, not stupid. I knew things weren't right early on when your abilities didn't match your record, though I didn't realize how deep that went. But now there's this supposed coup, and the PAC command scuttling Jamestown and going into hiding. And you, in the thick of it all. Appearing, disappearing. Showing up with these friends of yours who look like they eat rocks and belch fire. There's no other answer but that you're one of the people involved in everything that's happening. And…and your head. That's part of it all, isn't it?"

Fallon didn't answer. Didn't feel like she owed Wren any answers at the moment. "Do you still believe Colb?"

"I did. I thought he cared about you and wanted to protect you. But I trust you more than I trust gravity. So tell me what I should believe and I will."

Oh, Prelin. Wren's innocence and blind trust stripped Fallon bare. She rose, went around the desk, and opened her arms.

Wren broke into sobs and clung to Fallon like a child. "I'm sorry," she croaked. "I was so stupid."

Fallon guided her to a sofa. "We're both sorry. We thought we could protect each other by keeping secrets."

They lay back with Wren's head against Fallon's shoulder. After many long minutes, Wren sat up and took a deep breath, her eyes red. "I didn't pursue you because he told me to."

"I know."

"You do?"

Fallon had to smile at her look of surprise. "You'd never do that."

"Of course not! That's horrible."

Fallon laughed. Somehow, this eager, gullible woman's disgust for duplicity seemed hilarious. In spite of what she'd done, she was a better person than Fallon would ever be. "I guess it's no wonder you freaked out and dumped me when you realized I was involved in covert operations."

Wren sighed. "I had no idea what to think. Colb was out of touch, and you had no memories."

"I can only come to one conclusion," Fallon said.

"What?" Wren's face was full of worry.

"That you are truly awful at picking wives."

Wren smiled. "I picked a great one. I just wasn't strong enough to…to watch the world burn so I could be with you."

Fallon found her own words romantic, when coming out of Wren's mouth.

"And now?"

Wren held Fallon's hands in hers. "Let's burn it all down. Whatever this is, I'm in it with you."

Fallon usually had a few different options marked out at any given time. Strategies. Plans. But looking into Wren's eyes, she made the only choice she could—she kissed her.

"GOOD NEWS," Fallon announced when she assembled Avian

Unit, Ross, and Hesta in her quarters that evening. "I know how Colb escaped."

"And the bad news?" Hesta asked.

"Wren broke him out."

A long pause allowed Hawk to get all the swearing out of his system.

When he was done, she held up a hand to the questions being thrown at her. "She thought he was the right side to trust, just as we did at one point. She thought she was doing the right thing. But I've worked it through, and this could work in our favor."

"How's that?" Ross asked.

"He doesn't know we've flipped her. Therefore, he should still trust her. We can work with that. All we need is an idea."

Silence fell, and she knew they saw the opportunity.

"What do we do about Wren?" Hesta asked.

"She now understands the basics of the situation, and I'm certain we can trust her."

"You're sure you're being entirely objective about that?" Peregrine looked curious rather than doubtful.

"As sure as I can be. You're all welcome to question her. In fact, I want you to." She gave them a moment to think about it before she moved on. "Arin's going to be training Kellis, now that I've brought him on board. He'll be invited to meetings like these in the future too. It's going to get tougher to get us all together, since someone's bound to be on duty at any given time."

"You know..." Hawk scratched at his beard. "I'm thinking of chucking all of this top secret shit and taking up farming on some little planet."

"No you aren't." Peregrine smirked at him.

"No, I'm not," he agreed. "But it sure sounds nice, every now and then."

"You'd be bored in no time," Fallon pointed out. "It sounds

like we have no ideas on how to reel Colb in. I want you all to think about it and we'll meet tomorrow to discuss it."

Nobody looked thrilled with their assignment.

"Cheer up," Fallon said. "This is good. We have a way in."

She wondered if they were thinking about Wren and her trustworthiness, but they'd just have to talk to her themselves. Then they could be sure.

Raptor was the last to leave, and he fixed her with a look before he did. He'd said nothing the entire meeting, and she could only wonder what he was thinking. She needed to talk to him to explain her previous need for space, but his look told her that he now wanted some distance. They were the same, the two of them. What always drew them together also pushed them apart. She hoped that soon, he'd be ready to talk.

FALLON WOKE up with Wren the next morning, feeling happy but guilty. On one hand, she had Wren, pink-cheeked and brimming with gaiety, peeping at her over a quick breakfast. On the other, her heart felt heavy about Raptor. Her relationship with Wren hadn't bothered him before, but she'd told him she needed to not have relationship stuff clouding her vision. Then she'd almost immediately taken her relationship with Wren to another level. Raptor deserved better, and she couldn't have felt more shitty about it.

"Busy day ahead, right?" Wren asked.

"You could say that. Bunch of spy shit. You know."

Wren laughed at her. "You're awful."

"You're probably right."

Wren shook a chopstick at her. "You're not supposed to agree."

"How about you?" Fallon asked. "A lot to get done today?"

"Routine stuff. Some basic maintenance on incoming ships."

"Well, maybe you'll get lucky and someone's ship will blow up, requiring you to make unusual and difficult repairs."

"Don't tease. But that would be nice," Wren admitted. "Not that I want anyone to get hurt."

"You just like the more interesting jobs. I know."

Wren smiled and took the last bite of her blistercake. "Want to watch a holo-vid tonight?"

"I'd love to, but I'll have to see how the day goes."

"Right. Spy shit, and all." Wren began clearing the table.

"That's my life." Fallon finished her own blistercake and gathered her dishes, taking them into the kitchenette.

"Yeah. I'm okay with it." Wren leaned back against the cabinet and pulled Fallon into a hug. "I'm sure I don't even know what that really means yet, but I'll learn."

"You're sure you want to deal with that?" Fallon didn't know what this conversation was leading to.

"Yes. I love you. Whether your name is Em or Fallon or Rikivontagu. I love *you*. Your heart, your humor, your way of being all hard on the outside but all soft on the inside. I'm in this long term. You've never been just an *amore* to me." Wren fixed her with an intense look. She clearly needed Fallon to know that their relationship had never been a casual affair to her.

There are some statements and questions that, no matter how you answer, you're screwed. Even taking too long to answer means you're screwed. And as much as Fallon didn't want to be quiet for too long, she wanted even more not to say the wrong thing that she could never take back.

But rather than be offended, Wren smiled and kissed Fallon's nose. "Relax. I'm not asking for anything. Married, not married, monogamous, free…I don't care about all that. You humans have the worst time appreciating what you have. You have to put all this energy into owning someone, or being owned. That's the one thing you never really understood about me. I thought you'd started to loosen up, considering that good-looking teammate of yours." She gently traced her fingers over the back of Fallon's neck. "I don't need any more than to know that we have this, and that we're going to keep having this."

"So what you're saying is that you have other people you don't want to stop seeing naked." Fallon couldn't say it without laughing, even though she'd intended to be deadpan.

Wren pressed closer and kissed Fallon's earlobe. "You're my favorite person to be naked with, the only one I love beyond reason, no questions asked. And if you really wanted to go back to monogamy we could. But I think we'd both be happier if we didn't. Don't you, Lady Spy Shit? With all of your stunts and intrigue, don't you want to be able to live on the edge without worrying about petty jealousy?"

"Well, when you put it that way, it does sound more convenient."

Wren leaned in for a feather-soft kiss. "Why do humans measure different loves against one another, then limit themselves to only one? Why not take all the passion you can get? Our lives are short. Shouldn't we enjoy all the love we can while we have the chance?"

It sounded kind of familiar, if Fallon replaced "love" with "adventure." And in some respects, the two weren't that different. "I guess I can work on it."

"Would anything you did mean you loved me any less?" Wren dropped a line of kisses along Fallon's jaw.

"No." Fallon's answer came out on a soft breath. She steadied herself and spoke deliberately. "Wren, you're a better person than I am. Always have been. You're kinder, warmer, and so full of love that you're like a pillow and a supernova all at once. And you're so strong. You've bounced right back from every hard thing that's ever come your way. You're everything I'm not, and being with you makes me better. Even Raptor said so."

Wren's lips parted and her eyes grew shiny. "You're better than you think. You could have refused to believe me after what I did. I should be in a brig, not here with you. Don't think I don't know that. You have more heart than you let on."

Fallon found the bottom seam of Wren's lounge shirt and slid her fingers beneath, feeling the soft warmth of her skin. "I don't think you have an accurate perception of me."

"I do," Wren breathed against her neck. She pressed her lips to Fallon's pulse. "And you know what else?"

"What?" Fallon was as fascinated as she was apprehensive.

"You're going to be late to work for the first time in your whole, damn, disciplined life." She cupped Fallon's face and drew her into a deep and entirely disorienting kiss.

And she was absolutely right about that one.

FALLON SKIPPED HER MORNING RUN, enabling her to make it to work only a few minutes late. She preferred to maintain a routine, but she lived in strange times when her enemy turned out to be her lover and the person who felt like her other half wasn't talking to her. Not to mention that her government was tearing itself apart, her uncle was a monster, and the captain who had hated her now chugged drinks with her at the pub. Up was down, down was sideways, and what the hell. She was just riding the tide.

She'd barely begun her morning tasks when she received a call from the Deck One security office.

"Chief, we're getting a strange request to dock. No flight plan filed, no previous intent to dock received, and this ship's registry isn't on record."

Fallon sat up straight. "What did the message say?"

Her officer's face scrunched up. "Just a docking request. No data, none of the normal protocol. It's like he's never done a docking before."

"A refugee?" Fallon suggested. They occasionally ended up at Dragonfire.

"Maybe." The officer frowned. "There was something about it that felt odd."

"Give him permission to dock, but don't open the airlock until I arrive."

"Understood." The officer gave a quick bow and her image blinked out.

Fallon stood and smoothed her uniform. "Well, this should be interesting."

FALLON SAT in Deck One's security office. Her staff stood nearby as she connected to the communications system of the mysterious cruiser. "This is Chief Fallon, head of security. What is your purpose for visiting Dragonfire Station?"

The response was immediate. "I'm looking for someone. I heard he might be there."

Someone tracking a criminal, maybe? A law enforcement official would know proper docking protocol, so perhaps a bounty hunter? "What's his name? Perhaps I can be of assistance."

"He doesn't seem to have a last name. People just call him Hawk."

Fallon kept her face expressionless. "Unidentified vessel, a security team will come and admit you through the airlock. Be aware that Dragonfire's security is second to none. We will tolerate no infractions."

"Believe me, Chief, the last thing I'm looking for is trouble."

Fallon closed the circuit, puzzled. "All right. Orowitz and Chen, you're with me."

They were two of her higher-ranking staff. Good weapon accuracy. Chen had a particularly high aptitude for code breaking, while Orowitz had a knack for languages.

They followed her down to Docking Bay Six. As she entered, she could see their visitor on the other side of the airlock, peering through. He appeared to be a few years older than her, human, and a little rough around the edges.

She touched the voicecom panel. "I'm going to open the airlock, Mr..." She let a pause draw out, inviting him to fill in his name.

"Lim."

"Mr. Lim. Then—"

"Just Lim. No Mr."

"Fine," she continued. "I'll let you through, Lim, and then you can tell me why you're here."

He nodded, and she activated the airlock's opening sequence.

He stepped through, his wariness clear in his stance and expression. He wore fine clothes, but his hair was unkempt and he had a generally haphazard look about him. Her instinct told her there was something peculiar about this guy.

She bowed.

"Oh, right. Bows." He bent at the waist, a little too deeply for the circumstances.

"Welcome to Dragonfire Station, Lim. I'm Security Chief Fallon, and these are two of my staff, Lieutenants Chen and Orowitz."

Lim nodded to them, but his eyes remained on her. "Just Fallon? No other name?"

"Yes. Why didn't you transmit your credentials prior to docking?"

"I lost them."

Fallon frowned at him. "Misplaced, or revoked from you by the government?"

His eyes flicked from her to the other two security officers. "My story's a little unusual."

"You'd be surprised how many unusual stories I've heard."

"Can we talk alone?" He fidgeted.

Fallon didn't want the situation to escalate into something adversarial. That would only make matters more complicated, and she had enough complications on her hands already.

"Do you mind being searched for weapons beforehand?"

Surprise replaced his wary expression. "No. I'm no threat to anybody."

Her officers did a thorough scan of him and performed a physical pat down. An archaic check, but a good one when you were watching out for spies.

"We can go to my office," she said, nodding at her officers to dismiss them.

She watched his eyes as they walked. They darted around, as if they'd never viewed a space station, noting every detail. He was in good shape. Athletic, and a few centimeters taller than her. He was a mix of genetic backgrounds that she had a hard time identifying. Part human, probably. She guessed him to be in his early twenties.

They said little on the trip up to her office. She watched him study the lift, the door to her office, and finally, its interior. There was a hypervigilance to him.

"So." She sat on one couch and indicated that he should do the same on the other. "What brings you to Dragonfire?"

"I'm looking for a guy named Hawk."

"You know him?"

"No. Someone told me that he'd help me."

"Who?" Fallon asked.

"I don't know who she was. A doctor, but I didn't know her name. She helped me out of a situation, told me to find Hawk."

"What makes you think he's here?"

He chewed on his lip before answering. "I've been looking for him for about a year and a half. It's not easy finding someone when you know nothing but a name."

"So what led you here?"

"I figured if the guy can help someone who's in trouble, he

might have been in trouble in the past, or at least know people who are. So I started thinking about multi-planet operations, the kind of stuff that isn't terribly legal. Smuggling. Bogus identification. Things people keep off the books."

Very smart. Fallon was impressed. The pieces fell right into place and made his story ring true so far.

He continued, "I did a little off-books trading. Nothing illegal, just untraceable. But I made some contacts and a little money to live on. Eventually I met a guy named Arcy. Said he knew Hawk and would tell me where he last knew Hawk to be if I did some work for him."

"What was the work?"

He shrugged. "Delivering a package. I didn't ask what it was. But he told me that I'd be able to find Hawk here."

Arcy and Hawk had a strong partnership. Either Arcy had screwed Hawk over to benefit himself, or he had decided that Lim was trustworthy. Since Lim seemed to have little to offer, she was betting that Arcy had vetted him and determined him to be legit. Which was interesting.

When she didn't respond right away, Lim asked, "Is he here?"

"What if he isn't?"

"I'll go find Arcy and shake him down for why he lied."

Fallon couldn't fault that plan. She'd do the same thing. "And if he is here?"

"I need to see him. Right away."

"Why?"

Lim's green eyes glowed with intensity. "I'm hoping he can tell me who I am."

Fallon dismissed her lieutenants and took Lim to her office to wait for Hawk. When he arrived, she could practically smell his suspicion.

Lim frowned at Fallon's hulk of a partner. "You're Hawk?"

"Yeah. Who are you?"

Lim ignored the question. "How do I know you're the guy I'm looking for?"

Hawk pushed back into the couch cushion and rubbed his jaw. "Hell if I know. How am I supposed to prove it when neither of us knows the other?"

Lim's shoulders slumped. "I guess I should have asked Arcy for some way to know for sure."

Hawk's eyes narrowed. "Arcy? Pale little guy? About a meter and a half?"

"No. Dark as night, and almost as tall as you, though his frame is smaller. Likes to swear in some language that seems to involve a lot of spitting."

"Sartrevian," Hawk answered. "Very difficult language. I never did manage to learn much of it. *Shtiptu mokovol flistivtu.*"

He did appear to spit a couple times in the process of speaking.

"That's it!" Lim's words vibrated with excitement. "That's what he said when he dropped a pipe wrench on his foot." He beamed. "You *are* Hawk." He relaxed back into the couch with a look of contentment, as if now that he'd found Hawk, his work was done.

"So what is it you want from me?" Hawk asked.

Lim glanced at Fallon and back to Hawk.

"You can trust her with anything you tell me," Hawk said. "She's my partner. One of 'em, anyway."

"There are more of you?" Lim looked pleased, as if more people increased his odds somehow.

"And some associates too. We're growing." Hawk smirked. "We've had to recruit, so to speak."

Lim chewed his lip. "I don't actually know why I was supposed to find you. The woman just told me that you'd make everything stop."

"Make what stop?" Hawk asked.

"I don't know."

"What *do* you know?" By this point, Hawk seemed more intrigued than annoyed.

"Not much, to tell the truth. I woke up in a jail cell. I didn't know where or who I was. I was taken to this guy called Admiral, who told me to assemble a plasma converter."

Hawk nodded, encouraging Lim to continue.

"I did it, but not as well as he wanted. He ordered my guards to take me to get some food. They fed me well, treated me okay. But I kept seeing pity when they looked at me, and it wasn't hard to figure out that I was doomed. And I was remembering these little bits. A security code, the face of a woman, just little flashes without any context. Then the guards said it was time for me to see the doctor, and I got the feeling it was the last thing I'd ever do. So I grabbed a stinger from one, knocked them out, and ran."

He looked from Hawk to Fallon.

"What happened?" Hawk asked.

He licked his lips. "Those little flashes were all I remembered, but they got me to a docking bay. I hadn't even known I was on a station. I got stuck, unable to get to the shuttle, but the woman from my memory showed up and helped me. She wouldn't come with me though. She said she had to help the next one, that it was all her fault. Then she said, 'Find Hawk. He'll make it all stop.'"

Fallon raised an eyebrow at Hawk, but he only shrugged. "What did she look like?" he asked.

"Bennite. Pretty. No Bennite accent, though. Medium height. Right-handed."

Fallon and Hawk exchanged another look.

"Ugh, stop with the looks!" Lim burst out. "Just say what you're thinking. Does any of this make sense to you?"

"Some of it sounds familiar," Fallon said slowly. "What can you tell me other than that experience? Anything from before."

"Nothing. I don't remember a thing before that day. Everything else is what I've experienced in the past eighteen months or so. Including learning how to pilot the shuttle. If it hadn't had autopilot when I escaped, I'd have been dead."

"You think they were going to kill you?" Hawk asked.

"Yeah." Lim looked to some far-off point in the room. "I definitely had that feeling, and I assume it was why the woman wanted me to escape."

Fallon moved closer to the couch Lim sat on. "So you haven't recovered any memories in the past year? No dreams that felt like they could be memories? No additional flashes of knowledge?"

For each question, he shook his head. If what had happened to him was related to what had happened to her, they'd had very different experiences.

"Here's my problem," she said. "I'm not going to bullshit you. You're in serious trouble. I don't know if your kind of trouble is our kind of trouble, but whoever sent you to Hawk was right—he and the rest of our team are trying to fix some things, and we'll look out for you. Provided you don't give us a reason not to."

Lim frowned. "I won't. So long as you are the good guys."

Fallon stifled a sigh. "Unfortunately, 'good guy' and 'bad guy' don't seem to mean as much as they used to." She stood. "Okay. So I'll assign you quarters. You'll be staying with Hawk. Hawk, you'll be moving to the next suite over, and Raptor and Ross will gain a whole lot of space."

He smirked at her. "Not all of us can fit into a suitcase."

She flashed him a grin. Lim seemed puzzled by their interaction. "You'll get used to it," she promised. "If you're around long enough."

Lim's mouth tightened. "I will be. If I don't belong here, I don't belong anywhere."

Hawk patted his shoulder on their way out. "Hold that thought, young'un. All of us might just belong nowhere."

On that cryptic note, Fallon locked up her office and followed Hawk and their new hope.

"So Hawk's over there, babysitting the guy?" Peregrine seemed less than impressed.

"Pretty much," admitted Fallon. "I wanted a chance to meet as a team before deciding what to do with him. And I didn't want to leave Lim on his own, even if he is only next door." She rested her hand on the arm of the couch in Raptor and Ross's quarters.

"Distrust, or concern for him?" Hesta asked.

"More the first. A little of the second." Fallon smoothed her hand over the leg of her uniform pants.

Ross and Raptor remained silent.

"Is there anything I can help out with?" asked Arin.

"Possibly. What do you all think about this?" Fallon looked from one face to the next.

"I think it doesn't much matter what we think," Hesta said. "You're the one who's been through what he seems to have been through. That makes you the only person who can decide if he's legit or not."

"Not exactly," Fallon said. "I think Brak and Jerin could help us out with that. A physical exam could tell us a lot."

"Perhaps," Hesta agreed. "But if it doesn't, it still comes down to you."

"One of these days, I'm going to need a vacation," Fallon mused.

"What would you do on vacation?" Ross asked.

Fallon wasn't sure, but Peregrine answered before she could. "Probably go diving off of cliffs or rock climbing up a ridiculously hard mountain face. Something risky and difficult and not at all relaxing."

Well. She wasn't exactly wrong, Fallon supposed. "So I'll arrange that physical exam, then proceed from there. Agreed?"

"And you'll keep him under surveillance? I don't need some

piece of shit wandering around my station like we had with Colb." Hesta scowled.

Fallon took a moment to enjoy the shocked look on Arin's face. He hadn't encountered this side of the captain yet. "Of course." Fallon wouldn't risk being wrong about Lim.

"Fine," Hesta agreed. "And since we're on that general subject, I want to bring up something else. Are you sure we can trust Wren? I'm still wary of ignoring the fact that she cut holes in my station and released a prisoner."

All eyes shot to Fallon. "I'm glad you brought it up. You're welcome to question her yourself until you're satisfied. But I'm convinced she thought she was working for the good of the PAC. Thing is, she didn't have our training. She proved to be a remarkably resourceful ally, but trusted the wrong guy. So did we, for a minute or two. And if we got it wrong, I don't think we can blame her for getting it wrong."

Nevitt looked undecided, but said nothing.

"Like I said. Talk to her yourself."

Peregrine spoke up. "If she's actually on our side, and is a good asset, should we consider bringing her in? Training her?"

Fallon had thought about that too. "She could do well at certain aspects of intelligence work, as an analyst. Maybe even some contained field work related to mechanics. But she's not the kind of person who could do what we do and be able to live with herself."

Fallon had known her team would trust her judgment. Nevitt and Arin were a different matter.

"I believe what you're saying about her," Nevitt said. "But I think I'll feel better about it if I talk to Wren. Nothing too harrowing, just a few questions."

Fallon nodded. Arin looked from his captain to his chief, clearly conflicted. No doubt he was also experiencing surprise and uncertainty, because of his friendship with Wren.

"Good. I want to be sure we're all in agreement." When no

one else spoke, she said, "Okay. If there's nothing else, we can adjourn for now. Bring anything you're suspicious or concerned about to me. Even if it seems like nothing."

She glanced around the room and her gaze tangled with Raptor's. He still hadn't spoken to her, and it wasn't a situation she could allow to continue. "Raptor, could you stay, please? I need to discuss something with you."

He had little choice but to remain, or else look like an ass to the others. Refusing to remain in his own quarters to talk to her would have been awfully strange. Ross followed the others out, which saved Fallon from needing to move to Raptor's bedroom to talk to him.

"What do you want?" Raptor demanded as soon as the doors closed, leaving them alone.

"To apologize. I'm so sorry, Raptor."

His expression was guarded, but he sat back down, no longer inching toward the door. "Can't say I'm shocked that you shut me out again."

"Disappointed. I know." She closed her eyes, trying to figure out how to explain. "Okay, here's the thing. My brain has always been unusual, even before Blackout messed with it. As a kid, I just had a lot of frustration. Anger, even. My father teaching me to fight was the best thing that ever happened to me. I learned to be disciplined. I learned that getting hurt doesn't really matter. I could take a hit and I'd heal. And while I was never proud of getting top marks in my classes because it was so easy, I had to *earn* my combat skills."

She paused, struggling to put her past into words. "I was proud when I mastered skills and won competitions. I was proud when I got recruited into the academy. I learned that the higher the stakes, the more I could *feel*. I was like a foot that had been asleep, suddenly burning with sensation. When I got to the academy, I felt truly alive in a way I'd never felt. And then I met you." She smiled, thinking of his younger self. "You weren't jealous of my successes. You were more like me than anyone I'd ever met, but you were better—easygoing and fun. You were the first person to make me really feel without having to put my life on the line."

She let out a long breath and risked a peek at Raptor. His coolness had faded, and he seemed interested in what she was saying.

She moved next to him. "I can't describe how deeply I felt about you. When you suggested we forget about going into Blackout, I wanted to say yes. But I couldn't imagine having a normal life. Working the day shift, then going to the theater in the evenings. Sleeping in on the weekends. I was afraid I'd go numb again without Blackout. That I wouldn't feel the big things anymore, including you. So I said no."

The set of his shoulders had eased. "Why didn't you tell me that back then?"

"I was too young to be able to put it into words. And would it have even made sense to you? I didn't want to end things with you. I just didn't see any alternative."

"So why did you ice me out a few days ago?" His voice held no accusation.

"I needed a little distance to make sure I could be objective. I'd just realized that Wren had been working for Colb. I was afraid my personal relationships were affecting my judgment." She rubbed her hand over her eyes. "For the first time, I really wanted to go back to being numb. I didn't want my feelings for you to blind me."

He sat looking at her for a long minute. "I get why you did what you did when we were young. But you can't just put me in a box now. If you need some space, just tell me. I thought you were ending it with me."

"You seem to have a complex about that." She struggled to hide a smile.

"For good reason! I always suspected you had some weird

baggage. I want to learn more about that, but for now you just need to figure your shit out."

She let her smile unfurl. "You're always right."

"Of course I am. I landed in Avian Unit with you so that I could equal out your dumbassness."

"That's not a word."

"It is now."

She was glad to see the warmth return to his face, and as always, he pulled her in like gravity. "So."

"So figure yourself out, dumbass." He snorted in disdain. "When you do, you know where I am. Just be up front with me about what you need. Whatever it is, we'll make it work." He leaned forward, looking at her closely. "You're back with Wren now, aren't you?"

"Yeah. Is that a problem?"

He pursed his lips thoughtfully. "No. It's just funny how she seems to be in control of all your disarm codes. She's the one who always pulls you back from trying to be alone."

"There's just something about her. I can't explain it."

"Doesn't matter. She makes you happy." He shrugged.

"So do you, in a completely different way." She ran her hand over her hair. "She said humans are silly for thinking we have to pick one kind of love and refuse all others."

"I've always thought Sarkavians were wise. Maybe all those sandy beaches encourage relaxation and deep thought."

She smiled. "They have some great high-speed boating and other water sports too. You and I would have some fun there."

"A vacation is pretty wishful thinking."

"Why not wish? What's your wish for when all this is done?"

"I really don't know. I'll have to give it some thought."

She hoped his wishes involved her. "I think Lim is going to be what we need to break everything wide open."

"You're convinced he's for real?"

"Completely. His reactions and behavior remind me of myself

after I lost my memory. It's too familiar to be a fake. And his story adds up. That would mean he was experimented on six months before I came to Dragonfire."

"Do you think Colb was planning that far ahead to try to implant you?"

She'd wondered the same thing. "I don't know. I'm ready to find out though, and I think Lim is going to help us."

"I hope so."

A silence fell between them. Fallon stood. "I'll get going. Ross will probably be back soon."

"Okay." He walked her to the exit. The doors swooshed open. "Good luck sorting out all the crap in your head."

She had to smile at his cheerful tone. "Thanks. I guess I'll need it. I'm really sorry about before. I never said I wasn't broken."

"Someday I'll tell you about my background and we can compare brokenness." He dropped a grandfatherly kiss on the top of her head. "Goodnight."

"Goodnight."

8

"I can't say I'm excited about letting people poke around at my brain." Lim fidgeted on the couch in the quarters he shared with Hawk.

Fallon sympathized with him. "Brak and Jerin poked around in my brain too. I ended up far better off for it. But they only want to get images and see what's going on in there. That's it. If it makes you feel better, I'll stay with you during the procedure."

"Yeah. That'd be good." He smiled sheepishly. "I don't trust strangers, so I'd feel better knowing you were looking out for me. I mean, I know we just met, but…"

"But at least I'm a familiar face." She didn't blame him for being nervous. Living in a galaxy of nothing but strangers could make a person paranoid. She knew that better than anyone.

"Okay. I don't want to rush you, but the *Onari* is going to deploy tomorrow to deal with a plague on a mining planet. There's no telling how long they'll be gone. I'd like them to get a look at you before they go. Are you game?"

"Yeah. Sure." He gave her a watery smile. "It's just a look, right?"

"Yes. I promise. You'll be awake the whole time, and they'll tell you exactly what they're doing. You'll like them."

"I hope so."

"I have no doubts." She waited for him to voice any concerns, but he didn't. "I'll be back in an hour, and I'll walk you down to the infirmary."

"My legs work fine. It's my brain that's taken a shore leave. I'll meet you down there."

She smiled. "Good. I'll see you then."

As she made her way to ops control to give the captain her morning report, she hoped an hour wasn't long enough for him to think too much about it and spook himself. Sometimes a person's worries could be his worst enemy.

FALLON REALIZED she hadn't told Lim that Brak was Briveen. He stared at her, his mouth open slightly. Words seemed to have escaped him. Jerin closed the door to the infirmary's private room.

"This is my very good friend Brak. I trust her completely." Fallon put a hand on his shoulder.

"Right. Of course. Pardon me." He bowed clumsily, like someone new to the practice.

"I take it you haven't met a Briveen before?" Brak's amusement was clear to Fallon, though she doubted Lim would recognize it.

"Not that I recall. But I don't recall much."

Jerin chuckled. "I can assure you that I've never seen her eat a single human."

Lim laughed. "Well, that's good to know. Is that something Briveen are known for?"

"No," Brak answered. "The doctor thinks she's funny."

"I'd have to agree with her," Fallon said.

The humor loosened Lim up enough that he was able to lie back on the techbed and remain still.

"I know you won't care for this," Jerin said from the controls behind his head. "But I will need to apply restraints, to ensure that the images aren't blurred. If at any time you want me to release them, just say so. Okay?"

"Sure." His jaw had clenched, and he said the word through his teeth.

"We'll get through this as quickly as we can," Brak assured him. "It won't take long to thoroughly map your brain."

Fallon stood next to him and put her hand on his forearm. It felt odd for her to be in the role of support. It was not her usual gig.

Brak and Jerin worked through the imaging, talking as they went to reassure Lim. His muscles remained tense beneath Fallon's hand, but he didn't complain.

After a few more minutes, Jerin said, "There we go. We're through." A moment later she added, "You can sit up."

Lim pulled himself up and looked toward Brak and Jerin. "What did you see in there?"

Fallon smelled ammonia, and knew it didn't bode well.

Brak's discomfort showed in her posture, too. Her back rounded and her shoulders pulled forward. "I'm sorry to say that your brain has experienced extensive damage. Your memory cortex has essentially been removed and replaced with an implant."

"Removed? Does that mean I'll never remember anything?"

"It's encouraging that you seem to have no difficulties in creating new memories and being able to recall them. That must be a mechanism of the implant, but without further study we won't be able to tell. You also have some basic skills. You can speak the PAC standard, for example."

"I can do some pretty extreme math," Lim offered.

"Really. Now that's interesting." Brak looked thoughtful.

"Does he have the same kind of implant I had?" Fallon asked.

"No. Very different. This is far less advanced. An early prototype."

"So I was a test subject?" Lim's fists curled in his lap.

"Possibly. Like I said, we'll need to run a lot more tests and analyze the data. I don't want to jump to conclusions."

"Did you see anything that might make sense of the 'put your head to the ground' thing?" Fallon asked.

"Not yet," Brak said. "I need to study that implant."

Jerin finished her work at the techbed controls and moved to join them. "You should stay here and work on that."

Brak clicked her teeth in irritation. "I'd planned to go with you. I'm sure the planet has numerous people in need of cybernetics adjustments and recalibrations."

Jerin nodded. "I know. But we'll make our way back there again soon. This is important to the well-being of the entire PAC. You need to stay."

"You're right," Brak agreed. "But please have nurses document the people who need my help."

"Of course."

"All right." Brak looked to Lim. "I'm going to compile a series of tests that I want you to take, so I can get some functional data on the performance of that implant. Can you return this afternoon?"

"Sure." He seemed relieved. "Taking some tests is no problem."

Fallon asked him, "Would you like me to walk you back to your quarters?"

"No, thank you. I'm starved. Didn't eat breakfast. I think I'll go to the boardwalk for an early lunch."

Fallon checked the chronometer on her comport. "Very early. Have a good meal."

"Thanks. And thanks for coming here with me." He gave her

another of his sheepish smiles, which she had begun to find endearing. "It's nice to have a friend to count on."

His sweet statement hit her hard. She remembered being in his position. She knew how much it meant to have someone in her corner when the entire universe seemed like a giant question mark.

She clasped his hand in both of hers and looked into his green eyes. "I'll be here whenever you need me."

He brightened, then surprised her with a hug. "Thank you. I've been wandering around for a year and haven't felt like I could trust anyone. It's a relief to finally have someone."

She returned his hug and he stepped back. "Right. I'm off to get some food."

After he left, Jerin shook her head regretfully. "He has a lot ahead of him. He's going to need a great deal."

Fallon wasn't daunted. "We'll work it through. I did, with the help of friends. I'll make sure he does, too."

DESPITE HER ATTEMPTS to handle business on the station as usual, Fallon found that her mind kept wandering. She felt like she'd regained her seat at the helm of the universe and was ready to navigate. All she wanted to do was drive.

She was glad when Kellis called on the voicecom and asked to visit. Fallon gave her a temporary passcode to get onto Deck Four and responded to a non-urgent message while she waited.

"How are you?" Fallon asked when Kellis arrived. She guided her to the sitting area of her office.

"Great. Excited. I've been waiting for the chance to do more ever since we hit the Tokyo base."

They engaged in more small talk before Kellis got around to asking what she really wanted to know.

"What's going on with the PAC? It's bad, isn't it?"

Fallon had to think about how much she should tell Kellis. She deserved at least a general idea. But she couldn't tell Kellis anything of strategic importance.

"PAC command is at war with itself. There are two factions battling for power. My team and I are working to keep the would-be usurper from getting control, but the actions already taken may be enough to plunge us into war. We believe we know who is at the heart of it all, and we're working to contain him."

"What if you can't?" Kellis didn't look as upset as Fallon would have expected. But Kellis was from a planet torn by war. She'd seen more greed and tragedy than most people.

"I'm guessing all of our treaties will be dissolved, and the PAC will splinter into hundreds of sovereign planets. Allegiances will undoubtedly form, while existing governments and economies will collapse. From there I'd say we're looking at a few decades of mass chaos, war, and poverty. Eventually, new governments and leaders and alliances will emerge. But not soon enough for the billions who will be long dead."

Kellis frowned, but her gaze stayed steady. "I guess we have to make sure that doesn't happen."

"That's the plan." Fallon was impressed with the nerve Kellis had. It reinforced her feeling that she could handle this kind of work. Kellis was green, but she had a certain quality that Fallon recognized. A hunger to do more, to be more.

"Until the *Onari* returns, I have no duties to attend to," Kellis said. "Arin only has so much time to work with me. Is there a way I can do more?"

Fallon smiled at the idea. "A spy boot camp?"

"What's a boot camp?"

"Never mind. Historical reference." Fallon thought about what else she needed to get done that day. "I need to do my rounds on the boardwalk. How about you walk with me? I'll show you what I'm looking at, how things appear to me. It will help you start thinking tactically. When we're done with that, we'll begin with some hand-to-hand combat. Sound good?"

Kellis nodded so hard her curls bounced. "Sounds perfect."

"WATCH MY WEIGHT SHIFTS," Fallon advised as she circled Kellis in a security staff training room. "Smaller people like you and I can't rely on brute strength. We have to fight smarter. You must know how to throw them off balance and use their strength against them."

"What weight shifts?" Kellis asked, turning slowly to keep Fallon in front of her. "You move like a cat."

"You'll learn that too. Keep your guard up. Be ready."

"It's a lot to remember." Kellis frowned in concentration.

"It will feel awful at first. Awkward, ungainly, and just plain impossible. But it will become natural. Eventually, you'll have a hard time not thinking and moving that way."

"If you say so."

Fallon lightly shoved Kellis' left hip, causing her to stumble. "There's your weight shift. Smooth your gait. Don't shift your weight until your foot is solid under you. Never let your weight be in between your steps."

Kellis adjusted and her movement became more fluid.

"Better." Fallon stepped closer and drew back her fist. She held that posture. "Now look here. I'm going to step forward with this punch. What does this tell you about my weight?" She stepped back and slowly pantomimed the motion. Kellis awkwardly stepped to the side to dodge, then brought her foot down on the back of Fallon's weight-bearing knee.

"Good." Fallon stepped back to reset. "That's an excellent tactic. If you're fast enough, you can also attack the other leg to make sure I go down. Or you can hit my body from the side. If you do that while I'm moving forward, I'm almost certainly going to go sprawling. It depends on your desired effect."

Fallon walked her through that exercise, showing her in slow motion how it would work. "Okay. Let's practice."

After she repeated the exercise for the hundredth time, Kellis had improved the timing and the confidence of her attack. Fallon was pleased to note that in spite of the significant exertion, Kellis was not exhausted. She clearly kept herself in excellent shape.

"That's enough for today." Fallon let her arms fall to her sides.

"No, show me something else. Teach me how to throw a punch."

Fallon couldn't say no to something like that. So she spent the next two hours teaching Kellis how to strike. Then Kellis asked for more.

But sometimes enough was enough. "You need a break. Food. If you want to do some more work later today, I'll hook you up with Ross. He's one of the finest instructors the academy has ever had. And I'm going to make him your personal trainer."

Rather than look daunted, Kellis brightened. "Really?"

Fallon laughed. Only someone with the heart of a BlackOp would be so pleased.

FALLON GOT on the lift with Kellis. They went up a deck, where Kellis got off, then Fallon went down to Deck One alone. Her shift had ended two hours earlier, and she was starved.

She lingered as she passed the Bennite restaurant but continued to the noodle place. She was in the mood for lots and lots of carbs. And soup. And slurping. The fact that the noodle shop had dim lighting was also a plus. She felt like being alone. She'd said more in the past weeks than she had the entire year before all of this had started. At least it felt that way.

She selected a bowl of noodles in a seafood broth that

reminded her of a dish her mother often made. When it arrived, she took time to savor the steamy aroma, so hearty and fresh smelling. Her chopsticks seemed to dig in of their own free will, though she remembered her manners enough to slurp the noodles properly.

She received some offers to join others, but politely declined. Yet when she finished eating, she found herself reluctant to leave. She liked the hum of voices and the clank of dishes. She liked seeing people she knew talking and laughing. This was life. One evening among many, as time wended its way forward. It was friends and family and work and everything she was fighting for.

She finally paid her tab and left the restaurant.

Wren's face lit up when the doors opened and she saw Fallon. "Hi. I didn't expect to see you tonight."

"Why not?"

Wren gestured her into the quarters and toward the couch. "Because I just saw you, and even though you've had some personal epiphanies, you're still you."

"You expected me to want some distance," Fallon translated.

"Bingo," Wren said in Earth standard.

Fallon laughed and sat down with her. "I don't think I've ever heard you say that. It sounds funny coming from you."

"I've been studying. I thought it would be nice if we could talk in your language."

Fallon felt a little bad about what she would say next. "Actually, I grew up speaking Japanese at home. I think of it as more mine than Earth standard."

"Oh. Well, I'll start working on that, then."

Fallon laughed. "We could speak your language," she said in perfectly accented Sarkavian.

Wren's mouth fell open. "You sound like a native! I didn't know you could do that!"

"It wasn't part of my cover."

"Well, what else don't I know about you?" Wren leaned back to peer into Fallon's face.

"There is one thing I've been wanting to tell you," Fallon admitted.

Wren's forehead crinkled with apprehension. "What?"

"That fish thing you make with the herb sauce. I don't like it. It gives me indigestion and I end up burping all night."

Wren laughed in relief. "Why didn't you tell me before?"

"You made it the first time and told me it was your favorite. I didn't want to hurt your feelings, so I said I liked it. But then you kept making it, and I could hardly admit to not liking it at that point."

"So you kept eating it anyway?" Wren giggled and Fallon felt the vibration through her chest and stomach.

"Yeah."

"That proves it. You definitely love me. Nobody eats food they hate on a regular basis to spare the feelings of someone they don't love."

"Maybe Sarkavians wouldn't. But Japanese will put up with a tremendous amount of displeasure in the interest of being polite."

"Really?"

"Really."

"Hm. I guess I'll have to study being Japanese."

Fallon smiled. "Nah. Not really. I haven't kept many of the traditions out here."

"You might want to take me there to visit sometime, though. You could show me where you grew up, where your parents lived. I'd want to be able to behave myself appropriately."

"Oh. Well, actually, that reminds me of something. You know you thought my parents were dead?"

Wren nodded.

"They aren't."

"You have *parents*?" Wren sat up in surprise.

"A brother too."

"Oh, wow! I definitely want to meet them. And hear all about them. I mean, if you want me to meet them. Someday." Wren went from enthusiastic to uncertain.

"I'd like you to meet them." She was sure her parents would like Wren. Everyone did.

Wren gave her a knowing look. "Let me guess. Japanese people are a monogamous bunch."

"Not everyone is as enlightened as you Sarkavians."

"A shame. Think of how peaceful life would be."

"You might convert me, and that could be the beginning of the revolution."

Wren laughed and snuggled up with Fallon, wrapping her arms around her. They sat in cozy silence for several minutes, then Wren straightened and asked, straight-faced, "Are you converted yet?"

"I'm working on it. It's a difficult convention to break free of."

"Hmm. Maybe I should set up a meeting. You, me, Raptor, and we talk it all out. Think that'd do it?" The wicked glint in Wren's eye made Fallon laugh.

"I don't think so. This is just in my head. A frame of mind I need to adjust. I mean, I never minded that Sarkavians aren't monogamous. I think your dad's boyfriend is lovely. Great at chess."

Wren made a dismissive gesture. "Oh, he's not seeing him anymore. He's in between *amores* at the moment."

"Has your mom found a new one? She'd ended things with one, last I heard."

"Not yet. She's very picky. She sometimes goes years between."

Fallon stretched her legs out, resting her feet on the table.

"Since we're on the subject, have your parents' *amores* ever caused trouble between them?"

Wren stretched out too and wriggled her toes. "Only once that I know of. My mom was seeing a guy that my dad thought was an obnoxious jerk. And she admitted to me in private that she thought so too. But she said his personality was worth putting up with because he could use his tongue to—"

"Nooo, that's enough, I don't need to hear that. I'm working on the other thing, but you're never going to convince me it's not squicky for parents and kids to talk about their sex lives." Fallon cringed, refusing to even contemplate that with her own parents.

Wren snickered. "You humans are so sexually repressed."

"Only some of us. I happen to be from a particularly ancient and traditional culture."

"It's a fine culture, I'm sure."

"It is. Beautiful. We have music that will touch your soul. Art more engrossing than any holo-vid. Stories that will make you weep."

"See, Sarkavians are distinctly lacking in stories. We have tons of poetry. But we don't have a great tradition of literature."

"So it's a trade-off." Fallon couldn't remember ever having a conversation quite like this with Wren.

"All things are." Wren nodded sagely.

"What's your trade-off for being with me?" Fallon wasn't sure whether she was a good thing with a negative trade-off, or vice versa.

Wren sat up and turned to face Fallon, her expression serious. "That we're mortal, and one day, you might die and leave me alone."

From Raptor, those words would have simply been pragmatic. From Wren, they were romantic.

FALLON DIDN'T STAY the night. She needed to hit the ground running the next day, and knew she'd have a hard time doing that in the coziness of Wren's quarters.

So when her alarm sounded, she jumped out of bed and got going. Excitement crackled through her. She was getting close to finding Krazinski, she was sure. And close to setting the trap to bring Colb in. Then she could finally fix the PAC, and life could go on the way it should.

She met Brak for their run, bursting with questions. Once they got up to the track and began, she restrained herself to one word. "Well?"

"Good news and bad news. I asked Lim to meet us in an hour in the infirmary."

Fallon knew she'd have to wait for specifics. "That's cryptic. And doesn't give me much time to exercise and deliver my morning report to the captain."

Brak shot her a sidelong look. "I guess we'd better run faster."

LIM WORE an odd expression that seemed to be a combination of eagerness and dread. It turned out that he was right to feel both.

In the private room of the infirmary, Brak pulled up brain images on the voicecom terminal. "On the left side, we see Fallon's brain. On the right, we see Lim's."

Fallon squinted at the images. "Reading brain images is not my strong suit."

"Mine either," Lim echoed.

"Okay. See this small dark spot?" Brak pointed to Fallon's brain. "That's the implant I put in." Then she pointed to an area in Lim's brain. "This large gray area is Lim's implant."

It was huge. Fallon stared at the expanse of brain that had been taken away from him. Prelin's ass. Her stomach clenched.

"What does this mean for me?" Lim asked in a soft voice.

"With the implant, you're able to retain as much new information as any highly intelligent person. Your IQ is very high, and your mathematical skills are fantastic. Further, you're not in danger of losing anything you've experienced in the past eighteen months."

"Why do I sense a 'but' coming?" he asked in a stronger voice.

"A great deal of tissue has been removed. I could possibly regenerate some of it, but it wouldn't return any prior memories. I'm very sorry."

Lim's back bowed, and he stared at his lap. "I see."

"I can upgrade your implant, though. The one you have isn't meant for long-term use. I can give you one that's made to last, and will transfer the memory you already have. The new implant will be smaller, which means there will be room for me to see how much of your brain tissue I can regenerate."

"I like the idea of getting my brain back, but changing out the implant sounds scary. I don't want to start over again." Lim didn't look optimistic.

"I know, but it's actually a simple process. Just a copy and transfer of data from one device to another."

"Is there a risk of me losing my memory, though? That's my main worry."

"No. You already have a device. I won't be doing anything that hasn't already been done in that regard. I'll just be improving the technology. As for the brain matter, it's essentially like any wound repair. The tissue will be brand new. The great thing about brains is their remarkable ability to rewire themselves in the event of damage. My hope is that once you have that tissue back, you can transfer what's in your implant into your actual brain matter. If that happens, we can eventually remove the implant entirely."

"I do like the sound of that." He seemed slightly more encouraged by the idea. "Will it be painful?"

"You can expect to feel fine after, except maybe a slight headache from the surgery itself."

"When does it have to be done?"

Brak tilted her head. "There's no rush. I wouldn't recommend waiting more than three months, though. Like I said, that implant wasn't built to last."

"Right." Lim sat up straight. "When can you have the new implant ready?"

"Probably four days if I start immediately. That will give me time to manufacture it and run extensive testing. Plus, Jerin will be back to lead the regeneration of your lost tissue. Hardware is more my specialty, while the squishy bits are hers."

"Squishy bits." Lim smirked. "Right. So message me with the time you'll want me here. The sooner this is done, the sooner I can move forward with my life. Such as it is."

"Of course. If you have any questions—"

He cut her off, jumping to his feet. "No. You do what you do, and I'll do...well, I'm working on figuring out what I do. But I'll leave this part to you." He took a breath, seeming to rally himself. "I know I'm incredibly lucky to have your help. And I appreciate it."

"I could not be more glad that I'm able to help," Brak answered.

He bowed to them, then left.

"He took the news well, considering." Fallon wasn't sure how she'd have handled knowing that she'd never get her past back. Especially since Lim seemed to have none of the retained skills she had.

"They made him into a blank slate. Wiped clean. Probably multiple times. It's horrifying."

"I can't imagine."

Brak growled softly. "I'd like to take the doctors who did this, tear their heads off, and feed them to mandren."

Fallon blinked. "Wow." She'd never heard Brak say anything violent or threatening. "So how can we help him?"

"Make sure his health is good. Support him emotionally. Help him rediscover himself. Or develop a new self."

Fallon suspected she knew the answer to her next question, but she had to ask it. "Could you give him back his lost memories if we could reconstruct them from fact? If we found out who he is?"

"I could give him data. Facts. Images. I couldn't give him skills. But I don't believe it's ethical to give someone memories, even if they're based on fact."

"He'd experience those things as real memories?"

"Yes. But as I said." Brak clearly didn't like this line of thinking.

"I'm talking theory right now. That's all."

"It's a slippery slope. It worries me." Brak's discomfort was clear by the way she ducked her head.

"I know. Don't worry. I'm just curious about the mechanics. Strictly hypothetical."

Brak's jaw clenched and released. "Okay. Theoretically, yes, it might be possible to plant believable images. But they might also appear as nightmarish and be ultimately traumatic."

"Let's definitely not do that, then."

"Believe me, we won't." Brak returned to the voicecom display. "There's something else. I didn't want to talk about it with Lim here."

Fallon stared at the display. "What is it?"

"I know how to put your head to the ground."

FALLON WAITED, but Brak said nothing more. "Well, how? You can't say that and leave me hanging."

"I wasn't sure if you'd want to call everyone together first."

"Nope. I'll fill them in. I want to know now."

"Okay." Brak pointed at a dark area on the image of Lim's implant. "See that? That rounded dark bit?"

"Kind of." Fallon tilted her head, as if a different angle would make it more apparent to her.

"That's a router for a private network. It encrypts data, encapsulates it so that the data has a means of travel, then sends it across the network. The hardware is all right there. My guess is that this implant has a built-in way of communicating outside of the datastreams, to keep it completely secure. It's turned off right now, but I'm guessing it was used to load information into Lim's brain, like you'd upload any other data."

Fallon felt light-headed. "Did I have one of these? In the implant Colb gave me?" If so, Krazinski would expect her to have access to it.

"Based on the research you took from the lab, I'd guess that you did. All the successive designs included that feature."

Fallon had a moment of clarity. Krazinski knew about Colb's attempt to implant her. Krazinski expected her to have a means of communicating with him inside her head. Without it, she'd never be able to find him.

"Can you copy the network component of Lim's device and add it to the implant you created for me?" A thought occurred to her. "Or better yet, use the research records we took from the lab to create a more advanced one?"

Brak clicked her teeth. Clearly she didn't like the idea. "The creation of the device would not be very difficult. Since it's very small, adding it to your inducer implant would be relatively simple. But creating an open gateway *in your brain* could have any number of unintended consequences. Remember what happened the first time someone put something in your head."

Fallon ignored that. She was solving a puzzle. If she took time to think about it from a personal perspective, it would only make doing what she needed to do difficult. "How would the information be transmitted without a hardline between me and Krazinski? How would I get it where it needs to go?"

"I don't know. All I have is the hardware. But if what you say is true, I'd expect that Krazinski knows exactly what he's looking for, and you'd just need to supply it."

Fallon hoped so. "Right. I'm guessing the message travels via photonic energy."

"Why?"

Fallon touched the side of her head, thinking about the implant inside. It wasn't the implant Krazinski expected her to have, but she hoped it could do what she needed it to. "Because that's how I'd do it. Assuming there were no black holes or other interference in the path, it could work. Which means that Krazinski can't be too far away, if he's expecting me to be able to contact him."

"I don't care to cut open a person's head on the basis of that much conjecture."

Fallon had gotten so caught up in her discovery that she hadn't considered that Brak might not cooperate. "Are you saying you won't do it?"

"Why not use Lim's implant? He already has it."

"Krazinski's waiting to hear from me. He may not even know who Lim is. He hasn't turned up in any searches we've done."

Brak turned her back to the image of Lim's brain. "How can you even consider this, after everything you've been through?"

"Two things. First, it's my job to do what needs to be done. Second, I trust you to do what you do. You'll get it right."

"Shouldn't you consult with your team?"

Fallon didn't even have to think about that. "No. It will cause unnecessary delay, and opinions will be mixed. In the end, I'll end up making the decision anyway."

"But they're your team. Your family, for all intents and purposes. Shouldn't they get a say?"

"Sometimes. Not this time. Being in command sometimes means making unilateral decisions that may prove unpopular."

Brak rubbed at the scales on her head. Fallon had never seen her so agitated. "You're sure there's no other way around this?"

"Can you make an implant that doesn't need to be inside a brain to work? Because that'd be nice."

Brak shook her head. "No. They require neural feedback and electricity to be fully functional."

"Then I don't see any other way."

Brak looked like she was about to refuse. Fallon held up a hand before she could. "Look at it from my perspective. I have my team to protect. Plus all of Dragonfire. Plus all of the PAC. If I'm the only one who can get this done, then I'm going to do it." She closed her eyes, letting herself think about Brak's concerns. "I know it's a risk to me. I don't want anything else happening to my brain. But I really need to not think about that because if I do, it will make what I have to do a lot harder." She opened her eyes and fixed them on Brak. "I'm not going to watch the PAC fall apart and spend whatever's left of my life knowing I could have helped, if I hadn't been so worried about myself, or how the people who matter to me will feel about it. Please. Help me do this."

Brak stared at her, unblinking, for several long moments. "I can't believe I'm saying this, but I'll do it. On one condition."

"What?"

"Once all this is over, you have to get PAC intelligence to issue me an official commendation for saving the PAC with my cybernetics expertise."

The demand was so unexpected, Fallon laughed. "Okay. Why?"

"I want to take the commendation home to Briv and show it to my parents. Either they will recognize my honor, or they will shun me, but it'll be my chance to be a part of my family and my world again."

"Wow. All right. Pull this off and I'll do whatever I can to get you that commendation."

Brak dipped her chin in agreement. "I can have the device ready in a day. Two, if we want to be sure it won't make your head explode."

"Let's make it two." Fallon had always appreciated Brak's brutal sense of humor. "This won't delay your work for Lim?"

"No."

"Good." Fallon didn't want to prolong his wait. "We won't mention this to anyone."

"You're going to pay for that later, but I'll go along with it."

Fallon's amusement faded. "I'm always paying for something. It might as well be for something that might save us all."

IN THE TEAM meeting the next day, Fallon explained that Brak would create a duplicate of the router in Lim's brain. The others seemed encouraged by the possible step toward contacting Krazinski. She said nothing of her additional plans to have it put in her head. She let them think it might be possible to activate it in some other way.

After the meeting, she tapped several people to befriend Lim. She knew that he had the temperament and eye for detail of a BlackOp. He wouldn't have survived the past year and a half if he hadn't. But she also knew from her own experience that Lim needed people he could trust. He needed to feel like someone cared that he existed.

So she asked Arin and Kellis to seek him out. Both had overcome difficulties in their pasts, and that could serve as a bridge to common ground. They also were in the early stages of BlackOp recruitment, and if, as Fallon suspected, Lim had been a young BlackOp before his memory loss, he'd have two contemporaries. If he chose to continue in that line of work, anyway.

She also tapped Wren to befriend him. Fallon couldn't think of anyone with a bigger heart, or more love to give. Since Wren had experienced a situation similar to Lim's but from the other side, she was in a unique position to offer support.

Another day passed, and when it came time for her to lie down on the techbed, she did it without reservations.

"You're sure about this? It's a much simpler procedure than your last one, but there's still a risk." Though Brak remained perfectly professional, Fallon saw her personal concern as well.

"Completely." She positioned herself and waited for the restraints. She'd been through this drill before and looked forward to waking up to some results.

Jerin looked like she wanted to say something, but she didn't. She'd only just returned to Dragonfire, and had gotten an earful of a briefing upon arrival. Fallon knew she had reservations about this procedure, but Jerin merely rested her hand on Fallon's forearm for a moment, then stepped to the techbed controls.

Brak joined her and a moment later said, "Applying the restraints." Then she added, "Administering the sedative."

"See you on the other side," Fallon said before the stuff took effect.

"Count on it," Brak answered.

CONFUSION SWIRLED THROUGH FALLON. Lights and sound were a jumble. She opened her eyes, unsure where she was. She saw a Briveen face above her, watching. Just behind her, Jerin stood, looking unusually concerned. But she'd looked that way before the surgery too, and Fallon decided not to take it as a bad sign.

"How do you feel?" Brak asked.

"Groggy, but it's fading." Fallon struggled to pull herself together. "How did it go?"

"As planned. All that remains is to rest until you're fully alert and give the router a try."

"So soon?" Fallon had thought they'd need to wait for her to heal, or something.

"Yup."

"In that case, bring me some coffee," Fallon joked.

"No stimulants. Give the sedative some time to leave your system." Jerin's voice was gentle but stern.

"Sure. I'll hang out. Catch up on some deep thinking." Fallon stared up at the ceiling tiles and remembered counting and mentally measuring them before and after her previous surgeries. She seemed to be developing quite a history of having her brain operated on.

Fallon had no way to measure time, but after a while Brak asked, "How do you feel now?"

"Fine. Clearer."

"Good. Wren and Raptor are outside."

"What?" Fallon bolted upright.

"Just kidding. But you seem alert to me."

"Dirty trick." Fallon had to smile. It had been a good dirty trick. "So what do I do now?"

"You should be able to intentionally access the router and send a message. The message will automatically be encrypted and encapsulated. Once it goes out, all you can do is wait for a response on that same network."

What did she want to say? Well, not much. If someone had commandeered Krazinski's side of the gateway, she didn't want to be throwing information at them.

Head to the ground, she thought. *The chief is online.*

She scrunched her forehead. How did she send the message? "How does a person initialize a neural implant?"

"Electrical impulses go across the fibers and activate the implant. It shouldn't take any more effort than thinking."

"I don't feel like anything's happening." Fallon hadn't expected to be unable to access the thing once it was installed.

"I can see activity in that part of your brain, and everything looks like it should. I have no way of knowing what you might be thinking or sending."

"Right. That's the whole point of a private network." Fallon dangled her feet over the side of the techbed. "Am I allowed to stand?"

Jerin moved to offer her a hand. "Sure. Take it easy though. Standard advice—no blows to the head, no extreme exertion, tell me if you have nausea, vertigo, headaches, and all that. You'll probably be unusually tired, but back to yourself in a day or so."

"Yeah." Fallon got to her feet and tested her balance. "My brain's been sliced and diced a time or two before. This is getting to be a habit."

"Not something to brag about." Jerin did not seem amused.

"Probably not. But I seem fine. I guess I'll go about my day as usual. Unless the mother planet beams a transmission from the supreme commander into my brain."

Amusement and concern were an odd mix to smell from Brak, but Fallon took it as a good sign.

Aloud, Brak said, "Sounds like you watched old-fashioned space vids when you were growing up. I didn't see any until I was in university and a classmate had a party with a space-vid theme."

"They're good fun. Who doesn't enjoy a cheesy holo-vid now and then?"

Brak turned off the techbed, returning it to power-saving readiness. She gave Fallon a warning look. "I'll say it again: Take it easy. Call me if you notice anything unusual, even if it seems like nothing. When will you tell everyone about this?"

"I think I'll wait until I have proof that the network implant works. I just have to figure out how to make that happen."

"Good luck with that," Jerin said drily.

"I'll do it. I have to."

"I meant with telling your team what you've done. But yes, good luck with the other thing too."

Since Fallon wasn't eager to spend an extended amount of time with the people she was hiding something from, she finally got around to doing something she'd put off for too long.

"What can I do for you, Chief? I was just closing up." Cabot indicated the door of his shop, then bowed. "But of course I'm happy to reopen if there's something you need."

"Actually, it's something I want to do for you. I'd like to take you to dinner."

His blink of surprise made her smile. "I'd be delighted. And since the shop is closed for the evening, I'm available whenever you like."

"How about now?"

"Perfect." He gave her a wink. "Where were you thinking we'd go?"

"Wherever you like."

"How about the Tea Leaf? I've had a craving for nut milk tea all afternoon."

"Zerellian, or Bennite?" she asked.

"Zerellian. The Bennite is good too, but tends to put me to sleep."

"The Tea Leaf it is."

"You know," he said as they walked along, "if you were Rescan, you'd offer me your wrist."

"Offer it for what?"

Cabot chuckled. "Like this." He held his arm, palm up, in front of him. "I'd rest my palm on your wrist, and this would indicate that you are giving me the honor of acting as my host."

"Interesting. I've never heard of that."

"Oh, no one cares about Rescan traditions. Not even Rescans."

"It's come to my attention recently that I haven't done enough to experience other people's ways of living. So here." She lifted her arm as he'd demonstrated, offering him her wrist.

A slow smile spread across his face. "Chief, you continue to surprise me."

He rested his hand lightly on her wrist, and they proceeded that way. Fallon had to admit, it made her feel more stately. She wasn't sure that would help her in life, but at least she was keeping an open mind.

Day shift had only just ended, and soon the Tea Leaf would fill with diners or people just relaxing with a cup of Baronian chamomile. For the moment, the café was fairly quiet. They chose a secluded table in a corner and perused their menuboards.

Fallon quickly selected a sandwich, cold cucumber soup, and a pot of Japanese green tea. Cabot considered his options for a little longer before making his selections. As he set his menuboard aside, he smiled at her.

"I'm so glad you invited me." He folded his hands together on the table.

"So am I. I meant to do it sooner, but I've been caught up in recent events."

He nodded knowingly, which made her wonder about his perspective on said events. "What's the general feeling on the station? Are people anxious? Fearful?"

"There's certainly more anxiety than usual. An air of nervous excitement. PAC command going into seclusion has only happened a few times, and never in the past century. So of course it's going to stir people up. But overall, I'd say there's a..." The corners of his mouth drew down thoughtfully. "An overabundance of faith that things will work out. People are more fascinated than they are frightened."

"That's good to know. Why do you think the faith is excessive? You don't believe the PAC is strong enough to overcome a threat?"

He smiled, but it was a world-weary expression rather than a happy one. "I pay attention to the galaxies, Chief. Our own and all the others within communication distance. I'm also a student of history. I know all too well that no government lasts forever. All societies go through periods of governmental demise and renewal. Most of the time, they end up better for it, but living through the change can be painful—or fatal, for millions of people. So I look at an event like this as, perhaps, the tip of the asteroid. The harbinger of a new era."

"That's surprisingly pessimistic of you. I always saw you as someone who had more faith in happy endings."

"Happy endings happen all the time. But so do tragic ones. It isn't pessimism, Chief, it's realism. Is your outlook so different?"

She lifted her chin in acknowledgement. "No, but I've seen more bad than most people. I'm hardwired to look for undesirable outcomes so I can try to prevent them."

"And that's part of why I like you so much." His smile returned. "You're one of the good ones, the idealists fighting to make things better for everyone."

She shrugged off his praise. "It's only part idealism."

"What's the other part?"

"Hedonism. It's what makes me feel alive."

His eyes crinkled with delight. "See? You're a self-aware realist, like me."

A server arrived carrying their order on a tray, then carefully laid out each dish in front of them before retreating.

Fallon reached for her teapot but Cabot rested his hand on it first. "Shall I?" he asked. "As I understand it, it's polite to pour your tea for you."

"I didn't realize you were familiar with Japanese etiquette. Thank you." She watched tendrils of steam curl and waft away as he poured.

"I used to deal with a Japanese trader. Very traditional fellow. I found that I got much better deals when I observed his etiquette impeccably." He gave her a cheeky grin.

She poured his tea for him. "Funny. Not many people adhere to those traditions. Only on formal occasions back on Earth."

"That's what I like about what I do. I see so much variety. There's always something new and interesting right around the corner."

She'd always wondered about his background, and this seemed like an excellent opportunity to ask. "Do you come from a family of traders?"

"No. Believe it or not, my parents are scholars on the homeworld. They teach at university. But I knew early on that I wanted to have a front-row seat to everything going on in the galaxies. And I happened to have a knack for business that my parents never did. So here I am."

She smiled. "Well, I'm glad. I've valued your friendship greatly."

He leaned forward. "Shh. Don't say that too loudly. If anyone asks, I'm going to tell them that I'm trying to broker a deal between you and the manufacturers of a brand-new type of security scanner. A person in my line of business doesn't admit to making friends." His ale-brown eyes twinkled.

"Your secret's safe with me." She smiled and sipped her tea, careful not to burn her mouth.

"I don't doubt it." He picked up a bite-sized crustacean and popped it into his mouth.

"There are a lot of secrets around here lately." Her words were light and conversational, but she fixed him with a meaningful look.

"There are always secrets. Some are just more important to a larger number of people."

"Should we trade secrets?" She raised her eyebrows in a challenge.

"Oh, I never trade secrets," he said with a wave of his hand. "Bad for business."

"I see."

He leaned forward and whispered, "I would consider sharing a confidence with a friend, though. But I'd never pry if my friend wasn't ready to share in return."

"So your friend would need to speak up," she translated.

"Of course." He ate another crustacean.

That sounded like he had some help to offer if she asked the right question. Or prompted the right one.

She bit into her sandwich, thinking as she chewed. He probably suspected something about the recent goings-on, but would never ask her about it. Yet she couldn't answer his question without knowing what it was.

"Is there something about recent events that has you troubled?"

His eyes gleamed. He understood that she was offering information. "Now that you mention it, I've been concerned about a rumor I heard. Just a rumor, mind you, but sometimes these things stick in your mind and take root. So I've been wondering if it's possible that your job might be in jeopardy. You know we'd hate to lose you here."

But he wasn't talking about her job on Dragonfire, and they both knew it. He was asking whether she was part of what was going on with Jamestown and PAC command.

"I have absolutely no intention of leaving here. Anyone who tries to give me a new assignment will get an earful. I've invested a great deal in this station, and I'm going to see it through."

In other words, yes, she was fighting against someone in PAC command and intended to take him down. She watched him to see if he understood. As coded messages went, it was pretty shrouded.

"I'm glad to hear it. As it happens, I'm owed a few favors that I could always call in, if there's something that might be helpful to you. I've come to think of this station as my home, and I'd be happy to invest in it."

She smiled. She wasn't sure what he was capable of, but it was an interesting suggestion. "If something comes up, I'll be sure to let you know. I appreciate the offer."

"Least I can do, Chief. I hope I can be of service."

She refilled his teacup and changed the subject. "After we're done here, would you like to take a walk in the arboretum? I'd love to hear more about Rescan traditions."

"I'd be delighted. Although, the last time we enjoyed the arboretum, it didn't end so pleasantly."

Understanding passed between them. He knew that the man who had attacked her was connected to what was going on with PAC command. She'd killed the man, then later found out that he was a BlackOp from a different unit. Once she'd regained her memories, she'd realized that Granite had once been her friend. She still had a lot of scores to settle, and Cabot knew it.

"All the more reason to go and have a pleasant time. We have to take the good times where we can get them."

"Yes." He looked sad for a moment, then shook it off with an easy smile. "A walk sounds delightful. I'll tell you about Rescan wedding traditions. There are a few things that might surprise you."

"I look forward to hearing about them."

THE LEISURELY WALK through the arboretum proved to be remarkably enjoyable. Fallon smelled flowers, admired trees, and learned about Rescan society. Plus, Cabot seemed awfully pleased to talk about his people. There'd been no more coded conversation—they'd simply enjoyed their time together as friends.

She felt relaxed as she walked down the corridor to her quarters, then changed her mind and went two doors farther. She touched the chime.

"Hi." Lim seemed surprised to see her. "Something wrong?"

"No. I thought I'd see how you were doing."

They settled in the common living space of the quarters, which was nearly a mirror to her own.

"Okay, considering I may never get my past back." He made himself comfortable and seemed thoughtful, but not depressed.

"Yeah. I know how much that sucks. I faced that same possibility." She related her experience to him, while leaving out a lot of personal details and her revelations about Blackout.

He seemed deeply thoughtful. "What would you have done if you'd never gotten your memory back?"

"I'd have kept on with what I'd been doing. Your lack of memory doesn't mean you're less of a person. You still have your whole life ahead of you."

"But what does that look like?" he asked. "What can I do? I don't know where I belong."

"What *can* you do?" she countered. "You tell me."

"Math. Kellis seemed impressed when I showed her. She said with skills like that, I could get any number of jobs, wherever I wanted to go. The trouble is, where would I want to go?"

Fallon nodded, but said nothing. She wanted him to keep talking. Hearing his own words might help him figure himself out. She'd suggested he visit Grayith Barlow for some professional counseling, but so far Lim had been uninterested in that. Truthfully, she didn't blame him. She wasn't much for counseling, herself. She either worked things through on her own or talked them out with those closest to her.

After a long pause, he spoke again. "Is it foolish to hope I can recover some part of my old self? There was something that allowed me to remember enough to escape, and maybe the tissue regeneration will...I don't know. Give me a chance, somehow."

"What do you mean? About remembering enough to escape?"

"Well, I don't know how long I was in that place, but I got the impression that it had been a while. I got angry at how I was being treated and that should have made it harder for me to think things through, but I felt more alert when I was mad. More capable. And when I felt like they were about to kill me or something, I fought back. I had these bits of information in my head that I couldn't remember learning. A security code, how to use an emergency kit to force open bay doors, the way through the station. Stuff like that. It was like I'd saved the specific memories I'd need to escape."

"Wait, those memories were from before that day? I thought they were all from your last day there, before you escaped. Did you tell Brak about this?"

He looked embarrassed. "No. She'd already told me that my brain didn't have the necessary parts to store those memories. I didn't want her to think I was lying about how I escaped."

She tamped down her impatience by reminding herself of how paranoid she'd been—and rightfully so—when she'd had no memories. "You can trust her, and I promise she won't think you're lying. We need to take this to her right away."

"Wren said you'd say that." His voice held amusement and embarrassment.

That made her pause. "You talked to Wren about this?"

"She's been visiting me the last couple days. She's really easy to talk to. I told her about those flashes of memory and she told me that I needed to tell you."

"Well, she was right. I don't know what it means, but it must mean something."

"It's kind of late," he said. "Shouldn't we wait until morning?"

"Nope." She pointed at the door. "I promise you, Brak would kick my ass if I knew about this and didn't tell her, even for a few hours."

"You're sure she won't think I'm lying?"

"Yes. Besides, she's Briveen. If you were lying, she'd be able to smell it."

"Really?" His eyes got big.

"Yep. Let's go."

Brak clicked her teeth in agitation. "I wouldn't have thought you were lying about remembering things. We need to get to the infirmary, now."

Lim's voice grew small. "You think I'm in danger?"

"No. But I don't want to wait until tomorrow to figure this out."

Since Brak still had temporary guest quarters on Deck One, the trip to the infirmary didn't take long. Once there, Brak waved distractedly to the medical staff on duty and tersely explained that she needed the private room for her patient.

Fallon was impressed. She'd never seen Brak so driven. She backed into the corner of the room and made herself unobtrusive.

Brak guided Lim to the techbed. "Remain still. I don't need to use restraints unless you get fidgety. Let me get a functional scan set up." She paused on her way to the controls. "Don't worry. This won't hurt."

"But...you already did a functional scan," Lim said hesitantly. "What is there to see that you haven't already?"

"I was focusing on your long-term and short-term memories, which are stored in different locations. This time I'm going to look at your entire brain."

Lim seemed to want to ask more questions, but he fell silent. His obvious confusion brought Fallon out of the corner and to his side. She laced her fingers through his and smiled at him. It was an odd feeling for her to be so familiar with someone she barely knew. But it was something Wren would have done, which told her it was the right thing to do.

He smiled back, and the worry eased from his face.

"Okay." Brak moved to where Lim could see her. She handed him an infoboard. "I want you to look at the images that appear. Each one will remain for a few seconds, then be replaced by another. Just relax and think whatever you want to think when you look at them."

Fallon watched him look at pictures of animals, planets, body parts, blood, faces of people wearing various expressions and engaged in a variety of activities. Finally, instead of a picture, the sound of instrumental music came from the board.

"Fallon, please tell him something about your experiences of memory loss. How it felt, how you dealt with it. Something along those lines." Brak stared at the techbed display.

"Uh, sure." Fallon thought back to when she'd woken up with no memory. "When I didn't know what was going on, I was on alert. Paranoid. I was willing to do whatever I had to do in order to get my life back. That hole inside of me made me feel like there was far more of me missing than whatever I had left."

Lim nodded and she continued, "I know our situations are different, but your past isn't the most valuable thing about you. Your future is far more important. Everything you do tomorrow and the next day and the day after that. You still have all that ahead of you. And you already have friends. So no matter what these tests show, there's a lot of good stuff still to come. Okay?"

He smiled. "Yeah. Thanks."

After a long silence Brak said, "Lim, please think about your escape from that station. Step by step, from the moment you first thought of getting away."

Lim closed his eyes, and his mouth tightened.

Brak muttered something in Briveen, then growled. A moment later she growled again. Fallon looked at Lim's curious expression and shrugged. Brak's scents and body language were all muddled into an odd mix, making them difficult for her to interpret.

Finally, Brak left the controls to face Lim. "So we discussed brain anatomy before. That the memory cortex involves a number of different structures in the brain, which is why your long-term memory could be wiped and leave your short-term memory intact. It also explains why you might retain some skills and cultural awareness."

Lim nodded.

"You're missing nearly everything memory related in your frontal and temporal lobes except for your amygdala—which is the emotion center of the brain."

She paused and Lim said, "Okay." He looked entirely mystified.

"Both of you, come back here and take a look at Lim's amygdala." Brak waved them toward the techbed controls.

Fallon watched two almond-shaped blobs display a flashing sequence of activity.

"That's what it looked like when Lim thought about his escape. Any other time, his amygdala exhibited normal activity. It seems like Lim used his fear and desperation, or whatever he was feeling at the time, to imprint specific high-emotion information into his amygdala. It's brilliant. He hid a message to himself in his own brain."

A strong cinnamon aroma wafted around Fallon. She'd never smelled cinnamon from Brak before. Clearly she was incandescently happy. Ecstatic.

"I've never seen anything like it. This is fantastic!" Brak patted Lim on the back as if congratulating him.

"Uh. Thanks?" Lim seemed underwhelmed. "I'm guessing this doesn't change my memory situation, though."

Brak toned down her enthusiasm. "No. But it could open up new avenues in the study of memory. Imagine if we could intentionally load our own brains with memory engrams. We could make certain we'd never forget something truly important. And this could lead to new therapies for memory-destroying diseases."

Brak pressed her hand to her chest, looking emotional.

And Fallon thought *she* loved her work. "Did you need us for anything else?"

Brak pulled herself together. "No. But thank you both. I know this doesn't help your situation, Lim, but you've made a significant contribution to science."

He lifted his shoulder and let it drop, in a noncommittal gesture that looked a lot like the Briveen sign for contrition. "I'm glad if it helps someone. But for my own sake, it's nice to know that I have friends who will believe me if I say something crazy."

"Of course we believe you," Brak said. "As to the upgrade to your new implant, I'll be ready to do that tomorrow. Noon, if that works for you."

"Well, it's ahead of schedule. Can't say I'm sorry for it to be sooner rather than later." Lim smiled weakly.

"How about we go by the pub and I buy you a drink?" Fallon offered, giving his shoulder a pat.

"Sure, if I'm allowed to drink before brain surgery." Lim laughed.

Brak nodded distractedly and gave them a "go" gesture. Fallon suspected she'd work all night.

"All right. Let's see what you think of Zerellian ale."

9

Lim was not at all an ale person. After a cautious taste, he grimaced and asked, "Is there something that doesn't taste like sour, burning water?"

On a hunch, Fallon ordered him a Sarkavian brandy.

"Ahh. Now that's good." Lim wiped his mouth on a napkin with satisfaction. "It's strange, not even knowing what I like."

"I remember that. I ended up eating a rastor dumpling, only to find I absolutely hate them. It was like rotten dirty socks with a spicy sauce."

"I'll stay clear." Lim chuckled.

"Never know. They might be your favorite."

He sighed. "Yeah. I guess so. I'm going to have to try everything to see if I like it or not."

"Yep. But look at the bright side. You get to try everything." She smiled at him.

"Another good point." He took a drink of his brandy, seeming more upbeat.

A moment later, he asked, "You're going to take down the guy who did this to me, right?"

Fallon stared at him thoughtfully.

"What?" he asked, looking nervous.

"You saw him, right? The admiral who ordered this stuff be done to you? And you remember what he looks like?" With everything else going on, she'd failed to clamp onto that detail.

"Yeah."

She yanked her comport off her belt and pulled up an image of Colb, and one of Krazinski. One of her father too, to add another face to the mix. She handed her comport to Lim. "Is it one of these guys?"

"That one." His finger pointed to the one on the far right.

Her breath caught.

She'd never felt so validated as when she saw him pointing at Colb. So it *had* been him all along. She'd been sure of it, but in this world of hers, full of twists and turns and betrayals, it felt good to have actual visual confirmation.

"I'm buying you another brandy."

LIM TURNED out to be a lightweight, returning to his quarters early, so Fallon called Hawk. She expected him to turn her down, but he quickly agreed to come meet her in the pub. She had a whisky waiting for him when he arrived.

"That's the girl I love," he said, tossing the whisky back all at once. "Could have gotten two, though. I see you've had a head start on me."

"Yeah. Well. I figured if I had enough drinks, it might activate my brain."

He laughed. "I'm pretty sure alcohol works the opposite way, but even if it didn't, why start now?"

She elbowed him. "In other news, our new friend confirmed that our old friend, who is no longer our friend, is *definitely* not our friend."

"I think I actually understood that. Which means I'm ordering two more whiskies."

A good-looking guy walked past their table a little too slowly with his eyes fastened on Hawk. She recognized him as an entry-level maintenance worker. Some message passed between him and Hawk, and his pace increased once he passed the table.

"New pal?" she asked.

"You know me. A regular social butterfly."

"Right. You're a people person." She smirked.

Normally, they would have continued on with the witty repartee, insulting each other until one of them issued a challenge of some kind. Hawk pursed his lips thoughtfully. "What's bothering you? I'm guessing you didn't invite me here just to shoot the shit."

She sighed, frowning into her cup. He was right. She needed to confide in someone, and he was the one she leaned on in such situations. "I did a semi-reckless thing and so far it hasn't done shit for me. I kind of thought I'd have some big holo-vid moment that would have me solving everything, so we could get back out there where we belong—zooming through the stars, blowing shit up, and winning one for the good guys."

He squinted at her empty glass. "How many have you had?"

"Not enough." She punched an order for another into her menuboard.

"So what did you do?" he asked. "I have a feeling this is going to be a good one."

She thought for a long moment before speaking. He watched her, patiently waiting.

"Do you remember that time on the Verthain moon?" she asked. "We were tracking that woman but her trail went cold. You headed to the bar, got entirely piss drunk, and when I came to find you, we both almost got turned into hamburger?"

He closed one eye, peering at her. "What's your point?"

"I saved our asses and promised never to tell anyone about it. Remember?"

"Ya. I remember."

"I'm cashing that one in."

"Oh Prelin's ass, what have you done now?" He grimaced.

"Well, it's possible that I might have had Brak put something in my head so I can find our missing friend." She wasn't about to mention Krazinski's name in public.

"Are you kidding me?"

"No."

Instead of cursing a stream of inventive filth, he laughed. "You are so screwed. Raptor and Peregrine are going to be pissed."

"Not if I can come up with the break we need. Success comes with a lot of forgiveness."

"And how's that working for you?"

"I've got nothing," she admitted. "I don't even know how to activate it."

He laughed again. "Yep. Screwed."

She sighed. "You could stop being delighted and try to help me find a solution."

"Count your blessings. I'd be livid right now if you hadn't cashed in your Verthain chip and I didn't have three whiskies in me."

"Four," she corrected.

"Whatever."

She scowled at him.

"Look," he said. "First, I'd need to actually know exactly what you're talking about. And since I'm no tech wizard, I probably can't help anyway. Unless you need me to break your brain out of jail or something."

"Maybe I do. It hasn't been doing anything helpful."

"All right." He finished his drink. "Let's go."

"Where?"

"Your quarters."

"Why?" She'd never known Hawk to leave a bar this early.

"So you can tell me what we're talking about, and we can try to figure it out so you don't get your ass kicked by Peregrine and Raptor."

"Fine." She slid off her bar stool.

"You have drinks at your place, right?"

It didn't take long to get Hawk up to speed.

He jiggled his nearly empty glass, causing ice to clink against the sides. Frowning, he watched the cubes tumble around. "Like you said, we have to assume you're supposed to be able to use the network. It's designed for two-way traffic, right?"

"Yeah. And believe me, I've tried everything I can think of. Closing my eyes and imagining my brain, picturing the thing working, and all that. I might have strained my face a little just trying."

"We need the password for the drawbridge."

"The what?" Fallon decided she'd water down Hawk's next drink. He was no good to her if he got all-out drunk and started talking nonsense.

"It's a joke based on an old fairy tale. Not important. We just need to find the trigger."

"Believe me, I've tried. I've been tempted to bang my head on the wall to see if that would work."

"I could always punch you in the head, if that would help," he offered.

She fixed him with a glare. "It's amazing how many times in recent months my teammates have cheerfully offered to brain me."

He grinned at her. "Outside of that, I dunno. Brak didn't think she could activate the thing mechanically? Maybe some type of electronic pulse?"

"She tried numerous things before implanting it. She said it required actual brain waves."

"Okay." He tried taking another swig of his drink, only to remember it was already empty when an ice cube bonked him in the nose. He set the glass aside. "So how about ways you can use your brain that you usually don't?"

"What, like doing theoretical physics or something? It can't be anything too obscure. Krazinski expects us to figure it out."

Hawk rubbed his beard as he thought. He was due for a trim, so he mussed his facial hair in a way that made him look like a deranged badger. "Okay. When your memory was missing, I did a lot of reading. I read about a thing called brain wave entrainment. It's the electrical response in the brain caused by some rhythmic stimulus, like sound or light or touch. What if there's a stimulus that can create the specific brain wave needed to activate the network implant?"

Fallon stared at him in surprise. She'd wanted him to help her brainstorm, but hadn't expected him to say anything so on point.

"What? I'm too dumb to have learned stuff?" He rolled his eyes comically.

"No, I just hadn't realized you'd researched that stuff. The entrainment thing makes sense." She bit her top lip, thinking. "What type of stimulus would it be? Something Krazinski would expect us to associate with communication."

A thought occurred to her and gelled into an idea. Answering her own question, she said, "A hail. A hailing frequency."

Hawk's gaze locked onto hers. "Yeah. Yeah!"

"So…how do I experience a hailing frequency in some sensory way?"

He pushed the voicecom display toward her. "I bet Brak knows."

She leaned close to him and raked her fingers through his beard, so he no longer looked like a disheveled woolly mammoth.

"What?" he asked. "Did I have food caught in there again?"

"Gross. No, I was just fixing your face. It was all mussed up."

"Oh, okay. Now call your friend so we can go fix your brain."

"That's an intriguing idea," Brak said. "And easy to implement. I can create an audio representation of a hailing frequency. After you've heard it, simply remembering it should be all you need. I would not have thought of using entrainment in this way. What made you think of it?" Brak gazed at Hawk as if seeing him for the first time.

Hawk shrugged. "I'd like to pretend I'm a man of many hidden depths, with genius being among them. But the truth is, it's one of the few things that stuck with me after reading all that brain stuff."

"Given the specificity of a hailing frequency, it would be nearly impossible to accidentally experience that sensory sequence. It's quite clever."

"If it works," Fallon put in.

"If it works," Brak agreed.

"It'll work," Hawk insisted. When they both looked at him, he shrugged. "I'm trying on optimism, as a change of pace."

"When can we try the frequency?" Fallon asked.

"Tomorrow afternoon, right after Lim's surgery," Brak said.

"You won't need time to rest?"

"Are you kidding? It's going to be like a hatch-day celebration, but better."

Fallon had to smile. "You're the only person I know who likes her work as much as we do." She glanced at Hawk and thought of Peregrine. "Well, as much as we usually do. Recent events notwithstanding."

"There's a lot to be said for doing what you love," Brak agreed. "Now you two need to let me sleep so my mind will be fresh tomorrow."

Out in the corridor, Hawk looked down at Fallon. "You'd better hope she makes that thing work. Otherwise you're going to have to tell Raptor, Peregrine, and Nevitt what you did, and not have a thing to show for it."

Fallon grimaced. She just had to hope tomorrow proved to be a successful day.

FALLON STOOD with Brak and Jerin in the private room of the infirmary. She watched Lim's young, guileless face as he slept, vividly remembering her own surgeries. In a way, he was more like her than anyone, and she wanted more for him than just a successful surgery. She hoped she'd someday get to help him discover his past, and forge a future too. But first she had to sort out the present.

Brak remained at the techbed controls, watching the readouts. Finally, she nodded to Jerin.

Jerin touched his hand. "Lim? Lim, can you hear me?"

His head turned. "Yeah. I'm here." He sounded slightly groggy, but aware. His eyes opened and focused on them.

"Everything went well," Jerin explained. "More successfully than I'd anticipated, actually. I was able to regenerate ninety percent of the brain tissue that had been removed."

"Ninety percent of the man I used to be. Not too bad." Lim's smile was crooked.

"The anesthetic is lingering a little," Brak reported. "I'm going to wait it out. Given the tissue regeneration, I don't want to give him a stimulant."

"Agreed." Jerin returned her attention to Lim. "How are you feeling?"

His eyes became more focused. "Fine, I guess. Maybe a little nauseated?"

"We'll give you something for that." Jerin nodded to Brak. "Otherwise? Any headache?"

"Not exactly. The light's bothering me a little."

"That's normal, and will pass in a day or two. I recommend you spend the time resting in your quarters. You'll be tired. You might have some balance issues in the short term but your brain will figure itself out remarkably quickly." Jerin smiled at him encouragingly.

"So it went well?" He seemed unaware that he was repeating what had already been said.

"Yes. Very well, Lim. Why don't you rest while we tidy up?"

"Okay." He closed his eyes and went silent.

Fallon moved closer to Jerin. "Why is he so out of it?"

"Some people are slower to come around after brain surgery. Some take longer to recover from anesthetic. Perfectly normal. Don't worry."

Jerin joined Brak at the techbed controls and they murmured to each other in what sounded to Fallon like satisfied tones. She had nothing to do here but sit and watch Lim doze.

A half hour later, he was still dozing.

"He may sleep for another hour or so," Brak said to her. "If you want to go, we can contact you when he's awake."

"No. He asked me to be here. I don't want him to wake up and think I've abandoned him. I'll wait."

Fifty minutes later, he roused. He still looked tired, but he'd lost his air of confusion. Jerin and Brak explained the situation to him again as he became more and more alert.

"Great," he said. "Thanks."

"You can stay here as long as you like," Jerin told him.

"No. I'm good. I think I'd like to go back to my quarters and rest. Maybe watch a holo-vid."

"Perfect," Brak said. "We want you to take it very easy for the next few days. You won't be able to tell, but your brain is going to be very busy. Let it do its thing."

"Sure," he agreed.

"I'll help you to your quarters," Fallon said, moving to assist him when he sat up.

"That's nice of you," he said. "Thank you."

"It's nothing." She moved close as he stood, but he stayed steady under his own power. He just seemed terribly tired.

"When should I come back for my turn?" she asked Jerin and Brak before leaving.

"Two hours will give us time to get some lunch and rest a little." Jerin smiled at her.

"Two hours, then."

She saw Lim to his quarters, kept him company for a little while, then left him under Hawk's supervision.

"You'll let me know as soon as you leave the infirmary?" Hawk asked.

"I'll come straight back here. You'll be the first to know, after Jerin and Brak."

"And you," he added.

"Right. And if we're lucky, Krazinski will know very soon too."

"Are you ready?" Brak peered down at Fallon.

"I couldn't be more ready."

"Okay. I've programmed the techbed with a repeating audio frequency, as well as a physical pulse, just to be sure. Have you prepared the message you intend to send?"

"Yes." Fallon would keep the message short. She only needed to let Krazinski know that she was listening.

"Lie back and relax. I'm going to lower the lights so that you can focus more completely on the audio and sensory input. Tell me when you're ready to start."

Fallon glanced at Jerin, who smiled encouragingly, before closing her eyes. "Now."

She heard an electronic buzzing and felt a corresponding vibration beneath her. She focused on it as it repeated. She imagined herself aligning with the pattern, becoming part of it.

She felt something odd, and opened her eyes. It was like someone taking her outstretched hand in theirs. But it was in her mind. She must have made the connection. There was nothing left to do but send her message.

"I'm here," she thought.

"That's it." Fallon sat up. "It's sent." She focused on letting go of the connection, and after a moment the feeling went away.

Jerin nodded, and Brak said, "I'll discontinue the stimulus."

"Do you feel okay?" Jerin asked.

"Fine. It's interesting, actually. Like there's a tunnel inside my head."

"Can you open and close it at will?" Jerin asked.

"Yes." Fallon imagined the sound of the frequency and felt the sensation of connection again, then let go of it. "I just turned it on and off again. Kind of neat. Like flexing a muscle."

"I suggest you turn it off to sleep," Brak advised.

"Yeah. Good plan. Otherwise, I plan to keep it open as much as possible, so I'll know as soon as Krazinski replies." She looked to Brak. "Unless there's some reason I shouldn't?"

Brak gave a slight shake of the head. "Not that I'm aware of. You can receive messages, but the device can only be activated by your own brain. How long do you think it will take to get a reply?"

"Depends on how far away they are. My message will have to travel to them, then their response will have to cover the same distance. Since there won't be any relays along the way to boost the signal, I'd guess a couple days or more, if they're relatively nearby."

"That's a long time to wait," Jerin said.

"It's a far cry from the datastream," Fallon agreed. "This is a pretty old-school means of communication."

"When are you going to tell your team about this?" Jerin asked.

"Hawk already knows. But I'll tell the rest of them tonight. I want them to be prepared to act as soon as I get a response."

FALLON SAT next to Hawk in her quarters when she told the rest of their team, including Hesta and Ross. Afterward, she watched them intently as they thought it over.

After a long silence, Hesta said, "Okay, then. What next?"

The tedium of yet more meetings and discussions was tempered by her surprise at their lack of passionate response. She'd expected a verbal beatdown, and in its absence, a strategy meeting was downright tolerable. "We need to find Colb. Or get him to come to us."

"Colb doesn't know what we know and what we don't," Hesta pointed out. "Could we just pretend we know where the people of PAC command are hiding out?"

"A bluff." Fallon liked the idea. "It's a great play, but if he doesn't fall for it, we've given away the fact that we know he's watching."

"So we'd have to make sure the bait was too good for him to resist." Peregrine chewed on the pad of her thumb.

"I'm not sure what that would be," Fallon admitted. "That's why I've been focused on getting to Krazinski so we can use his resources and intel."

No one responded, so it seemed no one else knew a surefire way to lure Colb out, either.

"We can think about it," Ross said.

But Hesta's suggestion had gotten her thinking, and an idea struck Fallon. "Wait. I might have a way. Or know someone who will. Let me see what I can find out tomorrow and I'll let you know."

Hawk nudged her leg with his. "That's it? You can't give us any details?"

"No. Not yet. I might be chasing starshine and I want to be sure."

"Okay," said Peregrine. "Then I think we're done here. At least, I am."

Relief washed over Fallon. They weren't going to make a big deal about her decision to have the networking device added to her implant.

"Don't think you're off the hook." Peregrine smiled at her sweetly while stretching her back. On Peregrine, an expression like that was downright terrifying. "You have two people who will be distinctly unhappy with your decision. I'm certain they'll do a far better job at raking you over the coals than I will. That means I can save myself the trouble." She ran a hand down her ponytail.

Hesta stood. "I think that sounds about right." She directed her attention to Peregrine. "Can I buy you a drink at the pub?"

"Absolutely."

Ross and Hawk exchanged a glance. "I think we're out of here too, cupcake." Hawk kissed her cheek on his way out.

Which left Fallon alone with Raptor.

"If I thought yelling or cursing at you would do me any good, I'd do it," Raptor said. "I won't waste my energy."

"One second." She ignored his bewilderment as she turned and marched to her bedroom. She pulled her knife case from the closet and expanded it. From the second row, third column, she removed a sleek black knife with a carved handle. She had a hard time saying it out loud, but she hoped this would show him how she felt about him.

She returned the case to her closet and straightened just as the doors opened.

"What are you doing?" He frowned at her, looking puzzled and angry.

She closed the space between them and held out the knife. "Giving you this." She laid it carefully in his palm.

"This is the knife you won when you took the championship at the academy." He ran his thumb over the engraving, which spelled out her name and the words Grand Champion, along with their class year.

"It's always been my favorite, though it doesn't have the finest blade, or the most expensive inlay. I earned this one. And I want you to have it."

"Why?"

"Because you know what it means to me, and that I'd only ever give it to someone I truly love."

He slow-blinked at her.

She steeled herself. "That's right, I said it. I—*oof.*"

Raptor had picked her up and was squishing the air out of her. She had to wonder where that knife had gone, but it was a nice kind of squish. All warm and cozy and full of distracting Raptor kisses.

Apparently he had also decided to go with showing instead of telling.

"You didn't accidentally transmit any of that, did you?" Raptor tickled her playfully the next morning, to no effect. They both knew she wasn't ticklish.

"Nope. It's not like it's an open link to my thoughts. Telepathy, or mind sharing, or whatever you want to call it, has not been invented inside my head. Now I need to get to work." She started to roll out of bed, but he caught her around the waist and held her back.

"What if you go, and then we have another fight?"

She relaxed against him. "We're always going to fight. I wouldn't know what to do if you stopped fighting with me. But we're done fighting about whether or not we're together. Well, unless you decide you want out. And if that's the case I'll have to kick your ass."

"I'm not going to want out."

"Good, because I'm working at being all enlightened, here, and it would suck if you ruined it."

He gave her a push and she nearly fell off the bed. She got her feet under her and popped up beside it to see him grinning at her. She grabbed a pillow and threw it at him on her way to the shower.

Prelin's ass, she loved that man.

FALLON SEEMED to be making a habit of skipping her morning run. Instead, she asked Cabot to meet her at his shop before it opened.

Once they were inside with the door closed, she wasted no time. "You suggested that if there was a way you could help, I should let you know."

"Yes. What can I do for you, Chief?" Cabot's usual good humor had been eclipsed by seriousness.

"I need a way to make someone think that something big is happening here. I'm sure he's watching, and we just need to give him something to see. Something worth coming after."

"Well, to know if I can arrange that, I'd need to know what would interest this person."

"The transport of a few hundred people to the station would definitely get his attention."

Cabot rubbed his hands together thoughtfully. "Would we need actual people, or the mere assumption of people?"

Fallon smiled. Cabot had the right idea and that boded well for this plan. "Just the assumption."

"So a couple of personnel transports. Should these ships be capable of withstanding an attack?"

"Yes. We're presenting him with a target. A target that he'd love to destroy. So these ships need to be prepared. Of course, if there's any damage, I'll cover the cost of repair." And if the repairs were interesting, at least Wren would be entertained.

"Hmm. When would you want those ships to arrive?"

"The actual arrival isn't important. It's the approach I care about. I'd like them to take no longer than a week to arrive, but the sooner they got under way the better, so I could start laying the groundwork to draw out our snake."

Cabot pressed his lips together. "That's quick. Large transports tend to be booked out in advance to ensure capacity."

"If you can't help—"

He cut in. "I didn't say I couldn't. I just need to make some inquiries. See what's available."

"I'll let you get started." She paused at the door. "Thanks, Cabot. If you can help me out with this, I'll owe you one. Not just me, either. A lot of people will owe you one."

"Oh, I do love to be owed favors from important people." His jauntiness had returned. "I suspect this is going to be quite the interesting adventure."

He had no idea. Or...maybe he did.

ON THE BOARDWALK the next afternoon, Cabot waved Fallon over and ushered her into his shop for a private chat.

As she waited for him to finish up with his customer, she looked around, noticing what items were new or missing compared to the previous day. She recalled her bet with Hawk, and her need to pick out something special for him to give to Hesta, but she saw nothing bizarre enough. Another day.

Cabot escorted his happy customer, who carried a small cube-shaped container, to the door. He quickly locked up and joined Fallon.

"I can have two ships with a combined capacity of eight hundred here in about eight days. Is that sufficient?" he asked. "With just a few crew on each."

"It's faster than I expected, though slower than I hoped. So I guess it's just right."

He smiled. "Good. I already told them to get under way."

"That was presumptuous. But smart. Thank you." She calculated what she'd need to arrange. Timing would be critical, but a week gave her more than enough time to have everything in place.

"Anything I can do to help." Cabot wore his customary pleasant expression, but the look in his eyes was dead serious.

"I'll hold you to that." She smiled to show her gratitude, but she wasn't joking either.

She rode the lift back up to her office. As she stepped out, an odd sensation caused her to slap her hand to the wall to keep herself steady. She felt light-headed, and her perception of her surroundings dimmed for a moment.

The sensation passed quickly, and she straightened. She now had long numbers in her head, which she immediately recognized as coordinates. Krazinski had told her where to find him.

It was go time.

BACK IN THE pilot seat of the *Nefarious*, Fallon felt invincible. She wished she never had to leave this spot, existing in a time loop where she was forever embarking on a mission with her team.

She felt fairly certain Hawk, Peregrine, Raptor, and Ross felt the same.

The small Sarkavian moon her coordinates were leading her to seemed an unlikely place for Krazinski to be hiding out. But then the best hideouts were usually the unlikely ones.

Landing on the moon gave her a strange sense of having come full circle. She'd planned her rebellion from the outside, and here she was, bringing her team back into the fold so they could join forces to take out the real enemy. After two years of being diverted, she was returning to what she should have been doing all along.

Yet if she hadn't had these past years, she wouldn't have Dragonfire, the crew of the *Onari*, or her current relationship with Raptor. She wouldn't have even met Wren.

She wouldn't wish those things away, even if she could.

The coordinates she'd received led them to a bunker. Its opening was wedged into the side of a crater. Fallon didn't care for wearing a pressure suit, but there was no way around it. An airlock on the surface would have given the bunker away.

Raptor entered the code Krazinski had sent them, and the hatch opened. Though the passage below was lit, the steep stairs leading downward had an ominous feel.

"Creepy-ass entrance," Raptor observed. "Never would have known it was here. But that's the point, right?" His words came through their open channel sounding hollow.

"Why have a secret hideout unless you can make it seem like some space monster is about to come out and eat you?" She appreciated the ominous feeling of the place.

"Not what I meant, but I can't disagree."

She descended first. The sound of her boots clanging on the metal steps came up through her suit. *Bang, bang, shuffle, bang.*

Finally they reached the bottom. Fallon waited for Raptor to join her, and then they stepped into the airlock together.

"I have to admit, I don't feel awesome about this," Raptor said as he secured the hatch behind them. "It's like we're trapping ourselves for someone else's convenience."

"Yeah." She activated the pressurization sequence. "But even if someone did have plans for us, they'd know that we have friends in a nice big ship ready to tear the side of this moon off to get to us." She hit the airlock's voicecom circuit. "Isn't that right?" She had no doubt they were being monitored on an internal line.

"Save your energy for the real enemy, Fallon," Krazinski's voice advised, sounding amused. "There's nobody here but me."

"I've had a hard time telling who the real enemy is lately," she said to the faceless voice. "So you'll forgive my suspicion, I'm sure."

"How long have you been here? And why are you alone?" Raptor asked.

"Ever since we received Fallon's transmission. We'd just about given up hope. We've enacted an emergency protocol that requires the use of point-to-point closed networks. So I'm right here at the terminus as the relay between you and the rest of command."

"How many relay stations like this are there between us and them?" Raptor sat on a rock ledge that seemed designed for the purpose. Even through a pressure suit, Fallon could read his impatience.

"Four. The other members of PAC command aren't as far away as they could be, but they aren't right around the corner, either. It's not easy to hide that many people, as you can imagine."

"So they're together?" Fallon asked. "Seems like splitting them up would have made it easier to hide them."

"And easier for someone to sneak a communication through," Krazinski said. "We're not taking any risks. Everyone is securely locked down, with all disaster protocols observed."

"Everyone but you, and those four other point-to-point stations," Fallon noted.

"Yes," Krazinski agreed. "Not my first choice of duty station, but someone completely trustworthy had to do it. The clash on Jamestown forced us to neutralize everyone Colb had recruited. Most of them were good people who were duped into committing treason. But regardless of their delusions, I'm having a hard time with trust after seeing officers I'd had complete faith in killing their colleagues. That's why I came myself, and assigned only my closest comrades to the other spots."

"What exactly happened on Jamestown?" Raptor asked.

Krazinski's heavy sigh said much about regret. "Colb's people were planning an uprising to take over the station. We surprised them by attacking first. Our initial intent was to use nonlethal force, but that was a mistake. We suffered more casualties than we would have if I'd permitted lethal action at the outset. But that's my burden to bear. There will be a lot of holes to fill once we get back to Jamestown, left by the traitors and loyal officers both."

A beep signaled the completion of the pressurization. Fallon removed her helmet, drawing in a deep breath of air. Across from her, Raptor did the same.

Since putting a pressure suit on required at least fifteen minutes to properly attach and align the systems, she and Raptor only removed their gloves. Krazinski's voice said, "Might as well remove all of it. We have a lot to talk about, and you'll be more comfortable."

She looked at Raptor, but he only shrugged and reached behind his neck.

"Here, I'll get it." She moved behind him and depressurized the suit, then began helping him peel it off. When she moved to face him, she saw his humor and a hint of wickedness. He wouldn't say it out loud given their circumstances, but his expression said that he found the actions similar to a very different scenario.

She rolled her eyes, but couldn't help but smile. When they switched roles, he helped her out of her suit while giving her some enthusiastic leering. It was so incongruent with the situation she almost laughed out loud.

Finally they stepped through the airlock into a short corridor. At the end of it Raptor opened a door, and they entered a tiny room that reminded Fallon of a crisis ops control center. Krazinski stood waiting for them. He looked paler and thinner than Fallon remembered him.

He smiled. "I can't tell you how good it is to see you two. I feel like finally, the end to all this is near." He stepped closer and gave them a deep, deep bow of respect and gratitude.

Whatever Fallon had expected, it hadn't been that. Raptor's startled expression no doubt mirrored her own.

"I hope it is," she said quickly, trying to cover her surprise.

He nodded. "Let's get to work and make sure of it."

RAPTOR AND FALLON checked in with Avian Unit, then turned to making sure Krazinski's story checked out on all points before doing anything more. Like Krazinski's, their trust was in short supply lately.

"When exactly did you realize Colb was doing illegal research?" Raptor asked. He sat on a small modular chair that was identical to the ones Fallon and Krazinski sat on. This little hideout was far from plush.

"Not nearly soon enough." Krazinski's face was lined with regret. "We gave each other wide leeway to do our jobs. He handled his teams, I handled mine. But I've worked with him for over twenty years, and we'd run Blackout together seamlessly. I wish I could say that in retrospect, I could see the signs of his betrayal. But he seemed no less sincere, no less committed to the PAC." He sipped from a packet of water. "When Andra died a few years back, he grieved, but privately. Her loss did not affect his work. Or so I thought."

Krazinski lapsed into silence, no doubt picking through the past, trying to see if hindsight could give him a new view of events. But he shook his head. "It wasn't until I heard some whispers in the tech industry and followed one anomaly to the next that I noticed something bigger emerging. Even then I didn't realize it was him."

"That was when you tried to blackmail Brak to create that kind of technology," Fallon said.

"No, by the time I did that, I did suspect Colb. I just couldn't find any proof. I hoped Brak would be a link to the people involved, but it was very clear that she knew nothing of any of it. Even then I hoped I was wrong about Colb. That I was overly suspicious. An old man seeing shadows and thinking they were monsters. I even thought it might be time to retire. I was no use to anyone if I'd lost my edge. But then I connected a supplier to a scientist. Once I investigated the scientist, I realized the nature of what was happening. Implants. Illegal technology. Treaty violations."

"And of course by that point, the team you normally would have sent out had already been sidelined." Fallon frowned.

"Avian Unit was the best Blackout team, in my opinion. I never understood why Colb seemed to favor Stone Unit over you. And I objected when he sent you out on individual deep-cover missions. I wanted you back, but he insisted he had you on critical assignments. He backed it up with details, but I still felt another team should be doing that work."

Fallon's attention caught on the mention of Stone Unit. "Do you know that I killed Granite? I didn't know who he was at the time. I intended to question him but I injured him too badly."

Krazinski winced. "Yes. I did know."

He said nothing more, but Fallon distinctly sensed that he blamed himself for not seeing it all much sooner.

Disasters and betrayals were always like that. They seemed impossible right up until they happened.

"Any idea why Fallon was singled out to get an implant?" Raptor asked. "Colb had a lot of BlackOps to choose from."

"I can only speculate. Either he wanted to separate your unit to keep you from being able to work against him, or he did it specifically to get access to Fallon. Maybe because of her extraordinary memory?"

Fallon only nodded. She was disappointed he didn't have more to add about what had happened to her, but clearly those answers could only come from Colb himself.

Krazinski continued, "When he knew I suspected him, he began to squeeze me out. Tried to discredit me. Prove that I was unreliable. He connected some of his own dealings to me, making it seem I was the cause of it all. He managed to confuse the others in Blackout long enough to get his ass to Zerellus and make himself conspicuous." Anger darkened his face. "Of course we could do nothing at that point but try to keep him isolated."

"Because a public death or apprehension would have brought all the treaty violations to light," Fallon finished.

"Yes. And it gets worse," Krazinski said.

"Oh good, I was hoping you'd say that." Raptor sighed.

Krazinski ignored him. "The Barony Coalition has begun strategic attacks on small outposts on the fringes of the PAC zone. Testing our strength and tolerance. They're aware of at least some of the treaty violations—thanks to Colb, I'm guessing—and their goal will be to shift the balance of power so that they can take over the PAC."

"They'll be strip-mining entire planets and raising prices to the point that less prosperous planets begin to starve." Outrage flooded through Fallon. The Barony Coalition was barely contained under the best of circumstances. They followed the very letter of the law, but exploited any gray area. Fallon didn't want to find out how far they'd go to take advantage of the PAC's difficulties.

"Do they know that command is under more stress than just a terrorist threat?" Raptor asked.

"We have to assume they at least suspect so." Krazinski seemed reluctant to admit it. "We've done remarkably well, all things considered, at selling that story, but I never expected the Coalition to buy it. Still, I'd hoped to keep them pacified and uncertain long enough to allow us to handle Colb and reassert ourselves."

"Which means we need to contain Colb so that he can't do any further damage, shore up all of our treaties in good faith, and then soothe or scare the Barony Coalition back into compliance." Fallon frowned. It was more than she'd bargained on.

"I'd say that sums it up," Krazinski said.

Raptor stood. "Well, we've already started on a plan to get our hands on Colb. How do we handle the rest?"

KRAZINSKI SENT a final message out to the point-to-point network before joining Fallon and Raptor on the *Nefarious*.

They'd debated having Krazinski remain on the moon to maintain the communication relay, but ultimately decided that he could be put to better use in ensuring that Colb got snared in the web they were weaving. John Krazinski was a hell of an officer, and they needed all the help they could get.

After a quick debriefing, Fallon got herself to the bridge and began the sequence to get them off this dark little moon.

Peregrine sat in the chair beside her, looking pensive. "Ever hear of the warrior's dilemma? Realizing that what you're fighting for isn't the fight for right that you first thought it was?"

Fallon had heard of it, but wondered why Peregrine would be asking about it at this moment.

She lifted them off the moon's surface before she answered. "You mean us, right? When Colb was trying to use us against the

PAC. You're wondering what would have happened if we'd blindly followed our orders. If Raptor hadn't gotten our team back together so we could fight back."

"Yes." Peregrine sounded thoughtful. More philosophical than Fallon had ever heard her. "Would we have been like Stone Unit? They were good people. Probably still are. They're just on the wrong side of the fight."

Fallon understood what Peregrine was getting at. "In war, nobody ever thinks they're the evil one."

"Yeah, and it could have been us. Colb thought we'd be his secret weapon, but we backfired on him."

Fallon turned sideways to face Peregrine directly. "Is that how you see it?"

"Of course. Don't you? It's your head he carved into. Your life he wiped away. And here we are, about to be the ones to take him down." Instead of sounding fired up, Peregrine sounded frustrated. The prospect of being used to do wrong had clearly been weighing on her.

Fallon established a flight path, and engaged the autopilot for a moment. She moved to the edge of her seat, leaned way over, and kissed Peregrine on the forehead. "We did what we were born to do. We figured it out, and got to work on fixing it. If you think about it, we *had* to be the ones all this happened to. Who else could have gotten underneath it all so we could stop it?"

Peregrine chewed on her thumb, thinking. "I guess you're right. When you put it that way, of course it had to be us." A tiny grin appeared on her face. "Nobody's as good as Avian Unit."

Per's rare grin let Fallon know that her partner had put things back into perspective.

Fallon returned to the controls. "Not even close. We're going to kick Colb's ass harder than any other team could dream of doing."

"And Hawk will tell the story at all the bars, and we'll get free drinks for life."

Obviously he couldn't tell the real story, but he could probably cobble together enough of it to make that happen.

"I could use a few drinks. Once we get Colb, let's make Hawk buy us a few rounds."

Per's mood had lightened, and she seemed like the Peregrine that Fallon knew, sure of herself and ready to take on anything. "You know, once all this is over our unlimited stolen funding from Blackout will end."

Fallon hadn't yet thought of that. She'd have to go back to requesting funds the official way. Pisser. "Guess we'll have to make sure we enjoy our drinks extra hard, then."

"A last hurrah?"

"Or a first one, while we contemplate our future."

They both knew they had to survive their current endeavor to get to that point, so they fell into a companionable silence.

THE NEXT TWO days of waiting on the *Nefarious* to make their rendezvous passed with surprising calm. Fallon felt an odd sense of normalcy leading up to something that would be anything but normal. The end of this ordeal was coming. She could feel it.

She could only wonder how far-reaching the effects would be, once they'd captured Colb and ended his efforts.

Fallon and the others spent a fair amount of time talking to Krazinski, both giving and receiving details of the past couple of years. It made Fallon think again about the strange trajectory she'd been on all this time. How none of it should have ever happened, and how if it hadn't, she'd have continued her regularly scheduled life.

As she listened to Raptor breathe in the darkness of her quarters, she knew she probably would have spent the occasional night with him, but that too would have been very different. They wouldn't have an easy affection developing between them, or the open acknowledgement of the soul-deep connection they'd spent a decade denying. Yes, that had been her fault. She looked forward to spending the rest of her life making up for it.

She'd never been one to want an adventure to end, but this time she did. She wanted the PAC to be secure, and she wanted Colb to never see the stars again. Whether that meant imprisonment or death, she didn't care. She just wanted everyone to be safe.

Only then could she lean in to Raptor's sleepy warmth and not feel guilty to be glad for the way her life had been altered.

FALLON WOKE ALONE and lay in Raptor's bunk debating whether to work out or get some breakfast. Her rumbling stomach won out.

She heard no sound as she approached the mess, making her think it must be empty. But when she entered, she saw Krazinski sitting at a small table, staring out a porthole.

"Good evening, Fallon. Though I guess for you it's morning. I always find it difficult to keep track of the time of day when I'm on a ship. Strange, since a station isn't so different."

She grabbed two protein packs and a fresh tango fruit before sitting across from him. "It feels different though, doesn't it? A large station is like a tiny planet. It has its own community, its own culture. Even between Dragonfire and Blackthorn, there are differences. And Jamestown is its own thing altogether." She left off there, hoping to draw Krazinski out. He seemed melancholy, which was a bad mindset to have right before a battle.

"I'm an old man. I thought I'd managed to live my entire life without experiencing a major disaster. I flattered myself, thinking I'd had a part in that. And now look at us. Command in hiding, Jamestown critically disabled. The PAC in jeopardy. I didn't do such a good job, after all, did I?"

Self-pity did not look good on him. "Old man, my ass. You're as fit as my father, and he can throw down like a member of my team."

He smiled sadly. "I failed in recruiting Hiro into Blackout. I tried for years. He'd have none of it. Didn't even want to know it existed."

"And then I joined up. Ironic."

"He couldn't have been prouder of you. Worried, sure. But he knew you'd never be happy doing anything else."

That made her wonder about his own daughter. "How's Hollinare?"

"Just before we evacuated it, she came to Jamestown to discuss a proposed new process for streamlining the admission of new planets into the cooperative. I didn't like her being there during the battle with Colb's people, but no part of that was what I would have wanted, even though we ultimately succeeded. Anyway, she's with command, and at the moment there's no safer place for her to be. It's a great relief to me, but I feel guilty thinking about all the parents out there who can't protect their children the same way."

"The universe is an unfair place," she observed.

"It is. The PAC is supposed to level the playing field, to help ensure a future for everyone's children. And it may fall. On my watch."

"Which part hurts more? The possible fall, or your part in it?"

"Depends on whether it happens or not. Even if it doesn't, I'll go to my grave knowing how close we came." He ran a hand through his steely but thick hair. He claimed to be an old man but Fallon didn't see it. He was fit and strong, albeit jaded.

"I'm not in the habit of comforting admirals." She crumpled the wrapper of a protein pack between her palms. "Shouldn't you be the voice of experience, telling me it will be all right?"

"That'd be nice. The PAC has certainly overcome many obstacles. But nothing like this. So unfortunately I don't have any experience to offer on this one."

She leaned back in her chair and crossed one leg over the other, feigning a nonchalance she didn't feel. "Your pep talk sucks."

His startled look gave way to a sudden laugh. "I guess it does. Sorry."

She spread her arms expansively, then let them drop. "Here's how I see it. You've been out of the field for a long time now. Tucked away at headquarters, pushing buttons behind the scenes. It's been too long since you knew how it felt to be the tip of the sword."

His forehead creased, as if he was unsure what to think.

She continued, "Your chance is coming up. Be the sword. Remember what it feels like to win. And use that to lead us the hell out of this mess."

His mouth curved into a real smile. "You might be right. I'll give it my best."

"Screw that defeatist talk. You've forgotten how to ego-trip yourself into a false sense of immortality. A critical skill in this occupation." Her voice rose as she talked, becoming louder and more forceful.

"Uh, right. So...we'll win! We'll kick Colb's ass, then kick the asses of anyone who thinks they can threaten the PAC." His back straightened and he made a fist, and Fallon perceived a glimmer of the young officer he had once been.

"That's right!" she barked. "Those pieces of shit are nothing compared to the PAC. They'll be sorry they even thought about taking us on."

Krazinski stood and said in a stage whisper, "I think this is working." He continued loudly, "We'll smash those bastards and send their ashes home in envelopes!"

She froze. "Oh dude, no, too far."

"Really?" Krazinski frowned.

"Just kidding! When we're done with them, there won't even be any ashes to send!"

"And...and we'll confiscate all of their holdings and use them for the very thing they hate most—the PAC!"

It was the worst bit of trash talk ever, but Krazinski seemed enthusiastic now, so whatever. If it was helping him, she'd play along. "Yeah! We'll liquidate *all* their assets!"

Raptor appeared, looking perplexed by the things he'd heard as he entered the mess hall. He looked from Fallon to Krazinski and back, then shrugged. "Tried your comport but you didn't answer. We've got the ships on long-range scanners, if you want to see them."

She was already on her feet.

Peregrine watched as Raptor and Krazinski followed Fallon onto the bridge, but Fallon had eyes only for the screen. There she saw them—two large people carriers, being very obvious about what and where they were. Just as they'd been directed to do.

She leaned over Hawk's shoulder to see their ETA. Eight hours. Longer than she'd have liked. She felt like a kid at an amusement park, always in the line waiting to get on the ride. But she could see it now. They were close.

"All right." She decided to let Ross sleep, since he'd just come off his shift and would need the rest. She'd fill him in later. "Let's go over it again."

KRAZINSKI'S PRESENCE on the *Nefarious* made for the perfect opportunity.

He was the one who sent the message, relayed through one of the transport ships, to Dragonfire Station. It would make sense to Colb that PAC command would set up there as they prepared to repair and occupy Jamestown. Fallon was already established there, and the proximity was as good as they'd get.

And Colb knew that command would take risks to return themselves to Jamestown, in order to soothe their allies and restore confidence. He also knew that protocol in such a situation was not to have escort ships with heavy firepower that would only draw attention to the VIPs within.

Colb would recognize this as the perfect opportunity to take out the entire PAC command at once.

In retrospect, Fallon would have gone with smaller, less conspicuous ships. She'd expected to have to use smoke and mirrors to imply the presence of important people. Krazinski had made all that unnecessary, and now she worried that her ships were too obvious.

Well, she could do nothing about all that now. She could only play the game with the pieces already on the board.

When a trio of ships crossed their vector a mere ten thousand kilometers away, the crew of the *Nefarious* braced themselves. But the ships were only rusty trawlers that puttered right by.

Nothing.

They arrived at Dragonfire as scheduled. So they followed out the farce. They gave all the proper docking signals and informed the station of three hundred passengers to board.

Avian Unit remained in the *Nefarious* for two days, docked and ready to meet an enemy at any moment.

But still nothing. Fallon and her team, including Krazinski now, finally had to admit that the plan hadn't worked. They boarded Dragonfire and met with Hesta to decide what to do next.

"Either Colb saw through it, or he decided not to risk taking us on in that situation," Krazinski said, sitting at the head of the table in an executive boardroom.

Hesta's decision to make their meetings more formal due to Krazinski's presence amused Fallon, but she kept that to herself.

Rank didn't mean as much to Fallon as it once had, but she couldn't blame Hesta for not feeling the same way.

"We need another plan to draw him out," Hawk said.

"No. That didn't work before. Repeating the process won't be any more effective." Fallon traced a whorl in the design of the tabletop, then froze. Details shifted around in her mind to take on a new pattern.

"He doesn't want to destroy the PAC. He wants to run it." She continued to stare at the curving lines of the whorl, letting the new mental image coalesce. "He thinks he has a better way. One that somehow involves illegal technology."

She ignored the voices around her. Kept them at a distance, a murmur in the background. She was busy chasing the logic, letting it lead her to the truth. She blinked slowly. The universe shrank down to include just her and the whorl.

Colb didn't want the people of PAC command dead. And if he didn't want to destroy the PAC, he had to be concerned about the Barony Coalition, which was its biggest immediate threat. That meant Colb must want the same thing that the rest of them did—to reestablish PAC command at headquarters. Keeping the allies from knowing there was a true danger. Preventing everything in the PAC zone from going to shit.

"He's at Jamestown," she said. "He's gotten around your safeguards and he's repairing it. If he succeeds, he'll be the only person who can offer us a chance to keep the peace. We'd have to take it. Which would mean letting him run command his way."

She ran through the logic a second time, looking for flaws. But nope. It was the only thing that made sense.

Krazinski said, "Jamestown will take months to repair. Even with an army of engineers he can't hope to bring it back to full function and pretend nothing happened."

Hesta spoke up. "He doesn't need full function. He only needs to make it appear restored, and to lock you out. To make himself the face of salvation."

"And give us no choice but to work for him," Peregrine added.

"It makes sense." Hawk didn't seem happy about it, but he appeared entirely convinced. At least he wasn't swearing.

Fallon assessed her people. Raptor, Peregrine, and Hawk looked ready to burst into action. She hadn't been sure how Krazinski, Ross, and Hesta would take her conclusions. She didn't have the same bond of trust with them. She hadn't saved their lives repeatedly, as many times as they'd saved her life. She hadn't worn their blood, or they hers.

But they sat up straight, with their shoulders back. Ready to roll.

Hesta was the first to speak. "Sounds like you all need to get your asses back to Jamestown Station."

Fallon stood. "I'm ready. How about the rest of you?"

They stood.

"Good. Ross, you begin preflight on the *Nefarious*. Hawk and Peregrine, you'll be in charge of getting your hands on any repair tools and parts that might be useful."

Hawk frowned. "How do we know what gear we can grab, and what might be of use? We could use some engineering help."

Fallon smiled. "I'm way ahead of you."

Fallon sent Raptor to collect Kellis and Arin.

Krazinski's job was to order any PAC vessels with firepower, whether military or not, that were within a day's distance to maximum burn their way to Jamestown. Since he no longer had a direct connection to central command, that meant trying to track down individual ships that were within range. It was slow work, and Fallon could only hope Krazinski managed to rally some support.

Fallon didn't know what kind of support Colb had behind him. There were far more unknowns than Fallon preferred for a mission. Precision strikes were more her style. But she had a target, and a final chance to save the PAC, and Prelin's ass, she'd take it.

Which put her right back where it all started. In Wren's maintenance bay. Wren wasn't lying under some rust heap this time. She turned the moment Fallon walked in. Fallon watched Wren study her face. A crinkle appeared between Wren's eyes as she stopped in front of her.

"What's wrong?"

Three mechanics tried to pretend not to be listening. Fallon ignored them. "I need your help."

Wren stiffened her spine and said, "Let's go."

WREN WAS ALREADY YANKING things out of their tidy spots and piling them onto an anti-grav unit when Fallon left the shop. The other mechanics had been given the afternoon off and Hawk and Peregrine would arrive in minutes. That allowed Fallon to see to her other pre-mission errand.

"Do you have any other dirty tricks?" she asked.

To Cabot's great credit, he didn't bat an eye. He hadn't minded ushering a customer out in the middle of a negotiation, either. The favors she owed him were stacking up.

"What kind of dirty tricks are you in the market for?" he inquired.

"The kind of thing that the hero uses to save the day and live to fight again, while saving the universe."

"Oh, that kind of thing." He nodded knowingly. "Unfortunately, I sold my last one the other day, but let me think what else I might have."

The man was positively unflappable. He'd have made an excellent BlackOp.

"There might be something, depending on your specific needs. Would you like to follow me to my warehouse?" he asked.

Even under the circumstances, Fallon froze, staring at him. Cabot was notoriously secretive about his stockroom.

"Oh, come on now, Chief. It's not like there are many secrets between us at this point." He walked to the back of the store without even looking to see if she followed.

"There might be one or two."

He waved a hand dismissively. She followed him behind the counter and into his secret sanctum. It didn't look like much. Impressively organized rows of shelving stood stacked neatly with various boxes and items. Cabot strolled down the third row, stopped, and removed a box the size of a small suitcase. He returned to where she stood, next to a table, and set the box down. He gestured to it with a little flourish.

She unlatched the lid and removed it. "What the hell are you doing with two crystal-matrix converters?" The mechanisms that allowed the conversion to power interstellar flight were incredibly expensive. She hadn't realized how successful a trader Cabot was.

"Waiting for the right buyer. I also have high-quality energy-transfer units to go with them. Both brand new, zero degradation. As you can imagine, it takes a special buyer to make this kind of purchase." He smiled benignly.

"Yeah, I'd say so." A ship's value was largely based on its propulsion system, and this was pristine, high-quality equipment.

He rested a hand on the side of the box and nudged it toward her. "Take them. If speed is important. And if it isn't, you can use one of these to create a rather impressive bomb. The same engineer who could install them into a ship could make them quite...incendiary."

"I sure hope we don't have to blow anything up." Fallon couldn't imagine what would cause her to destroy the very thing she was trying to rescue. Still. Better safe than sorry. "But thank you." She curled her fingers around the box.

"I'll get the transfer units." He strode in one direction, then paused and changed course. After picking up a small box, he resumed his original path and retrieved another case.

"Here. I acquired this just the other day, thinking it might be your kind of thing. All-purpose, you might say." He pushed the box at her.

Inside she found a weapon case. Lifting its lid, she saw a projectile weapon. "A harpoon pistol?"

He made the scoffing sound of someone who'd been insulted. "A priyanomine harpoon pistol, thank you very much." He touched the handle. "Priyanomine harpoons, as you may know, are much more deadly than any bullet. They're noncombustible, nonconductive, and durable enough to withstand an explosion—or pierce a bulkhead. So watch your aim, unless you're trying to depressurize a ship or a station."

Under any other circumstance, she'd be highly irate at him having such an item on her station. But she could use every advantage she could get right now.

"Yeah, that could be useful all right." She'd never used one. On the one hand, she hoped she got the chance, and on the other, she knew that would require a dire situation. "We can settle the price when I get back."

His benevolent expression faded, changing into something far more shrewd and grim. "If what you're going off to do is anything like what I suspect, I'm the one who'll owe you. Along with all the other citizens of the PAC."

"When I return, we're also going to have a very frank, in-depth discussion."

Rather than seeming perturbed, he smiled. "I'm looking forward to it. You hurry back."

"I'll do my best."

10

"So how does it feel?" Hawk asked.

Fallon spared him a brief glance before returning her attention to navigating the *Nefarious*. "How does what feel?"

"Flying your team into battle, along with an admiral, and a few civilians. Plus, the fact that you see two of those people naked on a regular basis."

This time she turned her head to give him a frosty glare. "Fine. It feels fine." After a pause she added, "And shut up."

He laughed. "Come on, Chief, this is our biggest adventure yet. Got to laugh about it."

She smirked. She liked that her team had adopted her Dragonfire title. "I'll laugh when someone says something funny. Why don't you go see how Wren and Kellis are doing in the engineering room?" Sadly, this was the closest her ship had ever come to having a proper crew. It still fell short, but at least she had an engineering team.

"I could just call them."

"But then you'd still be here," she pointed out.

He laughed. "All right. Don't mind stretching my legs." He

ruffled her hair on his way off the bridge.

She smiled after he left. He *was* funny. She just didn't want to encourage him.

At the moment, she wanted a little time to think. To work through the details and possible scenarios. To plan how best, in every situation, to protect her team. And salvage the PAC.

Her deep thought was interrupted by Raptor's "Hey," as he took the seat recently vacated by Hawk.

"Hey," she answered.

"Thought I'd keep you company. While you think."

He sat silently beside her for hours as they blasted through space at the highest speed she'd ever flown the *Nefarious*. She was risking mechanical damage, but she had replacement parts and two brilliant engineers. She watched many millions of dark kilometers blast by as she thought ahead to what was to come.

And still he sat there. Just silent and there. For her. Neither of them left their post and when they finally saw Jamestown appear on the viewscreen, rotating the wrong direction and way too fast, she turned her seat to face him.

"Thank you," she said.

"You're welcome."

She hesitated, fighting an internal battle. She felt like he deserved to hear a declaration of feelings, but for her it felt like scraping all her guts out and dumping them on the floor. But screw it. She'd get it out, quick and clean. Like getting a hand lopped off by a samurai sword. "I love you."

He looked surprised, then scowled. "Prelin's ass, we're all going to die, aren't we?"

"I hope not."

"Well, don't go saying a thing like that in a situation like this. It doesn't sound right, coming from you, and I don't like it." He gave a quick head shake. "I mean I do, it's great, but still. Just *no*."

She laughed. "Okay, I take it back."

"Can't take it back." He grinned at her. "But you should probably go say it to that wife of yours. She might be freaking out about now."

"You think I'd marry a freak-out type? No way. You have a lot to learn about Wren. Also, she's not my wife."

He said nothing. Just smiled and made a shooing gesture at her.

She relented. "Fine. I should check on everyone anyway, and get ready. Call Ross up to take over the *Nefarious*. I'll see you on Jamestown."

"Aye, Captain." He sat in the pilot's seat when she vacated it. "Hey."

She turned around. "Yeah?"

"I love you too. And I know saying it isn't your thing, so in the future, don't. I already know. Always did."

She smiled. There was only one thing to say to that. "Blood and bone."

His return smile said everything that would ever need to be said. "Blood and bone."

IT PLEASED Fallon tremendously to see the two best engineers she'd ever met in her engineering room. She walked in behind Kellis and Wren as they both stood looking at the propulsion chamber.

"Did you break it already?"

They turned quickly, amused.

"We were just admiring it. This is one fine ship you've got," Wren said. Her eyes shone, and she looked absolutely lovely.

"Enjoying the change of pace?" Fallon asked her.

"Absolutely. And it's very interesting to get a glimpse into your life." Wren glanced at Kellis to include her in the conversation. "And what a surprise to learn that this one had already gotten a glimpse."

"More than a glimpse," Fallon said. "She stormed a PAC base with us."

Kellis made a self-deprecating gesture. "I didn't do much. Just tagged along, really. Cut through a bulkhead."

"Still, the idea of seeing all this in action is fascinating." Wren showed none of the nervousness Raptor had anticipated. Hah. She'd have to rub that in later.

"Let's hope you still think so once we get on the station. Do either of you have any questions?" Fallon had thought hard about which engineer to take to Jamestown and which to leave on the ship. She'd decided that since Kellis was more accustomed to working on board a ship while Wren had more experience on a station, there was no reason for them to switch that up.

"You're sure I shouldn't come with you on the *Outlaw*?" Wren asked.

"No. It's a great ship, but you'll be safer here. Plus you'll have more people to protect you during boarding. I don't expect Colb to let us waltz right in. The only question is how much protection he has."

"Do you have any idea what kind of ships we can expect?" Kellis asked.

"No. He had time to get to a mercenary station, which means he had the opportunity to hire mercenary ships. Those could be anything from slag heaps to warships. So we're planning on warships. Classes and models, I have no idea. We'll have to adjust as we go."

"Right."

"Anything else?" Fallon asked, looking from one to the other, but they both shook their heads, looking determined.

"Good. I'm off to the cargo bay to get ready."

"Can I walk you there?" Wren asked.

She remembered what Raptor had told her, and nodded. "That'd be great."

It felt strange yet nice to walk with Wren down the corridors of the *Nefarious*. Wren was finally seeing who Fallon truly was.

Fallon was proud of her ship, her partners, and the rest of her crew. She wasn't glad that Wren would be mixed up in whatever was about to happen, but she was very glad to know she could rely on the best engineer in any galaxy to handle whatever the station would throw at them.

In the cargo bay, Fallon ran a hand over the flank of her little race-car ship. "This is it. Gets some amazing speed and maneuvers like a dream."

Wren laughed. "It's funny to see you so excited about flying. I didn't know that about you."

"There's still a lot you don't know. Sorry you ever asked me out?"

Wren elbowed her. "Absolutely not. Best thing I ever did."

Wren faced her full-on, and Fallon braced herself for a teary farewell.

Wren leaned forward, gently pinching Fallon's nose. "Beep."

Fallon laughed. "I'm flying off to save the universe and you beep my nose?"

Wren grinned. "Not the universe, just a bunch of galaxies. And I know you don't want an emotional scene. So a beep seemed the safest course of action."

"I like it. Thanks." She wrapped her arms around Wren for a hug. Wren returned the hug tightly, belying her flippant words.

Fallon looked into her eyes. "Wren."

"*No.*" Wren stepped back, holding a hand up in front of her. "Nope. Say it when you get back. You've already done the 'dire circumstances' goodbye. No sense in repeating yourself."

"Are circumstances dire? You just said it's only some galaxies to save. I mean...*pfff*...no problem."

"Good. You remember that. Now up you go. Strap in nice and safe, and I'll see you when you get home." She turned and sauntered out as if she hadn't a care in the world.

Fallon was still smiling as she went through her pre-launch checklist.

"Fallon, are you seeing this?" Ross' voice filled the *Outlaw*'s small cockpit. She rested now, attached to the outside of the bigger ship, waiting for her moment. They'd practiced these maneuvers and she knew they were ready to do them for real.

"Yep." As they neared Jamestown, she saw five ships. Two were small, no match for the *Nefarious*. One was a mid-sized wild card—no telling if it was a real threat. Of the remaining two, both were worth a good portion of concern. The larger was a much older model than the *Nefarious* but clearly in excellent condition.

"Ross, you're going to take on the big guy. While you're working on that, I'll keep the others busy. See if I can get the little ones out of the way."

"Okay, but watch yourself. You won't be any use to us if you get yourself burned crispy like last time."

"Understood. Good luck, *Nefarious*."

"Back at you, *Outlaw*."

She wouldn't have admitted it to anyone, but she liked being called "Outlaw."

She watched her viewscreen, even as she felt the *Nefarious* shift almost imperceptibly. They dove in beneath the lead ship, and her team unleashed the standard weapons attacks and evasive patterns. Well, standard for a highly trained military team. Ross had improved greatly during the drills they'd done, and she had faith in him. She had to have faith, because she had her own job to do and it depended entirely on him doing his.

While the *Nefarious* angled its belly away from the other ships, Fallon detached the *Outlaw* from its hull and hid behind Ross' sensor shadow as long as she could. With the *Nefarious* occupying the lead ship, she streaked around it and unloaded some firepower at its aft section, where the life-support systems would be. Anything she could do to slow it down or disable it would give Ross a big advantage.

She sailed on by the lead ship, ignoring the two small vessels to focus on the second large one. If she let it get position on the *Nefarious*, the smaller ships could help at pinning Ross in, and it would only be a matter of time until their concerted efforts took him down.

Can't have that.

She came in fast—too fast, technically speaking. If she anticipated her target's movements incorrectly, or was too slow to correct her own craft, she'd ram the *Outlaw* right into it. She had no intentions of a suicide mission, but flying a little beyond tolerance was kind of her thing. Engineers always calculated tolerance conservatively.

Her target shifted slightly on its axis, protecting its aft belly from her. Just as it should.

The *Outlaw* wasn't big enough for torpedoes, but Wren and Kellis had created a little something special for her, retrofitted for the *Outlaw*'s rescue beacon. Sure, she had no beacon now, but if she ended up in the shit, it wouldn't be of any help anyway.

She made another pass, scraping close to the ship and launching the beacon. Except it wasn't a beacon that flew toward the other ship and lodged itself right on that tender spot on the belly. The device sat there, and within seconds the ship went dark.

She whooped with delight. Cabot probably hadn't expected her to use his electrical-killing "ancient good luck charm" this way, but it had sure worked. The ship was still a threat, but its crew would be occupied with restoring its oxygen flow and inertial dampening systems for the next, oh, fifteen minutes or so. Which was fine. She didn't need to destroy these ships—and would prefer not to. They were only mercenaries. Criminals, sure, but not the kind who deserved an instant death sentence without a trial. All she needed was time to get on board Jamestown. She needed to disable the small ships to pave her way, and that of the *Nefarious*, assuming it took out the lead ship. She'd circle back if necessary.

As she made for the wild-card ship, her voicecom came to life on an open channel. "*Outlaw*, this is the *Stinth*. I can handle these two small birds."

Fallon adjusted her trajectory, swooping out and around the ship. "That wouldn't be Arlen Stinth, would it?"

"You got it, Chief. Cabot Layne called in a favor, so I'm here to assist."

Fallon laughed. Now that was unexpected. Someone who had once gotten into a fight with two buffoons on Dragonfire's boardwalk was coming to her aid. Every now and then, the universe was funny like that.

"Understood, *Stinth*. I'll go help the *Nefarious*, and hopefully we'll manage to get our asses on Jamestown."

"Understood, Chief. Good luck."

Fallon closed the channel. As she circled back to the *Nefarious* she saw a new ship appear on her sensors, closing on their location.

That was good news though. The call sign of the P.A.C.S. *Roosevelt* was broadcast loud and clear. The military flagship would flush out the mercenaries with relative ease.

"*Outlaw* to *Nefarious* and *Roosevelt*. The *Stinth* is on our side, so please take care of it. I'm preparing to board Jamestown."

"See you there, *Outlaw*." Ross sounded entirely professional, but that didn't mean the ship had suffered no damage. She could only hope for the best.

"We'll keep you covered, *Outlaw*." The voice from the *Roosevelt* wasn't familiar, but there was no reason it should be.

"Grateful for that, *Roosevelt*. I'm your new biggest fan. *Outlaw* out."

She'd already maneuvered her ship wide of the melee, out of

weapons range. No sense in getting taken out by a potshot now. She focused on what she'd come to do—end this madness once and for all.

The docks were locked down. She'd expected that. Raptor had written a handy little program to gain access. The airlock pressurization had been disabled, but she'd come prepared, wearing a pressure suit.

She needed only a few minutes to force the airlock to open. Once on the other side, she had to put it into emergency containment mode so it would close itself again.

Her first discovery was finding that this part of the station had been repressurized. She wondered how much of Jamestown had been. The lights were on, in emergency mode to conserve energy. As she moved through the station, lights turned off behind her when they sensed an unoccupied area. It was an odd thing, the lights snapping to life ahead of her and clicking off behind. She existed in a small radius of light that adjusted itself to her as she made her way toward the heart of Jamestown.

As the first on board, her job was to get to engineering and assess the station's situation. Once the single-channel comport in her ear let her know her team had arrived, she'd switch tactics and head to crisis ops control. Colb was almost certainly hiding out there. It was where she'd be in his position—the most protected place on the station.

She was glad he'd pressurized it. It would make her work easier. It was chilly though. Temperature bled off quickly in space, only to be regained by time and great effort. In another ten degrees it would be comfortably livable.

Being on the empty station was eerie, but no more than during her first visit. At least it was more hospitable to life now. She was surprised when she made it to engineering with no issues. She'd expected to encounter resistance, but no one had blocked her way, and Colb apparently hadn't wanted to booby-trap the thing he was trying to repair.

She shed her pressure suit and replaced it with her stinger dissipator. Now she was ready for a fight.

A survey of the station's systems showed that the place remained a husk. No communications, no information systems. But Colb wouldn't have needed much more time to lock out the other PAC officials. Which would give him the upper hand with the PAC, allowing him to establish himself as the de facto leader of the entire alliance.

She'd been worried that she was already too late, but now she'd made it aboard and she wasn't leaving without him.

She studied the engineering readouts, trying to figure out what all he'd done and how she could thwart him. Lock him out somehow. But she was a fighter and a pilot, not an engineer. Security systems were nothing like systems operations. She needed an engineer.

Her earpiece came to life with Raptor's voice. "Docking now. Expect to receive Wren to engineering in ten minutes. Krazinski and I are headed to crisis ops."

She touched the broadcasting mechanism at the top of her ear. "Docking bays aren't pressurized, but the rest of the station is. Cold but tolerable without a pressure suit. Minimal but sufficient lighting."

"Understood. See you soon."

Colb would know the docking bays had been accessed. He wouldn't know where she and the others were, though, or how many. And he wouldn't be able to pick up their transmissions.

So far, she'd found no evidence of anyone being on the station. She'd expected to meet resistance in the form of some mercenaries or perhaps a team of subverted BlackOps once she got through the airlock. Either he was keeping his protection closer to his actual location, or he hadn't trusted even his own flunkies to board Jamestown.

Peregrine and Hawk arrived with Wren. They quickly peeled off their pressure suits.

"You all in good shape?"

Hawk grinned. "No problem. The *Roosevelt* came in and gave us the royal treatment. Kind of nice, for a change. You?"

"Not even a little crispy."

"You must be getting better."

Wren ignored their byplay, going immediately to the systems displays when she got her suit off. Her hands flew over the controls, and for a few minutes, the rest of them could do little but wait. Fallon had never seen such take-charge intensity in Wren before.

Finally Wren twisted around to face them. "Colb has managed to get the station into lockdown mode, which reroutes all commands, even engineering, to crisis ops. I can't make any changes from here."

"Can you do it from another location?" Peregrine asked.

"Yes. Any mechanized system has moving parts that I can physically alter. I just have to get to them."

Raptor's voice came over the comport again, quieter this time. "He's in lockdown mode. Crisis ops is like a fortress. Is there anything Wren can do?"

Fallon looked to her. Wren nodded, her mouth set in a determined line.

"We're on our way," Fallon said.

"Hand me the decoupler." A minute later, Wren added, "Now the laser torch."

Fallon waited in silence, encased in a small service conduit. As the smallest of the team, she'd been selected to serve as Wren's assistant while the others scouted out the rest of the station. So far they hadn't turned up a single person working for Colb. Unless he had someone locked inside crisis ops with him, he must have been too paranoid to trust anyone. Which was probably wise. Colb had as much interest as she did in preventing the public at large from finding out about the true state of affairs.

On the other hand, if he had no one to cover him, that worked just fine for Fallon.

"Think you could do something like when you busted Colb out of the brig?" Fallon asked Wren.

"Wow, thanks for reminding me about that. But unfortunately no. The Dragonfire brig was meant for keeping people from breaking out. We've got the opposite situation here." Wren's voice grew muffled halfway through.

Fallon knew that, but she'd hoped Wren could work some engineering magic for her. Plus, she'd grown tired of lying in a conduit listening to various scrapings and scufflings while Wren worked.

Wren grunted, and her feet shifted. "I can't get it. Do you think you can squeeze up here and help me?"

"Maybe. I'll have to crawl up over you. Probably won't be comfortable for you."

"Try it. I'll be as flat as I can."

Fallon turned onto her stomach and dragged herself up the conduit. Whoever had designed these things had not expected them to be accessed, it seemed. The security conduits on Dragonfire were cramped, but nothing like this.

She tried not to hurt Wren as she dragged herself over, then carefully lay on her. "Can you breathe?"

"Yes. You're not that heavy."

"This reminds me of going sledding with my brother when we were kids. I'd tickle you, but you'd probably thrash around and hurt us both." Fallon spoke softly. Sound was already too loud in such a small space, and her mouth was right behind Wren's head.

"Do you joke around this much when you're on a mission with your team?"

"Yes, actually. It cuts the tension. Peregrine doesn't joke as much as we do, but she's..." She didn't know how to finish that sentence in a way that wasn't unflattering to Per.

"As much fun as a bag of dead kittens?" Wren supplied.

"Definitely more fun than that. So what am I supposed to be doing here? Or did you just want to get all horizontal with me?"

She felt Wren sigh in exasperation.

"See this?" Wren wrapped her fingers around an air-intake grate above her.

"Yep."

"Help me pull it out."

Air supply seemed like a dicey thing to tinker with. "Assuming we get it out, will we still be able to breathe?"

"Yes. For about two minutes. We need to get out of here and hit the emergency stop in the containment tank before the system detects contamination."

Fallon kind of hated to ask the next question. "What happens if we don't?"

"The system will recognize that the intake has been polluted and begin a decontamination cycle. Unfortunately that'd be pretty deadly for us, with the acid gas and all." Wren seemed a little too chipper about explaining that.

"So let's definitely not do that," Fallon said.

"Agreed. Ready? On three. One...two...three."

They pulled. It was difficult to get much strength behind the pull from a prone position reaching ahead of them. Fallon gave it everything she had and all at once the grate gave way, coming at them so fast it hit them both in the face. But there was no time to rub her smarting nose or her elbows where they'd smacked into unforgiving conduit. She scrambled over Wren into the tank, which was probably the last place she ever wanted to be on a space station.

Fallon had no choice but to slide down the wall of the tank on her stomach. She was sure she left a layer of skin on the hard metal as she went. On the bright side, it was crazy cold, which soothed the ouch a little.

The tank was too deep for her to save Wren from the same fate, so she had to stand by and watch her slide down the same way, groaning as she went.

"How does maintenance on this stuff usually get done?" Fallon helped Wren up so they were both standing in a metal tank the size of a large house.

"Bots. Now we need to run!"

Fallon chased after Wren to the other side of the tank, where a red emergency button was next to an access ladder. She didn't know how much of the two minutes they had left when Wren smacked it, but she doubted it was much.

"There! Easy!" Wren said through gasps for breath. She wasn't much of an athlete.

"Now what?" Fallon eyed the ladder.

Sure enough, Wren pointed to it, too winded to talk.

"I'm guessing there's a time element involved with that too."

Wren nodded, waving at the ladder.

"Nope," Fallon answered. "You're going first."

Wren stepped onto the ladder and hauled herself up.

"You need to work out more. Hurry up, or I'll start poking your ass with my harpoon gun."

Finally they reached the top and stepped up onto a walkway. A small maintenance door stood between them and safety from whatever inhospitable reaction was about to occur in the tank.

Wren tried to activate the door but it remained closed. "Locked," she gasped.

Fallon stepped in and looked at it. The door wasn't exceptionally reinforced, and it had only a basic code unlock. "It's low security. I can probably crack it, but it may take more time than we have."

"I got it. Old engineer's trick. The wall alongside a door is usually far less reinforced than the door itself. That's definitely the case here." Wren dropped her backpack, rummaged around in it, and pulled out the laser torch Colb had given her. At least the thing had turned out to be useful to them.

Wren cut a roughly circular shape in the wall beside the door. The cutter went through with relatively little resistance. When she had a hole big enough to get her shoulders through, she returned the torch to her bag and pulled out a thermal blanket. She shoved the cutout circle to the other side, then laid the blanket over the bottom of the hole.

"Careful. It's hot, and the metal's sharp."

After pushing their backpacks and weapons out the other side, Fallon helped Wren go through head first, arms up so she could catch herself as she tumbled to the floor. Then it was Fallon's turn. She ignored the bite of the metal digging into her stomach, grateful for the durable fabric of her jumpsuit.

As she got to her feet on the other side, Fallon heard the whir of a turbine starting. A red light began flashing above the door.

Wren grabbed the blanket and dropped it, then reached for the metal cutout. "Hurry, help me!"

They shifted it around to find the right fit for the irregular shape, then slid it into the hole. Wren used the same laser cutter to fuse the metal. It warped and bubbled unevenly, but she achieved a seal on their side of the wall.

"There." Wren turned off the cutter.

"What would've happened if you hadn't sealed it?" Fallon put her weapon belt back on as she asked. She felt naked without it.

"That's the batch tank for the air supply. Since we averted a decontamination cycle when we hit the emergency button, it's now preparing a fresh supply of the perfect formula of air. If we hadn't sealed the hole, the unmixed gases would have leaked into this corridor, causing a potentially dangerous mix."

"Which would have set off an alarm and informed Colb of our location. Gotcha."

"Also, we might not have been able to breathe." Wren picked

up the blanket and returned it to her backpack, then put on the pack. "But yeah, the alarm thing too."

Fallon consulted the station's schematics in her head. "Where do we need to go next?"

"The service conduit next to the air distribution duct. You'll have to get past the security though. That's a highly restricted area, since it goes right to crisis ops."

"Right. That's this way." Fallon went to the left.

"So this is what you really do?" Wren asked as they went.

"More or less. There's often a lot more shooting involved."

"And you like that?"

Fallon took a left, and a right, which led them to the conduit they needed. "Yeah."

There were a lot of things she could say to add to that, but she stopped herself. Most of those details would probably not be helpful in seeing Wren through this experience.

They kneeled next to the entrance to the conduit. While Fallon worked on getting it open, Wren said, "We could adjust his air mix and kill him. That would make it easier to take crisis ops."

"It would." Fallon frowned at the code sequencer, which was proving harder to crack than she'd hoped, even with the small device running Raptor's program. "But if he's dead I can't get the answers I need about what he's done."

The right code finally came up and she sighed with relief as she got through that layer. Next, she input a master command authorization code, which Krazinski had given her. Nope. Colb had changed that too. She reset Raptor's device to work on that code.

"Not to mention that you want to ask him why," Wren added.

"Why what?"

"Why he'd do all this. Why he chose you."

Fallon frowned at the device, still running through thousands of possible codes every tenth of a second. "It would be nice, but it doesn't matter. What matters is that a lot of people are dead because of him. You saw some of the bodies, but there are a lot more that you didn't see. Most were probably good people who had been led astray by someone they trusted. Those were our people, and if they were largely innocent, their records should reflect that. And their families should know it."

"Yeah." Wren sounded sad.

"And he had an entire station of scientists doing research on illegal tech, hidden away on a little moon base. They fought, and they died. I want to know about them. To clear their names if they were coerced. To let their loved ones know what happened to them."

She wished the code-cracking device would hurry. For all she knew, Colb knew they were on the station and was preparing to destroy it and everyone on it.

"Does it matter if they were coerced or not?" Wren asked. "They were still doing things that broke our treaties."

Fallon kept her eyes locked on the device. "You broke some major PAC laws helping Colb. You'd be in a brig somewhere right now if not for your intentions, and someone to explain them for you."

Wren's voice was barely audible when she said, "Right."

"Don't let it get you down. You're making up for it now."

Wren pursed her lips and nodded.

The code clicked into place. "Yes! Got it." She removed a hair-width wire from her backpack and threaded it through the DNA scanner's input port. She backed away slightly, and with what sounded like a computerized sneeze, the scanner went dark. "Hah."

"What was that?" Wren asked.

"DNA scanners are extremely touchy devices. They're a weak point in any security system because of that. If they're disabled from the command side, they disengage and leave the rest of the security in place until they're recalibrated." The wire was one of her favorite Blackout tools. Fortunate for her that Krazinski had supplied her with some.

She opened the conduit, but before going in, she activated her comport. "Status request."

Raptor replied almost immediately. "No other souls found on board. Proceeding now toward crisis ops to try to force our way in."

"Hold off on that," Fallon ordered. "It's unlikely to work and the attempt would be incredibly loud. I'm hoping to be able to take him quietly by surprise. We're making our way in via conduit, where there's a hatch into control ops. Once we get inside and secure Colb, first order of business will be shutting down lockdown mode and opening the door for you."

"Any chance we can follow your route in?"

"Negative. You'd never fit through the conduits. They're meant for bots, not people."

"Understood. Waiting for your signal. Blood and bone."

"Blood and bone." She ignored Wren's curious look. "I'll go first this time."

HALF CRAWLING, half dragging herself through fifteen meters of conduit was not kind to Fallon's body. She knew Wren had to have it even harder. Though she had a slim build, Wren was a good bit taller.

Finally they made it to the hatch, which mercifully was surrounded by a wider space, giving Fallon enough room to pull herself into and sit up, if she kept her head down.

"The good news," Fallon whispered to Wren, who lay flat in the tighter part of the conduit, "is that this side is not secured. It's a regular old hatch. All we have to do is drop in on Colb. Literally." The opening was in the ceiling of crisis ops, which meant she'd have to lower herself from it, then drop another meter and a half to the floor. The plus side of that was that she could do it quickly and quietly, and hopefully take Colb by surprise.

Wren nodded.

"First, I'm going to get a look in there, to see what's going on." She put on a pair of glasses and removed a coil of wire attached to a tiny display from her backpack. Attached to the wire was a tiny camera. Carefully, to avoid any scraping sounds, Fallon fed it though the air delivery grate.

Rotating it slowly around, she saw that Colb was, in fact, not alone. Nine large toughs surrounded him where he sat in the command chair. Damn. Zooming in on faces, she recognized the surviving members of Stone Unit and three members of Ice Unit, plus three unknowns. Double damn. She could take on six average bruisers, but not six BlackOps plus three others.

She blew out a breath. Okay. Different tactic. She didn't need to beat them. She only needed to get crisis ops out of lockdown mode so her reinforcements on the other side could get in.

Right. No problem.

"Wrinkle in the plan," she whispered to Wren. "I was going to tell you to stay up here, but that clearly won't work. Since we're both dead if you don't come down with me, we're going to have to do that."

"Wow, great pep talk," Wren whispered back.

Fallon had to hand it to her. The woman had nerve. "Best you're going to get today. I'm going to drop in and keep the people down there busy. I need you to get crisis ops open to let the others in." She pulled a stinger from her belt. "You know how to use one of these, right?"

"Sure, it's like a laser torch. But instead of cutting metal, I cut people." She looked unhappily resigned to that idea.

"More or less. It's set to lethal force. You only have to hit them once, unless they're wearing dissipators. If they are, you'll need to switch to that torch of yours. Just don't hit me, and don't hit Colb.

Unless you have no choice but to take Colb out. But really, really don't hit me."

"Right. Take out everyone, including you. Got it."

If Wren didn't stop that, Fallon would start to think she was cut out for this kind of work.

"I'll need the torch for a minute." When Wren handed it to her, she carefully sliced the bolts holding the intake hatch in place.

After handing the torch to Wren, she turned backward to the opening on her knees. "This is going to happen fast, but time will probably feel like it's slowed down. At least that's how it happens for me. Good luck."

Wren scooted closer, getting ready to occupy the space when Fallon left it. "So I'm about to see the business end of what you really do."

"Fraid so. Can you handle it?" Fallon knew full well that most people couldn't deal with seeing that kind of action.

"Yeah. Blood and bone, or whatever it is you all say."

Fallon grinned at her. "Blood and bone."

She lifted the hatch and moved it aside, then palmed her second stinger. With her other hand she slid a knife from her belt. She nodded to Wren and dropped to the floor of crisis ops.

She hit one with her stinger center mass during her drop. No help there. They were wearing dissipators. Damn. That would make this job harder.

She threw the stinger at one and the knife at another. The blade stuck right into the throat of the closest BlackOp. At least the stinger distracted the other for a moment.

In the seconds it took for them to advance on her, she grabbed two more knives and launched them into two more throats. They landed true, and she was down to six opponents. Plus Colb, but she was barely aware of him while she tracked her bigger threats.

Two came into range of her within two seconds of her landing, with two more only steps away. The last two remained with Colb.

No more room for knife throwing. It would be close combat from here on out. On the plus side, they couldn't use ranged weapons either. No one had tried using a stinger so they either recognized her dissipator or just assumed she wore one.

Her first priority was to reverse positions with them. She needed them facing away from the hatch to give Wren a chance. She launched herself into the air. She tucked her knees in sideways to her body, executing a head-over-heels flip that had her landing on a voicecom terminal.

She dodged a punch from the man on her left and delivered a kick to his throat. Her stance on the console gave her a vantage point. He went down choking for breath. Unfortunately that left her open to the second person, who landed a solid punch to Fallon's chest, knocking her off the terminal. At least it pushed her closer to the far wall, drawing the others toward her and away from Wren.

She landed awkwardly on one foot, which required her to adjust to balance. It also caused her to take another hard hit, in the same spot as the last one. Her chest felt like it had caved in.

But now on level ground, she mounted her own offensive. She threw the most vicious combo she had in her arsenal. Kick, jab, cross, feint, and a left hook to the temple. The woman stumbled back, giving Fallon the advantage. Before she could follow it up, the one she'd kicked in the throat came at her back. She sensed him more than she heard or saw him. She bent at the waist, reaching for the floor. Using momentum and her increased reach, she kicked her right foot up, catching him in the chin and sending him falling backward.

And here came the one she'd hit with the stinger. Dammit. They were too many, too fast. Wren had dropped and begun working at a science station, and Fallon hoped she could work fast. She estimated they had less than half a minute.

She backed up, making as much noise as she could to keep their attention on her and not on what was going on behind them. She threw punches and dodged theirs, but she was only marking time. She was the bait, and she knew she'd get eaten eventually. They converged on her, and she knew she didn't have much time now. If only they would politely come at her one by one or in pairs, like in the holo-vids.

Another hit to the chest made her wonder how many broken ribs she had. A punch to the head muffled the sounds around her and made her vision dim. Yeah, that was bad. But she couldn't pull herself together enough to block the hits she saw coming her way. She felt the impacts as they came, but less and less as things grew blurrier. Huh. So this was how it felt to lose a fight. All she could do now was remain on her feet as long as possible.

Dimly she was aware of a pause in the hits, like a missed beat in a drum cadence. She shook her head, trying to process what was happening around her. The door had opened. Hawk flew in first and destroyed the two that came at him, like a chef tenderizing meat. Peregrine bolted past him to yank one of Fallon's assailants away and tackle her. Somewhere in the background Krazinski jumped in with Hawk while Ross took on the one she'd tried to shoot with the stinger. She watched it all, dumb and confused, as if it were a hazy dream.

Raptor took on the last of Colb's flunkies, the one Fallon had thought would end up killing her.

She staggered back against the wall, wiping her hand over her right eye. It came away with blood on it.

She closed both eyes for a moment, struggling to center herself in real time.

Finally remembering to look for Colb, she stepped away from the bulkhead. As soon as she focused on him, time slowed to a crawl. She saw his hand, holding a stinger pointed toward Wren. She couldn't see Wren, but her exact position was burned into Fallon's awareness.

She needed answers only Colb had. Needed them for herself and the entire PAC. But she'd watch everything burn before she'd let Wren die.

Her harpoon gun had appeared in her hand, and she didn't pause a microsecond before pulling the trigger. It flew across the brief space and landed in Colb's chest, the force of it causing him to fall backward. His stinger came alive as he fell, snaking a bright arc of energy in Wren's direction. He hit the ground and the stinger's blast cut off abruptly as the weapon tumbled out of his hand.

As much as she wanted to go to Wren, she had to finish the job. Her vision and mind clear now, she bolted to Colb, her gun still pointed at him even though she hadn't reloaded it.

"No need," he gasped. The old, familiar face of Uncle Masumi looked at her sadly. "I've got a minute. Maybe two."

"Why did you do all this?" she asked.

"You'll see when you get older. Spouses die. Friends move on. Children grow up and become strangers. You always end up... alone." He coughed hard and blood came up, coating his lip and chin. "Only the mark you leave on your civilization stays. I tried to ensure the PAC's survival."

"You've *threatened* its survival. We'll be lucky if we can avoid interstellar war. *That's* your legacy."

He coughed again and gasped hard for breath. "...wrong. Wait and see."

She leaned down to hear his weakening voice. "What do you mean?"

But the light in his eyes had gone out. She straightened.

Her heart froze. *Wren.* Oh, no. Was she too late? She turned and ran. As she approached, she saw eyes full of grief and sympathy.

Wren's pale eyes looked up at her, tortured. "I'm so sorry." She moved aside.

Fallon fell to her knees beside Raptor. His skin had gone a sickly color.

"He dove in front of me," Wren murmured.

Words poured out of Fallon's mouth. "No, no, no! *Raptor!*" Her throat burned as she framed his face with her hands. Traces of her blood smudged onto his skin. "Why did you do that?"

His eyes didn't open, but his lips moved slightly. "You love her."

He went limp.

"Oh, hell no!" Fallon yelled at Raptor. "You are not dying on me!" She looked around wildly. "Where's his backpack?"

Someone found it and brought it to her. She tore it open and grabbed the packages of nanopods and the injector. She slammed every damn nanopod they had into him.

"Fallon." Hawk touched her shoulder. "Don't torture him. That was a maximum-setting blast. He can't..." His words trailed off. "He's not breathing," he said carefully. He probably sensed that telling her that Raptor couldn't survive it would have a bad effect on her.

"Then someone had better fucking start breathing for him!" she shouted. "He wouldn't give up, if it were us, and we're not giving up on him." Her cheeks were wet. She impatiently swiped her hands over them but was surprised to see little blood on them.

It was Krazinski who knelt by Raptor's head and put a respirator over his face as she wiped her hands on her thighs.

"Per, inform the *Roosevelt* that we need medevac. Immediately." The docking of the *Roosevelt* would probably take more time than Raptor had. Maybe it was already too late. The rest of them thought so. But she wouldn't stop trying until a doctor forced her to.

She measured the time in the artificial breaths that Krazinski supplied. Wren put a flat silver disk on Raptor's chest and gave him regular shock-pulse charges, keeping his body's electrical system online and forcing his heart to contract. So Fallon counted those too. Breath, pulse charge, breath, pulse charge.

Wren was on her knees above Raptor's head, stroking his hair and whispering in his ear.

Fallon almost wished he was bleeding. That would give her something to do, trying to patch him up. But she could do nothing for him but count and wait.

Finally the *Roosevelt's* medical crew arrived and took over, saying a lot of medical words. Fallon recognized enough of the words to be terrified in a way she'd never felt in her whole life. She trailed the medical workers, refusing to be more than a few feet away from Raptor. As if she could keep him alive by sheer will, if only she were close enough.

On the *Roosevelt*, her team and the others went somewhere while she followed Raptor to the infirmary. Time passed. She had no awareness of how much.

She heard more medical words like broken ribs and internal bleeding and concussion and suddenly all the attention was on her. She wanted no part of those words. The only words she wanted were, "He's going to be fine."

She refused to leave him, so the medical staff had to work on her sitting up. She heard soft murmurings including her name in the far corners of the infirmary. She didn't care. Fuck their words. Fuck everything if Raptor wasn't with her. The medical staff changed out, then changed again. She never took her eyes off him.

She nearly fell off the stool when his eyes opened a crack. She stood and leaned in close to him. "Raptor?"

He whispered something but she couldn't hear it.

"What?"

He managed three louder, rusty-sounding words. "You

look awful."

She took what felt like the first breath she'd taken since he'd been shot. "So do you."

"You smell awful too."

"Well, you stink worse than I do."

"Good." A ghost of a smile haunted his mouth. "I'm going to sleep now. You go clean yourself up. Didn't anyone tell you it's unbecoming of an officer to look so shitty?"

She laughed. "Pretty sure that was the first thing we learned at the academy. I'll go clean up if you promise me you won't die while I'm gone."

"Deal. No dying today."

It was only after his eyes closed again that she realized how much her body ached.

"What I'd really like is some blistercakes." Fallon frowned at her soup. It didn't even have meat in it.

"Soup first," Wren insisted, taking a spoon from the tray she'd placed on the foot of Fallon's bed and handing it to her. "It's chock full of Bennite vegetables, and will help restore your energy. Brannin says you two can try a little walking tomorrow. If you try today, I'll send you right back to the infirmary."

Fallon scowled, but put a spoonful of soup into her mouth. Sure, it was delicious, but blistercakes would really hit the spot.

"I ate all my soup." Reclining next to her, Raptor sounded far too obedient. He held the bowl out for Wren, who took it and set it gently on the tray. "Can I have blistercakes?"

Wren beamed at him. "Yes! I'll go get them." She pointed at Fallon and said sternly, "Every drop or you'll get nothing else! You could take some lessons from Raptor on being a good patient." She and Raptor shared a look of mutual admiration.

Fallon turned her scowl on him after Wren left. "Why are you even in my quarters? You should be up already. You didn't even have any broken bones."

"Yeah, I nearly died, that's all." He scoffed at her. "You're such a baby with your broken ribs."

"And wrist and fingers. And a touch of fractured skull. But if it helps you to call me a baby, then fine."

He pretended to glare at her, then broke into a grin. "Tell you what. I'll sneak you a blistercake."

She smiled. "Sounds perfect. Don't tell Wren."

"I won't. We'd both get in trouble."

They laughed. Not because it was really that funny, but because this was how they talked, and they understood each other perfectly.

11

Fallon paused during her midday rounds on the boardwalk to just look at it. At all the different species, the throngs of visitors, and the fantastic people who lived right here in her little community. It couldn't have been more beautiful.

She missed Brak, who had left a week ago with her PAC commendation in hand to visit her homeworld. Fallon hoped it went the way Brak wanted. She looked forward to hearing all about it when Brak returned to take an advisory role with Blackout.

Krazinski and the rest of Blackout had taken residence on Dragonfire. It was a new but exciting change that had enlivened the entire station. They only knew PAC intelligence had moved in, but that was plenty thrilling all by itself.

The new citizens of Dragonfire had been housed on Deck Four. It gave her fewer accommodations to assign to ambassadors, admirals, and other VIPs, but she was fine with that. While Jamestown was being repaired, this was the perfect place for Blackout to operate. Fallon intended to campaign for keeping Blackout on the station permanently, separate from the rest of

PAC command. But later, after command had gotten used to Blackout being on Dragonfire. Sometimes, in battle, timing was everything.

Lim was still working out his new existence. He'd chosen to remain with Blackout, at least for the time being. He might find a new calling in life, but meanwhile he had become very popular on the station. Arin was trying to recruit him for security.

Most of Jamestown's remaining staff had been temporarily housed at the Tokyo base. That worked well, since a good deal of restaffing and restructuring was required. Tokyo was an excellent place to find replacements. Meanwhile, new oversight would be created, as well as new protocols for Blackout and all other branches of intelligence.

Fallon continued walking, only to pause again near the Tea Leaf. She stared at the table she and Wren preferred. She missed Wren. But the PAC could do no better than to have Wren on Jamestown, ensuring the repairs got done not just on schedule, but ahead of it.

Kellis was also helping, even while she received officer training. It was an unusual setup, but Kellis was an unusual and exceptional person.

Fallon was still surprised that Hesta had turned down an offer for a promotion and a position at headquarters once Jamestown was repaired. Hesta had counteroffered to be an asset for Blackout, and remain as the captain of Dragonfire.

Fallon had accepted a promotion of sorts on Dragonfire. She was now the chief of operations. It was a new position on the station, but it allowed her to appoint Arin as the chief of security. She would maintain oversight of the department, but daily operations would be up to him. Which freed her up to do more administrative work for the PAC. She'd taken the time, though, to set up an internship program for one Nixabrin Maringo. Young Nix gave Fallon hope for the future.

Jerin had also stepped up to serve the PAC. She brought her

whole crew to the party, too. Jerin, while captaining the *Onari* as before, had become a PAC health ambassador. She would help speed the entry of worlds into the PAC by helping them develop their health programs. She would get to continue helping those who most needed it, while saying goodbye to her financial issues. And her home port would remain Dragonfire Station.

Not everything was starshine and rainbows, though. The Barony Coalition had continued its efforts to undermine the PAC, and they'd had moderate success in whipping up dissent among PAC members regarding broken treaties.

These were dicey times. Fallon felt like the PAC was poised at the top of a huge hill, and it wouldn't take much for it to begin a long descent. She could envision two futures for the PAC. One where the difficulties were handled, and the PAC became stronger, safer, and more beneficial to all of its members. And one where tensions burned through the ties that had once bound, plunging planets and galaxies into war.

But both possibilities always existed, in every society. She could only hope that unity won out. She'd sure do whatever she could to make that happen, as would all the amazing people she'd met over the past two years. Along with the people she'd long had faith in. They were equal to the task, and she was proud to be among them.

She saw Cabot wave from inside his shop as she resumed her stroll down the concourse. She waved back, then shot him one of Trin's finger guns, just for fun.

He laughed and returned the gesture. Which seemed to imply that he knew Trin fairly well. Funny.

She returned to the quarters she still shared with Peregrine after her rounds. She was no longer chief of security, and her office now belonged to Arin. But she liked to maintain her tradition of walking the boardwalk every day. It felt like home to her, and she suspected that her daily habit contributed to the feeling of home for many of its residents.

Home. That reminded her of a message she'd been meaning to send.

She sat down at the voicecom display in her room.

"Hi, Dad. I'm thrilled that you and Mom are transferring to Jamestown. It will be fantastic to have you so nearby. And by the time you make it there, it will be better than new and almost entirely staffed. I think you'll like Jamestown. And Sarkan is near enough for shore leaves so you'll be able to get planetside on a regular basis. I can't wait to show it to you—you're going to love it. Especially Mom. You might never get her to leave the beach." She smiled at the thought.

"Let me know when you've arrived and I'll come see you at Jamestown. We have a lot of catching up to do. And there's someone I want you to meet. Well, two people, but you met one of them last time I saw you. Anyway, I look forward to hearing back from you."

She smiled, waved, then closed the channel. She started to call Hawk to invite him for a drink that evening. It had been a while since they'd done that and they were overdue. Before she could open a channel to him, an incoming message lit up her display. She answered it.

Raptor's face filled her screen. He looked fantastic, as if he'd never caught a stinger blast that should have killed him. "Hey. I've got a line on that doctor Lim said helped him escape. Want to come to my quarters?"

"Be there in a minute."

The screen went blank. She had to laugh. After everything she and her team had been through, there was always more to be done.

Thank goodness. They'd never be satisfied with anything else. Blood and bone.

MESSAGE FROM THE AUTHOR

Thank you for reading!

Please visit www.ZenDiPietro.com to sign up for my newsletter to receive updates on new releases.

Reviews are critical to an author's success. I would be grateful if you could write a review at Amazon and/or Goodreads. Just a couple minutes of your time would mean so much to me.

Ready for more Dragonfire Station? Cabot's Mercenary Warfare series is underway! Check out the first book, *Selling Out,* on Amazon.

You can also go back in time and see Avian unit's early days. They'll go to the PAC academy, Officer Training School, and then to the stars.

I hope to hear from you!

In gratitude,
    Zen DiPietro

ABOUT THE AUTHOR

Zen DiPietro is a lifelong bookworm, dreamer, and writer. Perhaps most importantly, a Browncoat Trekkie Whovian. Also red-haired, left-handed, and a vegetarian geek. Absolutely terrible at conforming. A recovering gamer, but we won't talk about that. Particular loves include badass heroines, British accents, and the smell of Band-Aids.

www.ZenDiPietro.com

Printed in Dunstable, United Kingdom